ONLY AND EVER THIS

ONLY AND EVER THIS

— A NOVEL —

J. A. TYLER

2580 Craig Rd.
Ann Arbor, MI 48103
www.dzancbooks.org

First Edition: February 2023
Cover design by Jade They
Interior design byMichelle Dotter
ISBN: 9781950539703

Excerpts previously appeared in *Diagram, Denver Quarterly, Hayden's Ferry Review*, and *Failbetter*

With much additional gratitude to early readers and supporters: Matt Bell, Jac Jemc, David Ohle, Selah Saterstrom, and Ken Sparling.

Printed in the United States of America

10 9 8 7 6 5 4 3 2 1

to my family,
who I hope I've returned to
soon enough

We live where water meets land. The rain hits our bodies, cold and crowding. The smell of wet spruce surrounds us. The sound of dripping runs down fern fronds. The soil is black. Our blood is black. The sky above us is gray. When we look into the sky, we see the ocean. Down at the shore, the waves are another sky, their static bleating in our ears. This is our home. This is our family. We have Our Mother and Our Father, both teetering on the edge of something else. Our Mother a ghost. Our Father a pirate. We aren't anything yet. But among the bicycles and the arcade, there's a map, and we will follow it. We have no choice. It is tattooed on our hearts.

o

Rain curls around and drips from the eaves, gathers in the gutters, soaks into the lawn. This morning, the world remains gray, steeped in the mist of low-crowding clouds and drizzle.

Our Father hunches over. His head trembles, blood rages in his temples. His molars ache. He does his best to blink away the tremors, impaired. As blurred figures of wife and sons, we limp him to the jeep's passenger seat. The rolled-down window sets fresh wind on his face as the road changes from dirt to pavement and back again, houses stacked like jigsaw pieces along each wet street, nestled in fern and spruce.

We stood in front of him yesterday, palms sweating and knees buckling, pushing our chests out and flexing our muscles, but he was too sick and blunted to see our pirate potential. Instead, he staggered to the bedroom and keeled onto the mattress, pleading for a stilled room, for a rest from the spinning, his vision doubled and rank. Through the sway and fever, he saw only boys being boys.

All day we'd snuck looks at him lying there, coated in sweat. A half-empty glass of water on the nightstand, sunlight desperate through the clouds, curtains blowing; photographs stared down from the wall, rain stuttered on the roof, the hallway clock ticked. How meager he looked with that damp cloth on his forehead. His boots off. His cutlass on the dresser. Chest pale and sunken, hollowed, breeches pooled, puddled with his blood-red headscarf and sash, the sad feather of his tossed-aside tricorne, his hair matted, beard wild and salted.

Our Father, the pirate.

We felt feverish too, finding him so unmasked and fragile, absorbed in his land-sickness, the way the shore consumes him.

Our Mother startled us, placing her hands on our necks, rupturing our spying like a ship on the shoals. She didn't say a word, only entered the room and watched Our Father's eyelids flutter. She smiled the empty smile of a ghost, exhausted, and tipped the half-full glass of water to Our Father's lips, holding his head as he sipped and sputtered, making small, tidal sounds.

We take after him. We are pirates at heart, dreaming of rubies, of worn pistol stocks, of loaded cannons thrust portside. We wake with masts tall like Our Father's. There aren't arcades or bicycles enough to hide our longing.

Our Mother doesn't want to be left for a world of water and buried treasure, broad skies and cutlasses. Our Mother doesn't want to wave to us, her twin boys, as we sail out to sea. Our Mother doesn't want to lose us as she's lost her husband, soaked in grief, the rain washing everything away.

This morning she dressed Our Father in his buccaneer finery, adjusted the bright feather of his tricorne and straightened his waistcoat. She strapped him with the pistol's sheath, dagger in the boot's mouth, bound him with the red sash and combed his hair with her fingers, tucking at the strays. This morning she kissed him aside his silver-toothed mouth, skin furious with heat, then we loaded him into the jeep and trounced down the wet roads to the gravel beach, where his jolly boat was waiting.

Our Father rows past the tide to the ship anchored deep in the bay. The ship is a hulk of brown and weathered wood, with mountainous masts and furled sails, all in silhouette out on the water. The jolly boat tips and jostles before it is lashed to the ship's side, the crew rejoicing in their captain's return, their curses battering across the water. Already, we can barely remember how it feels to wrap our arms around his waist, press our faces into his buccaneer layers.

We stand with Our Mother on the thick pebbled shore, watching Our Father sail away again, his ship headed slowly onto the horizon, gliding over the rim of forever. Our Mother holds an arm around each of us, pulling us to her, as if the contact will keep our sadness at bay.

We pretend the best we can.

Tomorrow we'll ride our bicycles to the arcade, brown sack lunches clenched to handlebars, pockets jangling with coins, tires racing water up our spines.

Today, we stand on the thick-pebbled shore, two boys, waves combing rocks. Our Mother's hands curve around our shoulders, clouded sunlight backlighting Our Father's ship, rain trestling our necks. If Our Mother is crying, it blends with the rain.

The anchor stowed, sails raised, Our Father gains his feet, back straightening, land-sickness abating, watching us watch him, each of us only a pinpoint of darkness on a distant shore. For a moment we imagine he might raise up a hooked hand, wave a steel goodbye before becoming a blot in the decaying light. But he doesn't, and before long, he is indistinguishable among the silhouettes, the familiar black spill of boat deck and horizon and sadness expanding.

We drive home, away from the sea. The widow at the end of our street is perched like a seagull on her balcony, her mouth open to the sky, teeth like mislaid stars. The rain fills her near to drowning before a grieving daughter guides her back inside.

By evening, the streets are deep black, dark as the soil beneath these spruce-covered hills. The sky is rife with clouds, the moon attempting to glow, pitiful in its obligation.

We leave our bicycles in the driveway. We lower taunts like cannons across the dinner table, call *I love you* from the staircase as we head to bed, leave a sea of clothes on the floor. We dirty the bathroom with wet towels and fogged smears. We perform as boys who aren't dying of sadness, though Our Mother sees through it.

o

Hardly perceptible sunlight trades with the moon, a dim bulb straining through the clouds, houses huddled together in the rain. Our grit-covered shoes are scattered near the rug. Our Mother settles at the sewing machine, switching on its tiny lamp. She takes hold of a swath of fabric, gripping the material like it's all there is to hold onto, the whir of the machine filling the living room. Her hands slide amidst the textures and patterns, threading and unthreading, like a dream being born.

Our Mother, the creator.

In our room, we turn the music up beyond the point of listening, to erase the sadness. And though we try to be just boys, our lust for buccaneering is oceans deep. Everything becomes swords, the echoing blasts of single-shot weapons and cannon fire, walking the plank of our bunk bed. We make spyglasses, check for ships off the bow, climb the crow's nest of our bed posts, commanding one another. We draw maps, ink routes, all those enemy eyes on our treasure. We plunge their chests, dagger their throats, bash their skulls in with the heavy shots jettisoned from our pistols. We Jolly Roger each other, tattoo our backs and chests, illustrate our bodies, thinly muscled arms like tightly tethered ropes. We blacken some of our teeth, as if they are holes to be replaced in silver. We paint beards on our faces with markers, draw scars and bruises, mock-wounds welting.

Our Mother works the fabric, attempting to stay her own execution by way of grief, until she hears the music trembling the floor, then the thudding and thumping, her boys unleashed. She abandons the blood-red dress she's been fitting for her widow's frame.

Completely lost in our pretend buccaneer life, we don't hear Our Mother take the stairs.

She opens the bedroom door and sees us pretending to be pirates. She sees our cutlasses and maps, the marker and ink we've tattooed on each other's arms and chests and backs, the beards we've colored on our faces. She sees the makeshift planks and our room strewn as an imagined sea. It's like she's boarded our ship, scented in sweat and finger-greased hair, shirtless and ragged. Our smiles fade. We swore we'd hide it better next time. The teeth we've blackened recede behind our lips.

The water is scalding, though the greater burn comes from her silence. We strip and climb into the bathtub, straining not to see it as some low plank. We would do anything to make our piracy disappear, to forget the dreams sailing in our hearts, to make Our Mother smile again. The scrubbing helps. Washcloth in hand, she reminds us how strong she is, grinding at the marker streaks. The water splashes like a million waves. The mirror fogs, each of us brothers looking at the other with guilt and regret for what we've become again, over and over, despite ourselves.

When she finishes, our bodies are raw, red and abused, none of the pirate ink remaining. We are back to being boys, sitting in water the color of tarnished silver, no waves breaking. Our Mother towels us and we revel in the warmth, a fanned ember of love.

She hugs each of us, as if admitting the sadness she knows is looming.

Our bodies heave into hers, the steam beading, sparkling in the bathroom light.

Toweling us, hugging us, Our Mother tells how Our Father tried to be a fisherman when we were swelling in her womb, her eyes aglow with dreams of little hands. They were on the shore, where pebbles meet waves, tide wetting their ankles, the sky sodden. The rain swayed and the cliffs rose. They were holding hands, looking out to the sea with her belly so round, seagulls changing direction in the wind, the air bleak.

Our Mother says Our Father is doing the best he can.

She says *Behind his promises of fish and nets and lines and bait, there were always rubies.* Our Mother swears, when she laid her head to his chest, she could hear the clang of cutlasses, the rip of pistol fire, the blunt thud of the cannons.

We ask how he tried to be a fisherman, and she says, *He was trying to be a good father, trying to make a seamstress happy, trying to raise his children right. And because of all that, Our Father attempted to become what he wasn't. He left the shore in a boat lined with nets and poles and hooks and returned with a pouch of rubies, and not one single fish.*

We've asked Our Father this same question. He tells it differently.

In bed, our hearts still wet, Our Mother sings us a song. It's a song she's been singing since we were born, a song about the sea and bats at dusk, about a moon clinging to this township's clouds. She knows how foolish it is to sing that song, especially to boys like us, boys longing for piracy, boys mourning the constant recurrent loss of a father, but she can't help it. We love the song. It lilts and wafts, simmers like a kettle on the stove, dances into the room along with the night and the light from the hall and the warmth of the bath hanging on our skin.

Her voice helps us imagine stars, her fingers smoothing our hair.

She tucks us in, rain falling outside, and when she stands the movement creates a small wind across our faces, another reminder of sails. She leaves the door ajar, the light from the hallway cutting across the floor, stretching as it reaches to the rain-streaked window. We can feel every drop on our eyelids.

Downstairs, Our Mother returns to dressmaking. The light of her sewing machine makes a halo in the darkness. The machine hums its own song. Outside, the rain gathers.

We fall asleep, and we dream of setting sail from this township. We dream of leaving this place where Our Father is plagued by land-sickness, dream of standing next to him on a ship's prow, watching out over the water, a legacy of generations following generations. We dream of his rough hands on our backs, steadying us as the ship croons and curls, the sea misting our faces. We dream, too, of escaping before Our Mother goes transparent, before she becomes a ghost. We dream of being able to hold her one last time before we depart, our arms not slipping through but landing on flesh still composed of motherhood. We dream the wind. We dream the sails. We dream the rain on the roof is the rain we will one day leave behind on this shore, pooling beside our at last relinquished grief.

o

After a hard sleep, we take the stairs cautiously, unsure if Our Mother will still be upset. The sewing machine hummed late into the night, the light from the hallway spilling into our bedroom, a strip like a world splitting, a chasm growing between us.

Breakfast is set, glasses full, and she is there, though only like a chair at the table. The rain is weak, brittle against the windows, sunlight prodding. Our Mother doesn't say *Good morning*, doesn't say *Hello boys* or *Breakfast is on the table*. She is only sitting, watching out the window as the hallway clock pegs across the kitchen.

We take our seats, chairs shifting against the wooden floor, spooning mouthfuls. We eat and the sun continues weakly behind the clouds and rain. There is a gust of wind and the resonance of our breathing. The house creaks somewhere in its frame. Eventually, Our Mother says *Would you like more?*

We decline and take our bowls and spoons and glasses to the sink. There is a tidy way to it, gravitating toward normalcy, boys pretending to be boys and imagining Our Mother as if she isn't already ghostly, as if Our Father isn't blown out to sea again.

Relieved by the routine, we take the stairs two at a time, playfully shoving each other on the way up. We dress and stuff our pockets with coins, leaping down the steps, socked-feet trampling. Our Mother is there with brown sack lunches when we turn the bottom steps, our hands on the newel post. We're too old for Our Mother to make our lunches, but she keeps on, holding onto those younger selves, hoping in every way to still us in our innocence. We take the lunches she's made and play our best at forgetting too.

Our bicycles are where we left them in the driveway. We clamp the brown sack lunches against our handlebars and kick off down the street, into the rain, another bout of baptism.

We ride the streets in curves around seaside hills, houses stacked one next to another, a palette of blues and yellows and greens. The lawns are roughly manicured, the porches draped in empty swings and rocking chairs. Newspapers soak at the end of driveways. Telephone lines sag from one pole to the next. Leaves shine and ferns cover the ground.

Bumping our tires across the sloped gutters, we stand to pedal then coast, twin brothers beside each other, tires spitting water up our identical backs. With half-closed eyes we ride, knowing these streets better than any map, knowing where every fisherman and pirate lives, the name of every family in every house, the sons and daughters whose bicycles are leaned against the sides of their own porches, or in the weeds next to their garages.

The arcade's hide is made of worn wood and dirty windows and a handful of machines slim-glowing within. We open the filthy glass door to musty air, exhausted floorboards, and uneven walls. The machines give off a faint heat, their games strewn and blipping. Our shoes scuff. Our coins rattle. A bell chimes brokenly when we enter, alerting no one to our arrival, the place empty. The place is always empty. No one except us ever comes here, as if it is a dream only we're privy to. For a long time, we expected to see other kids here, but each day it is as empty as the day before, until we've forgotten our expectations, and the place becomes wholly ours.

The floor creaks as the door closes.

Our lunches placed on the dusty windowsill, we slide coins into the machines' vertical mouths, down their mechanical throats. The arcade squelches and hums. The machines bleat and beg more coins and, while we play, we aren't imagining the weight of a weapon, the kick of a shot, the sway of a deck at sea, the sunshine on our faces and the feathers in our tricornes. We forget the bedtime absence of Our Father, Our Mother's husbandless room, the kitchen table where one chair is perpetually sullen and empty. At the arcade, our pirate lusts briefly mute, the sadness temporarily set aside.

At home, Our Mother is dicing vegetables and brewing stock for soup. The kitchen steams and the knife hits against the cutting board. Today, she does it with her mind elsewhere, thinking only of how we are growing sad much faster than she anticipated, how our pirate longing has come on harder and harsher than she ever thought possible.

Our Mother remembers when we were toddlers, all those early *Arrghs* and *Avasts*, our voices singing buccaneer hymns, but she never thought it would consume us so quickly, so greedily. She remembers us making our fingers into the shape of pistols, firing point blank at one another's heads. She remembers us pretending to walk the plank, wobbling off surfaces, limp with surrender. She remembers how the cooing from our crib was like waves against a hull. Our Mother remembers when we first came barreling out of her, how she held us to her chest, the sheets bloodied, an ocean of gems already accumulating in our eyes, and Our Father, even then, out to sea.

At the arcade, we play every game in turn, moving from one to the next then back again, each machine different hues of the same light. Midday we eat, our chins perched on the dirty windowsill, a portal of pane rubbed clean to look to the wet street, gutters slick with cloudburst. And when the arcade's magic begins wearing off, we play marbles on the warbled floorboards, a return to basic games, a life before machine life, before the need for coins in pockets, before there was a place like this arcade to keep us from tunneling into darkness.

We keep our marbles in pouches hung around our necks. Inside, along with a small collection of marbles, is a red thread Our Mother gave us long ago. It's tied in a circle and worn with use. We use it instead of chalking an outline. On the arcade floor, no marble travels straight, no trajectory predictable. The boards are bowed and cupped, splintered and nail-breached, as unsteady as our young lives.

When the marbles have been played and re-pouched around our necks, when lunch has been eaten and the coins exhausted, we ride our bicycles home under the clouds, the rain on our faces. We ride and sing a pirate hymn, a ballast to pray Our Father back from the sea, to shore up Our Mother. We sing together in twinned boy voices, pedaling our bicycles, the rain as much a part of us as breathing.

Home again, the hallway clock ticks, the sewing machine hums, its tiny light pooled around Our Mother, dregs of daylight filtering through. We holler *Arrgh* and *Avast* as we cross the doorsill, the curses our attempt at leavening. Our Mother doesn't flinch, and we can't force the right kind of smiles onto our faces.

We put our wet shoes on the rug. We ask Our Mother if it's time for supper and she nods, fingering a line of stitches, a needle pursed in the material, intent on the waves of fabric flayed about her.

Our heads are already refilling with treasure maps and masts. We try to focus on bicycles and arcades, but every pebble on our shore is another rubied dream, every wave a wave beneath a plank. Even our words aren't safe anymore, and the rain at the window becomes spray over a hull. We are unsalvageable. We ladle soup into our bowls, eating in a quiet only disturbed by the cooling blow on each spoonful, those small winds gathered from our hearts.

o

Before his land-sickness had grown immeasurable, on one of those rare occasions when Our Father was home and upright, groping at fatherhood like a torn sail, he told us this story:

Watch the clouds at dusk. Watch through the rain and fog. You'll see bats. And those bats, during the day, they're seagulls. Those seagulls calling from telephone poles, drifting near the shore, propped on roofs or walking along the beach, they transform at night. It's impossible to see it happen, because of the rain and the dark, because of the sun turning into the moon, because your eyes are tired by then, but it happens. You've seen those seagulls in the half-moonlight of evening, right?

The rain falls on the roof in rhythm with Our Father's words.

Those seagull bodies become leathern, and their beaks turn to small mouths. Their wings grow grasping claws and their flight becomes chaotic. Their bodies blacken until they are nearly invisible in the sky, all their feathers turned to ash. The real magic though, is that these seagulls forget everything that's come before. Their memories disappear.

The rain breathes for us. Our Father's silver tooth catches the room's lamplight. His raw knuckles rest on our blankets, his boots wide and black below his breech-covered calves.

These seagulls get to erase their days of scavenging, of calling out to the fisherman bundling their lines, of the mothers making lunches or the children riding bicycles or shooting marbles or playing in the rain. They get to erase it all, every night. When the bat in them comes out, when their bodies turn black, they forget the lot of it. It's like nothing ever came before. As bats, they dart into the moonlight and forge futures without guilt or remorse, without the feeling of loss or pity or grief. They are born anew.

Our Father's hand upon us is a blessing, a rapture.

On his ship, Our Father is captain. He wears plumage in his tricorne. His body is covered in layers of headscarf and doublet and waistcoat. He wields a sashed cutlass, the blade sharp enough to cut a man's voice, his smoke-black pistol set to fire into the temple of any treachery. He calls to his inked men, their rugged tans and brooding brows, and they sail. They pull lines and run the deck, quick to everything a crew should do. Wind fills the canvas. Our Father sets a route without map or compass spindling.

Our Father tells different stories to his crew. When they are at sea, night coming on, the crew with their knees flattening in hammocks, bodies mimicking the horizon, swaying in the netted rope of their slings, Our Father talks to them until their eyes quietly droop:

One night in every millennium, the moon comes up on the horizon, on the water, resting on the ocean itself. A golden orb kissing the water, a new planet coming close enough to touch. And when the moon is there, this one night in so many thousand, a channel opens, the gold of the moon parting like curtains. That one night, when the moon meets the lip of the world, a waterway opens, accessible only to a ship whose crew believes in forever, a crew with hearts like rubies. That crew, on that ship, with a captain like me, they are beckoned in, invited to sail onto those golden shores.

His crew doesn't think of the moon as the actual moon. They think of it like an island, an archipelago in the midst of some unknown world. A sudden change in circumstances. But Our Father means the moon.

Can you picture yourself sailing into it? On the stillest waters, an island of glowing, silhouetted ranges. And if that captain were your captain, there'd be a map written on his heart, so when the jolly boats take to the shore, he'd only have to close his eyes to feel the truth in his blood, guiding the crew over moonscape and litany, into the heart of a treasure the likes of which none of them could ever have imagined.

The ship is cradled by the sea, joists moaning, latch bolts slowly scraping, the nulled wrench of knots pulling tighter.

That captain will lead them into the shadows of the island, moonlight on their backs. They'll chase through vegetation and rock, over sand and through trees, magnetized to its end, until suddenly, without warning, they'll arrive, and the treasure will burst from every pore, each one of that crew becoming legendary, each one transformed into a pirate for the ages.

The crew falls asleep dreaming of an island like the moon, of Our Father leading them onto its golden shores, into a dark heart where treasure blooms. They can feel the weight of it, his words resonating in their heads. The buccaneers sleep, cradled in their hammocks. The ship crawls under the stars, pushed by the night's breeze.

When the last mate falls asleep, Our Father returns topside. He has a small hammock in his own cabin, though he doesn't recede to it. He likes to watch the stars while everyone else dreams, likes to hear the night in the sails, likes to walk the deck quietly telling himself one more story:

On that island, through the silhouettes of trees, through the crags and the volcanic ranges, there will be a cave, and in the heart of that cave will be a woman. She isn't Our Mother, and she isn't a woman fondled up from some port. The woman there will be a wonder of fanged magic, coated in the possibilities of forever. See the glimmering light of the moon parted like drapery. See the golden shore. See the island, so absolutely opposite to a rainy township. See the woman hidden in its darkest reaches. See her teeth like cutlass points.

The ship rasps, nudging Our Father to his captain's quarters, to his cross-hatched hammock, speaking the last of it:

I will find her. I will find her and I will hold my neck wide to take what she offers. I will trade my blood for magic and immortality will course through me. I will become forever.

o

For the first few nights after Our Father leaves, Our Mother waits until we are asleep and then returns to the kitchen. She stands at the window, watching the distant waves. She looks to the water, toward the depth of the bay, hoping for the shape of a ship to break its line.

Our Mother believes one day he'll regret what he's done. Our Father will miss us. He'll see all the holes he's left gaping like tears in a sail, and he'll come back. One day, she thinks, Our Father will decide to be a father instead of a pirate, a husband instead of a captain. One day, he'll finally let his heart admit love.

Those few nights, Our Mother's hope returns like an infection, her sadness multiplying. She goes back to making dresses, the sewing machine thrumming, the fabric unspooling, her grief ripening.

We eat dinner while listening to the rain pattering against the roof, Our Mother joining us at the table with no food in front of her, only a small cup of tea and the silence of that empty chair, where Our Father should be.

The stars were shining, Our Mother says, *the night clear and cloudless.* She takes a sip of tea. We take sips of soup. The rain patters. *He looked into me, like he was staring into a star that had come too close. He saw every stitch and seam of me, everything I was and wanted to be, and we danced, and he dipped me so low I felt like I was drowning in the sky.*

And us? we ask.

Back then, you two were only future memories buried in my heart.

She takes our hands in hers.

Our Father wasn't a pirate yet. He was only a boy who'd become a young man. And even young as he was, Our Father was also my husband, and the father of the children I knew we'd have. She takes another sip, the cup gently steaming, the rain filling each silence, each pause she leaves to collect herself, to gather the story to her like dainty feathers scattered in a gust. *He loved me. He loved me beyond everything, beyond riches and power and anything else. He loved me, and we danced.*

We already know the rest. Her heart has spilled this story so many times before.

My dress was red as rubies. Our Father's beard was close to his face, with only a hint of gray. He was wearing a cuffed shirt and shined shoes and none of his teeth shone silver. He was a sight. And boys, she looks right at us, into us, *Our Father smiled a smile you wouldn't believe.*

Our Mother's feet are shiftless on the floor, her body rife with remembering. Joy swarms her face, bright behind her eyes, jewels of faith glimmering. She exhales. She closes her eyes.

We danced and danced, and, for a moment, the rain stopped. For that moonlit moment the rain backed away and the clouds parted and the stars shone. Oh, my boys, the thousand stars that hide there, behind the clouds, they are a magic few have ever truly understood.

We like to imagine the story stops there, because when Our Mother tells it, she radiates. When she tells us about the stars it's like we are there with her, watching the clouds disappear, the sky shimmering. She glows and shimmers, brightness on her cheeks and a twinkle in her eye. But when Our Mother goes on, dipping toward the inevitable ending, her smile is swallowed by sadness, and the real ghost comes to the surface.

We danced under those stars, Our Father and me, but it was actually all of us, because both of you were there already, gestating, building in my body like clouds across the moon, like a rainstorm, like an armada. I had to tell Our Father. I had to say to him, as I did when he dipped me back, You are going to be a father.

There is the story's chasm, the pit we fall into, where there's no room left to breathe.

Every time Our Father heads back to sea, we crumple a little more. Like Our Mother, we pull at the past, desperate to huddle inside of it, to shape it around us as if it can shield us from what is coming, from what happens over and again. Our Father going dizzy, his throat parched, his stomach turning. Our father heading back to the sea. And though she denies it, Our Mother's grief is as rampant as ours. Her body is ghosting. When we say *You are going see-through*, she only laughs and wipes the table clean, crumbs falling through her palm and onto the floor. She pretends not to notice. Some nights, tucking us into bed, the crown of her head disappears in the light.

I saw it first in his eyes, then his smile dropped like a stone. It filled him like blood, like a gouge in a ship's hull, awful and drowning.

Rain fingers the windows, the wind wanting in.

When I asked him about it, he said it was just the reflection of my ruby-colored dress. He blamed it on the sky opening its clouds, our eyes unaccustomed to the stars. But when I asked why I saw masts and sails in his face, why I heard the booming of cannon fire in his chest, he only said, It's my heart. He didn't understand how that gave it all away.

This part of the story, it's when the wreckage of Our Mother becomes the most obvious. Tears accumulate like rain in Our Mother's eyes, though none fall, her weeping ghostly.

We finished our dance, Our Father pretending happiness, even though it was already too late. He held his body against mine, your two heartbeats glowing in the middle, but he couldn't hide the rest. He told me he'd become a fisherman. He whispered it in my ear. He said the scales of fish would heap on his deck, that he'd bait the ocean back to this shore and we'd spend the rest of the days nestled with our child, tethered to a joyous life. This was before everything doubled, before the time came and there were two of you instead of one. And though he did try to become a fisherman, he only returned with that pouch of rubies and a thirst for the sea, the tide no match for him.

o

We know these streets. The houses, the wet parked cars. We know the leaves on each hillside, the spruce boughs, the telephone poles listing and the gutters cradling rain, the streams as if made to float toothpick boats. We know this township like we know the house up the street, the one that has sat empty for so long.

Before it emptied, the house up the street held a confused man who left each morning clutching a briefcase, pleading for work. When he came back every evening, sunlight purpling behind clouds, he was still jobless. At night, his hands were as catastrophic as hooks. At night, fishing lines pulled his chest. At night, the moon looked to him like an island.

In time, his wife began to feel like a widow. It was a tender blight that spread until her legs faded and her arms were hardly visible, her head swimming in fears of their future, what little she'd be left with.

One morning we found them hurriedly packing, panicked. They stuffed belongings into boxes, the rain relentless, as if it meant to wash this township back into their hearts. They shut their eyes and pressed on, heaping everything into a furious jumble atop the car, tying goods to the roof and mounding them in the backseat, driving away as fast as possible, stains of sorrow plaguing their bodies as they disappeared.

For months, that house up the street stood empty, cavernous and hollow, with nails on the walls where pictures had hung, sheer curtains forgotten on the windows, not enough room in the car for the rods and the hooks, that pirate future barreling after them, chasing them through the rain.

Many houses in this township sit empty just like that, hugging the foggy boundaries, awaiting the next family to settle there in tentative belonging, holding palms out to gauge the rain, listening to the breeze blowing, trying not to be hypnotized by the waves forever sounding.

Occasionally, a family will appear from out of town, windshield wipers murmuring. They drive through, browsing the for-sale signs, watching us ride our bicycles to the arcade, lunch sacks clenched to our handlebars. They sit behind wet car windows, imagining how they would raise children here, imagining their own brood bicycling up and down in the rain, making forts under spruce boughs, splendid youth beneath perpetually wet clothes. A life like a great adventure. Only then they drive farther in, and they see widows pacing the walks, their desperate throats filling with rain. They see children pretending to lop off each other's heads. They smell the glossy copper of blood. They hear the hum of sewing machines as if someone is attempting to stitch a heart back together, halos of light behind paned glass, a heaviness all around. They feel the sadness in the sky. They drive around a bend to witness a pirate lugging home his laden body, the sea like cataracts in his eyes. Without even setting foot in our township, without even opening a car door or toeing the wet street, without stepping one step into the abandoned houses, the grief begins to overtake them. They begin to feel the glint of rubies behind their own eyes, the creep of scales beneath their own skin, the itch of a salted beard they'd grow and the exhaustion of late nights when one of them would go to ghosting, widowing alongside the rain. They feel the pulse of the waves in their veins, the taste of ocean on their tongues, the smell of entrails in the air. They feel their feet sprinting across the soaked lawns and battling across the boards of a ship, prow cutting through water, beyond this township where their relationships would cut like the thinnest thread. All of this creeps into them, soaks, until the car makes a U-turn and the family speeds away, hoping they haven't accidentally contracted this township's grief, something that would grow inside them like a tumor.

So empty houses here are common.

Mourning is thick in the town's bones.

Until this morning, the house up the street had stood empty just like that for a very long time. But now, riding up to it, we see a faint light emanating behind the leftover drapes. We slow our bicycles, straining to discover who moved in overnight. A figure passes behind the gauze of the curtains. A small, beautiful girl's body. She passes then returns, radiating. We tread wide circles in the street like bats looping, tires squelching against the wet pavement. There is only the slightest breeze. The girl's figure watches us before disappearing again, taking the light with her, only a failing glow left in the street.

We circle a time or two more, holding our bicycles as steady as possible, waiting for the girl to return. Rain comes, and when she doesn't show, we stop our bicycles dead in the street, use our legs as kickstands, eager to see what will happen next. We stare and don't speak. The spruce boughs glisten. The house is still. Then, in an upper window, a hand pulls back part of the sheer drapes and there she is again, masked in a veil of the curtains, looking like a ghost.

We saw our first ghost years ago. We'd wandered far away into the forest playing pirates, pretending ourselves into the nether regions of the world, landing an anchor in a wet bay, our swords level and our pistols ready. We'd made a map loaded with markers and omens, paces counted, and we'd held our fingers to the air, rain faulting our brows. We'd gestured and grimaced as if we didn't know where the treasure was, as if we hadn't buried it ourselves that morning.

We'd been on our hands and knees, digging in the mud and the leaves and the fern fronds, soil thick and difficult, then dusk came and went, and we were working by the sporadic light of the moon through clouds, using sticks as shovels. Suddenly, a new light shone out of nowhere, a wilted warmth where no light should have been. In our make-believe world we pretended it was the lantern of a rival crew, the light drifting and hovering, sinking and rising as if held by the wind, until we knew it wasn't a rival crew but a ghost that was upon us. The light barreled forward when we stopped digging to look, moving faster than we could think to stand or run. It pushed through tree trunks and wet branches at an unbelievable speed until it passed clean through both our bodies in one tremendous burst.

That night we'd shouldered for position at the bathroom mirror, searching for strands of stark white hair or a scar on our chests. We'd found nothing, though we knew, deep in those trees, where our treasure was still buried, that we'd seen our first ghost.

Today, standing astride our bicycles, we saw our second, lighting the window of the once empty house up the street, more beautiful than anything.

o

Our Father has pressed a blade to a man's throat. Our Father has stuck a dagger up to the hilt in a man's abdomen. Our Father has snapped a man's bones and watched the victim's cheeks discolor as his blood runs out. Our Father has thrown men overboard. Our Father has made men walk the plank into coral and shark shoals. Our Father has keelhauled men. Our Father has blown men's heads up with his words and his pistol. Our Father has shot a man with a cannon at such close range that the body disintegrated into a billion unrecognizable pieces. Our Father is a tremendous pirate.

Our Father has no maps and no compass. Our Father has only what he calls *the magnetism of belief.* He feels it in his chest, this compression, like the anticipation of violence. His pulse thrums, his lungs seethe. It's as if a gaff is hooked to his sternum, drawing him forward. The crew worries, having only ever been captained by men who sail to Xs drawn on aged parchment, compasses embedded in their helms. Our Father pacifies them by telling them again the story of an island in the moon: *A path opens only one night in every thousand, when the moon rests on the water.* The crew sets about humming his myth, believing as best they can, clinging to Our Father's mythical trajectory.

These misfits and vagabonds know as well as Our Father does that if any ship doesn't sail into treasure, the recourse is simple: mutiny. Pirates have the right, the privilege, to peel a captain limb from limb if they work for no reward. Mutiny is clear and unspoken. If there is no gain, this crew will do their best to pull Our Father's heart from his chest and set it on the deck, awash in the waves.

Standing at the kitchen window, Our Mother watches the bay,

the ships moored there, those flagrant vessels, none of which are Our Father's. Our Mother hates Our Father's ship. Hates its worn hull and unadorned prow, its masts and sails, the silhouette it makes against the sky, out in the bay, through the rain. She sees the wisps of light from other lanterns, other crews readying other decks, the rain in sheets between them. Our Mother imagines paying a gaggle of boys to swim beneath a ship like Our Father's, to bore holes in its broad belly, make it list and gurgle and drown. She imagines dressing a heap of gunpowder as a manikin of love, rowing it softly to the ship's edge at dusk, imagines how the crew would welcome the faux-lover onboard, realizing the trick and the explosion only as it happened, the ship bursting into a wreckage of stars.

When Our Mother's body became swollen with the last of her pregnancy, Our Father loaded a small boat with nets and hooks and lines, bundled bait and barbs. The house was quiet then, except for the hum of the sewing machine and rain running down the shingles. But he returned without fish, hooks clean and bright, only a leather pouch tipping open into her palm, a tiny cache of rubies slipping from its threaded mouth, each gem as red as blood.

Our Mother longed for Our Father to be a fisherman. She imagined his great beard and proud chest, a small ship plundering the seas for scales and fins, nets rising full with the writhing of huddled bodies. Our Mother dreamt this every day of her pregnancy, her body expanding like the clouds above the township, until Our Father returned with only that small pouch spilling like stigmata. From then on, Our Mother had nightmares instead of dreams. She nightmared about Our Father's body lifeless on the boards, his eyes forever open. She nightmared about his chest cut wide, a black pit where his heart used to be. She nightmared about the ship gently rocking, water sweeping across the deck, Our Father gone, the weight of everything left on her shoulders.

So much time passed, so much of us growing up, until these nightmares started coming to her in the daytime too, the blood brighter in each iteration, the gashes more livid, the water churning whiter and whiter. Our Mother closes her eyes to his heartless chest. She blinks and his sails wither. She breathes and there is the empty ship, nothing left to give, everything left under her care, her transparent hands attempting to hold it all together.

When we were younger, Our Father would throw fistfuls of dirt into the air at dusk to encourage swarms of bats. He would tell that story of seagulls transforming, flooding our heads with slick wings. We didn't know he dreamt of immortality, how he longed for the tingling prospect of magic, a lust for forever in his veins.

How alike Our Mother's and Our Father's dreams.

When the crew signed on, Our Father only asked one question: *Do you want to be legendary?* Since then, they've heard him talk of an island in the moon, and they've trod cautiously, and they've awaited the treasure, rewarded only with more sailing. They have more to give, would surely have granted Our Father many more days without a landing, but then they heard him walking the deck at night, chatting loudly to himself about immortality, about the magical ways a body could live forever.

Our Father thought the crew was asleep. He spoke of blood as red as rubies, the constant repeated integer of *forever*. The crew below was awake and listening. They thought he'd lost his mind, only a madman would be loaded down with such thoughts. They had no choice. Below deck, the crew gathered daggers and pistols, taking to the topside to stab and burst and bludgeon. They mutinied.

Our Father heard the clink and loading below, heard the crew's steps. Our Mother nightmares about his death, chest opened and heart removed, but Our Father doesn't believe in that ending. Our Father believes in eternity. He smiles thinking about it, smiles even as they come up in waves from the holds, thrusting and cutting, pistols cocked and exploding.

This is not Our Father's first mutiny.

He becomes a blur, stretching and receding like a coastline. He cuts through the first burst of them. Lashes out at a throat, a chest, an arm. Pierces a stomach. Muffles a pistol shot with someone else's body. Our Father leverages his cutlass to sever legs, gouge faces, open bodies, spill guts. Even when they attack all at once, hoping to overwhelm him, he only stands amidst their mauling bodies, outing their blood in a dozen ways, and none of the crew ever comes near enough to even scratch his skin. The deck is awash in red, and not a drop of it his.

The last of them square off less eagerly, hands tense, elbows wide, daggers at the ready, no pistols left in living hands. Our Father's silver tooth glints. These last go gently, with subtle moans and exhalations, hands reaching to Our Father's heart as he walks the deck. Stars hang dim in the morning light. Our Father, a gemmed heart, a tongue of myth, and now a new crew to be gathered before he can sail off into the island of the moon, a good reminder to keep himself to himself, even in the middle of the night, even when he thinks no one else is listening. Even then, Our Father remembers, a life can be changed into something else entirely.

o

Rain pattered on the gutters, built into rivulets, and we heard the mewling of a cat. We didn't creep downstairs to look. Instead we fell back asleep, dreaming of a cat's fur rubbing softly against us.

If we had made our way downstairs, we'd have only found Our Mother standing in the kitchen, the oven on, kettles boiling atop the stove, half-filled jars surrounding her, a book splayed open on the counter.

Our Mother with that book is so different than Our Mother with a needle and thread, the delicate pinch of ghostly finger and thumb on a single page, mid-turn.

That book is a tome. Thousands of pages. Images and diagrams and text. She chews the words, swallows the sentences. The book is

Chinchorro and in it she reads of the earliest mummifications. Where they found the bodies, the state of the skin, the makeup of the adjacent landscape. She learns the techniques, the culture, the materials at play. The difference between arid incidental mummification and purposeful incisions. The black manganese, the red ochre, the mud coatings. The bandaging and the stick-binding, the organ removal. Our Mother is entranced by this idea of forever.

She reads about the use of vegetable fibers, animal fur, leaves and dirt and stones. She reads about those children, the first mummies, treasures in sackcloth at their feet, children no longer made of the same bone or flesh, filled with stones and calcified ornaments, charms to ward off the last sunlight. When Our Mother looks into the faces on those pages, it's as if she's falling into the sky all over again.

In the morning, after a sleep of cat sounds and fuzzed dreams, we come downstairs to a shroud of steam. The jars on the counter are filled with unrecognizable substances. It doesn't look like stock or jelly. Steam fingers the air, Our Mother in its cloud, apron around her middle. *Eat,* she says, pointing to where our breakfast is set. We eat, consuming as we're consumed by curiosity, trying to name whatever she was cooking late last night, whatever is trapped now under lids, glass jars thick with gutted colors. We eat as she moves swiftly from kettle to pan, sink to cupboard, tightening rings on jar mouths. There are glimpses of what looks like dirt or stones, leaves or grass. Our spoons chime. Her shoulders are tense with concentration.

Next to the jars we see the book, that tome of paper and ink. She wavers between one page and another, her fingers perched as a bird on a pole, tracing the text, studying the images with a furrowed brow. She reads and rereads. She eyes the substances. One is dark red. Another is black. Another is mud brown. Another is the tint of sand, white floating on its surface. One is marigold, flecked with granules. One is green. One is gray. Each jar looks as if it has captured something, held it there, made it conform to a new set of rules. Our Mother cups her hands around the jars, bringing them close to the book, its spine flexed, as if she is comparing. She weighs the contents, stares at the settlements within. Rain advances in a rhythm we know by heart.

We strain to see if her arms are apparent, if her legs are beneath her or if it's only vacuous space. We watch for transparency in her knuckles. She turns one lid ring and pulls the top from its sticky circumference, placing the opened jar on the table in front of us, fear on our lips and faces. Our buccaneer courage shrinks. She sets a plate of toast and a knife on the tabletop. She waits and watches, a hand on her hip, where we'd swear the texture of her apron shows clear through. The scent hits then. Raspberry jam. We knife the red, spread it, and by the time we take our first bite, her attention is back to the other jars, the steam receding.

Last night, while we slept, this happened: she slit the cat's throat, a quick deep cut beneath its chin. She held the cat's body to her own like some furious bagpipe, its claws pricking through her clothing. Small blood spatters coated her forearms, the throat held above a roasting pan. When the last of the blood ran from its veins, she rested the cat on its back, legs falling open, exasperated atop the butcher paper. She severed each leg, limbs snapped, tendons and ligaments spurned, the furred skin striving to hold together. Where the first puncture was made, its head was nearly cut from the spine, so much new, unrectified space.

She'd spent the rest of the night completing the process. She shaved the fur from each leg in a dishpan of warm water, razored sheets of flesh from rounds of muscle. She flayed the skin in long, thin rectangles that were then flattened and dried in the oven. She scoured the bones first with a stout brush then burnished them in a shallow dish. The organs were lifted to awaiting kettles, their stringy ties cut from the opened cavity, some pureed and others baked and others stewed and others whipped into cold, billowy mousse. Blood coagulated in the pan.

Later, Our Mother reassembled the bones inside the body, still syrupy with liquids and clotted with ropes of sinew. She pushed the bones back into place, adding sticks and twine to reinforce their structures, then she filled the emptiness of each leg with landscape leavings and rain and wrapped the skin back over it, dried to rectangular plots like thick fabric. She sutured the incisions. Our Mother refilled the abdomen with sackcloth pouches of pureed and baked and stewed and whipped organs, sackcloth twined and reinserted, the surroundings stuffed with vegetable matter and fur, the blood cut into jellied cubes. She closed the abdominal cavity with needle and thread, careful stitches exacted from top to bottom.

When the body was done, the limbs rebound and closed, the chest clamped, Our Mother flopped the head back on its bodily stem. The face was as it had been when the cat curled its body under the eaves of the house. The same whiskers and wet forehead as when she'd found it there, on the porch, pitiful and soaked. She stared into its face as she worked up a mudded mixture of soil and rainwater. With a basting brush, Our Mother painted earthen mud along its remounted limbs and sutured body.

In the early hours of the morning, before we began to stir, she made notes in the margins of the book, folded corners and crossed out sentences, bracketed images and drew arrows and wrote annotations for the next time. She studied and detailed everything she'd done, start to finish, then wrapped the cat in a canvas shroud and placed it in the ground, buried like a treasure in the spruce hillsides, Our Mother barely aware of the rain on her skin as she shoveled the dirt over its hasty tomb.

In the end, all that remained were the contents of those jars, which she kept to observe, to compare with the book's illustrations, to prolong for the sake of study, to see which rotted and which was preserved, searching for the key to ceasing decay, the means to actual forever.

This was the moment of Our Mother's first mummification. Upstairs, we only heard the quick and quiet sounds of a cat pleading in the rain, awaking to those jars and Our Mother changed in a way we didn't yet understand.

o

Once we'd tasted the jam, we ignored the kettles and steam and jars on the counter. The rain helped. We returned instead to thoughts of Our Father's ship sailing away, so long gone already. We dwelled on the curve of the hull and his sails against the horizon. Our Mother watched us with a new menace, her eyes cutlasses.

We took our lunches on the way out the door, kissed Our Mother on the cheek, eliciting a wry smile behind dark clouds. The door closed but she stayed at the window, in the hallway's light, watching us ride away from the house.

We pedaled hard on the wet streets, pretending we could believe in forgetting. Clouds hung about the posts and poles and alleyways. Seagulls shadowed the air. Rain distended from the eaves, from spruce boughs, from fern fronds. Rain sank into the ground. Newspapers soaked at the end of driveways. We rode toward the once empty house up the street, where that ghost of a girl had wavered, where she'd stirred the drapes, where she'd looked straight into our hearts as if she could see our futures, where she'd sewn the seed of our rupture, our rivalry, our wreckage.

Slowing on the approach, we took to circling, cutting wide paths in the street, tires slick and no cars passing, until one of us called to the draperies in a half-voice, *Avast*, and the other said *Arrgh*.

Watching those windows, we felt brave, baiting her with buccaneer words. We waited, and while we did, a cat in a muddied body hobbled across the lawn. It was the most disheveled and crooked animal we'd ever seen, spilling clumps of mud and trailing segments of something that looked like canvas. The cat seemed to be fighting its own limbs, head barely attached, bandages like a shroud, fully entombed in mud, disappearing beyond the house.

The temptation of that cat was too much to resist.

We left our bicycles in the gutter and ran to the bushes, chasing its tail through the steady rain, shroud waving behind, shedding gobs of mud. Tumbling through the backyards of those tight-packed houses, winding through spruce boughs and fern fronds and rain, the cat outran us even on its rhythmless limbs. We followed as quickly as we could, stopping only to collect wet bits of the swatches loosed from its ragged back. When we lost it finally amidst a stand of spruce, we took to backtracking, until we caught another glimpse of its disconnected body, legs as if unattached, head as if severed. Rampaging through alleyways and over hillsides, we went on.

The cat was surprisingly quick, and eventually we lost it again, not able to find its muddy footprints or tangles of shroud this time, nothing left to lead the way. So we sat in the grass and the rain, looking over the bits of shroud we'd collected, trying to decipher their meaning. They were smeared with dirt and traces of grasses, loosed fur and specks of something dry like parchment. We sat between houses, telling each other how sure we were of the space between its head and neck. We said the word *Ghost.* We said the word *Mummy.*

The rain was cold walking back, but we didn't mind. The canvas in our back pockets was a great and unexpected treasure.

Back at the once empty house up the street, where our bicycles were still resting in the gutter, there was no ghost in the window. We took a quick breath before setting off toward the arcade. We rode under ledges of leaves and branches, rain spilling, clouds dampening the landscape, our hair wet, our shoes soaked, our pockets full of mysteries to be unraveled.

o

Mutiny leaves a hole.

This, a long time ago:

The table cleared of dishes, Our Mother cradled a small cup of tea. Our Father leaned back in his chair, one elbow cocked over the back. The clock ticked in the hallway. We were in a playpen in the living room where they could see our heads bobbing.

Our Father said, *When I close my eyes, I hear something. Beneath the sound of the waves and the seagulls, beneath the bats at dusk, beneath the boys up in their room crying for sleep, beneath your feet shuffling to comfort them. Beneath that lullaby, I hear something else.*

Our Father's arms are strong, his legs taut, his heart solid, though his words are holes. When we say, *We love you,* he doesn't say anything back. Those are the failings of Our Father's language. His lips and breath and tongue won't make the shapes. What we don't know is that Our Father longs for a buccaneer to snip away his tongue, so that he'll be freed of obligation to words. Tongueless, his silence would be revered instead of hated.

What is it you hear? Our Mother asked, steam rising into the lamp-shaded night. *It's a glimmering,* Our Father said, doing his best to explain how it drew him seaward, pulling at his heart. *I'm going to build an armada,* he said. Our Mother didn't understand. He couldn't spell out the bright red that overtook him from inside. Our Mother left the table without finishing her tea. Our Father sat listening to the rain, to our murmuring from the playpen, the ticking of the hallway clock, and beneath it the whisper of rubies across the sea.

Even back then, Our Father was prone to mutinies.

Now, in this current mutiny, not one crew member is left. Waves have washed the planks clean. It was effortless in Our Father's hands. And as with all the mutinies that have come before, next is a laboring journey to the nearest port, to cobble together a new crew.

He drops anchor in Port Honte, battening the rigs and rowing the jolly boat ashore. The moon is perched like a dim star. He makes his way down the main road, a hard-packed dirt road running like a seam through the middle of this harbinger of a town, a scape mixed with desire and desperation, defeat so thick on its skin the sky seems soured. Windows are alight with candles and lanterns, the voices within rowdy and cragged, men striving for piracy and women holding up the walls.

Though Our Father doesn't walk with a peg leg or a parrot on his shoulder, everyone can see he is a captain. It isn't the plume of his tricorne or the glint of his silver tooth. It's in his posture and his gait, how his cutlass sings with blood, the weight of the pistol at his side, the look in his eyes.

He walks past the taverns and brothels to the worn siding of a ramshackle inn. He takes a table near the door, laying out his parchment. Everyone knows what he's there for, and it takes no time for a line to form, Our Father writes down the names of the men who materialize, eager to enlist. Each is tanned and inked, marked with strength and grit. Our Father asks every one of them the same question: *Do you want to be legendary?* Men line the inn floor, longing to stand at his rails. None of them need the proof of map or compass. They already know the tales of Our Father. His stature precedes him.

Our Father did try to become a fisherman. He sailed a small boat laden with nets and hooks and bait out into open water. He cast about in the sea, seeking scales. Maybe no fish ever came. Or maybe fish loaded his deck but he turned them all loose overboard. Or maybe the fish would bite and he'd only string them along, never bringing them up. Or maybe he told everyone that he was dreaming of fish, even when his heart was pulled completely otherwise. Jewels were his only catch. His pirate christening, that first palmful of bold red gems.

At home, there were two of us instead of one, and Our Father stayed gone longer and longer.

Our Mother received shares of his plunder a handful at a time, those tidy moments when he could muster the courage and strength to return. She never understood the glimmering Our Father spoke of. Her treasure is us. And when Our Father returns home those few nights in every lifetime, he is doused with land-sickness, head spinning and stomach curdling. He becomes coffin-sized, and he doesn't see the prize we are.

Remember when you said the rubies called to you? she once asked, Our Father nodding, swells behind his eyes. *The ship is loaded with them*, he dourly answered, *so full I can't come any farther into the bay, afraid I'll split the bottom. Piles as tall as me, rubies enough to buy and sink this whole township.* She didn't believe a word of it. *Then why can't you come home? You said you were building an armada. Isn't this enough?* she asked, looking out the window, where the rain was falling. She spoke to him, but he was already out to sea.

After loading up on signatures, Our Father returns down the hardened paths of Port Honte toward the dock, through this shanty village where the houses waver and weary chandeliers cling to ceilings. He's snagged a new tagalong collection of inked men who trail him, their swords jostling. A woman who is not Our Mother watches him pass, a tattered hem of dusk draped on her ankles, and when she flares a grin at Our Father, he thinks he sees the cusp of fangs hidden there, and his heart goes rabid.

o

Our Mother hates Our Father's story of seagulls becoming bats, hates the way he tells it, tucking us into bed. She loves when he's there, seldom as it is, tipping the blankets under our chins, softly walking the room, the light in the hallway illuminating what could be. But that story. She whispers, *Don't believe everything he says*, knowing his tales are infectious. When he tells stories like that, his face goes wide and gleaming. When he tells stories to us, his heart shines. On the nights of his stories, we dream of white wings turning black, of beaks becoming toothsome mouths, of pirate hearts as enormous as Our Father's.

Our Mother longs to change every ruby into a broken heart, so many that he'll finally see, that he'll trail back here to her, to us. But she can't wait. It might take Our Father a lifetime to see it. In the meantime, she'll still us, use needle and thread to keep us as children, boys who will never grow up. She'll open us up to stop the sadness from crowding our hearts, to remove the dreams of sails and masts.

The rain in this township goes radiant when she thinks of it, her heart pure as any ghost.

She stands at the counter, her mood tidal. We come downstairs, coins ringing in our pockets, ready for sack lunches, and for a moment we catch her in a loss so large there is nothing else. She is hollowing out like a ghost, birthed into nothingness. Then her body goes dense again, back to bone and muscle and skin. After that, it is a morning like any other.

We ride our bicycles to the arcade. Games to help us forget Our Father for a little while. We're afraid that one time, he won't return, afraid his love for the ocean has eclipsed his love for us. We're afraid that no matter how we burst or bloom, he'll only ever see us as boys being boys.

Behind the front door, Our Mother takes a sack from the cupboard and removes the limp bodies of a bat and a seagull. Each set of wings droops and splays as she places the dead animals on the kitchen table.

Our Mother knows a seagull and a bat are not the same, knows Our Father is only full of stories. They aren't there on the table to deny his myths. They are there for learning, another lesson in the splitting open of bodies, the cadavering of insides, the continued discovery of a new kind of mummification, a means to her sons' salvation, and to her own.

Our Mother does as she did with the cat, her hands moving deftly. There are pans and tins and jars. She has continued reading up on those first mummies, *Chinchorro*, the red and the black and the mud. That tome reveals ancient ideas with every reading, opening her to better tactics and varied angles, a tighter wielding of the weaponry, Our Mother so much more now than an admirer.

She excavates a layer at a time, until she reaches their minute bones. Those she removes, scrapes clean, chars, polishes to yellow-white, wraps and reinforces with sticks and twine. The work is meticulous and unforgiving. She loads each chest with vegetable matter and black soil, with leaves and grass, drops of rain and whorls of seaside air. She separates and manipulates and supplants. She washes the gull's feathers and smooths the bat's skin, looking into those small black eyes, gently petting each quiet head, as if cooing to a newborn, so vulnerable. Our Mother takes great care, working more methodically than ever before, matching cut for cut deeper and deeper, down to the truth. Their bodies are unique, no way to believe Our Father's story now, though she swore she knew it all along.

When she turns her attention lastly to the two exhumed hearts side by side on the tabletop, she's suddenly forgotten which is which. She was thinking of Our Father and his mythologies, those stories that waver the world around them, and now the two hearts resting there seem identical, each as if it came from the same animal. Both chests are open, repackaged and awaiting the final element, but her hands are unsure which goes where. There is no difference in pallor or structure, no distinguishable features to exploit. Then there is only Our Father's voice grinning in her head, the way in which he lovingly touches each boy's forehead with the slightest rub of his gruff pirate hand.

On instinct she lifts one and tucks it into the bat's chest, attempting all the while to convince herself that she remembers, that she knows which is which, that she's making the right choice. The heart rests there, inside, as if it belongs. She does the same with the seagull. Rain batters the roof.

Before we return from the arcade, sun giving way to dusk, Our Mother finishes the last sutures, carefully threading each chest closed, and with the bat in one hand and the seagull in the other, she stands in the wet backyard. She holds their winged bodies to the sky. She lifts until all she can see are the knuckles of her own upraised hands under sheets of gray clouds, rain streaming her cheeks. She waits until the weight of each slight animal lifts and vanishes.

Our Mother stands in the backyard, eyes closed, hands raised, and the silhouettes of bat and seagull transcend the rain, impossibly twinned, two sets of wings disappearing into the ether.

She fears for those possibly misappropriated hearts, worried she'll never again be able to decipher a seagull from a bat at dusk. She worries how it means Our Father is maybe right, how difficult it is to tell a boy from a pirate, or a man who once loved her from a man like Our Father.

At dinner, Our Mother says, *I saw the piracy in your hearts a long time ago. As unmistakable as rubies.* We try not to smile, the sentiment filling us with pride even though we know Our Mother wants none of it. What she doesn't say is how that morning, when she reached for the golden leaf of an autumn tree, her fingers slipped through.

We look through the windows to the bay, and Our Father's ship isn't there. We spoon. We sit and eat without pirate words. Another ghostly silence suspended, Our Mother enshrined in a halo of light, her skin perilously thin, the sewing machine humming, the rain coming on.

o

We know a boy named Billy. He likes to ride his bicycle to the corner store. He rests it against the siding and steals nickel candy from the store's lowest shelves. Billy always has a pocket of horehound or lemongrass or butter mints, whatever the rest of us don't want anyway.

Billy says to us all kinds of evil things. He says: *Your mom will turn into a ghost. She'll get more see-through the longer he's a pirate, at sea. She'll start to crumble, you'll see. You'll find the wall through her face, the door through her arm. You'll see nothing where her heart should be. You'll only see the window behind her, where your father's ship isn't anchored. And when your mother becomes a ghost, you'll be all alone, no one left here to love you.*

We tell Our Mother how Billy says she'll leave us, how she'll become a ghost, and though we expect her to say something about the difference between truth and lies, she only says, *Ghosts never abandon their brood.*

Billy stalks. We'll be walking through the spruce forest and Billy will join without invitation, having seen our bicycles at the tree line. He'll pick up a stick and thrash his way behind us, talking as if he's been there all along: *You two are basically abandoned. Sons of a soon-to-be ghost. Sons of a pirate who never comes home. Someday you'll find your own ghost of a girl and you'll make your own sons and you'll abandon them too. You'll take off for the water just like your dad does, leaving a wife on the shore to go ghostly. You'll leave your sons just like you've been left, and the town won't look any different then either. It'll just rain and rain and rain.*

We tell Our Mother and she takes our hands in her own. We're at the kitchen table, a kettle patiently simmering, her breathing soundless while we wait for an answer to unspool. She only says, *See?* letting us push and prod her palms and fingers, measuring the truth with our own hands. We find her skin is as solid as ours, so we smile, and she smiles back.

Billy says, *There's a ghost in all of us,* but we've stopped listening. We know he only says these things so he won't be alone. We've never seen his mother or father. We've never heard him talk about them. They must have disappeared a long time ago. We forge ahead without him, and eventually it's like Billy has disappeared too. We ask around but no one knows where he's gone. It's like when our belief expired, he expired with it.

Our Mother is drying dishes, suns of lamplight stretching across the living room. When we ask her if we should be worried about Billy disappearing, she only says, *He'll turn up sooner or later*, rain sounding on the roof, *or he won't*. We think of that muddied cat, its ill-working limbs and severed head. We think of Our Father the pirate and Our Mother the ghost. We think of the ghostly girl in the once empty house up the street. We've never felt so ripe or caustic.

o

It has been days since we trailed that muddied cat through the bushes, collecting scraps to decipher the mystery of sky between head and neck, and we are up the street again, in front of the once empty house, waiting to see that ghost of a girl brightly shining.

Standing astride our bicycles, the rain mists our faces, the streets are darkened though not yet puddling. This morning, the house is shy. There is no light. The curtains hang motionless. The lawn is wet and unkempt. There is the call of early morning birds, the occasional cars down the damp streets, a shift in the boughs. We want to see her body in the window, want to feel her beaming light. We want the burden of falling in love. As we wait the mist turns to rain. Wind rushes our arms. The rain goes sideways until we're drenched, and the house still hasn't opened its eyes. We kick off on our bicycles. If she isn't going to appear, we need the arcade to balance our angst.

We lean our bicycles against the arcade's siding and the bell croons. We smudge free a circle in the panes and set our lunch sacks on the sill. Rain bites the roof as we put coins in the machines, nuzzling their electric balm. We pat each other's shoulders through the cold of our shirts. The arcade stints our hearts as we pretend living. We make believe we are boys being boys instead of pirates with no one to apprentice, no captain to stake our claim. When our lunches are gone and our pockets are emptied, marbles returned to their pouch, we return home.

On the way, we careen toward the once empty house one more time, slowing our bicycles, the rain wetting our shirts anew. There is the silhouette of a seagull or a bat against the clouds. We ride slow enough to get a good look at each window of the house, searching for her luminescing figure. There is nothing. The dusk rushes forward, the sky blackens, and we ride home to Our Mother, one more ghost to track down.

We leave our shoes in the entryway. At the table we spoon dinner, thinking of Our Father and Our Mother and all our familiar maladies.

But tonight, we also think of the once empty house up the street, how we're sure there's a ghost of a girl inside, livid with light, and how we'll continue to seek her until she appears, continue to push with words from the street until she steps from that house, until she walks fully into our lives. We finish supper with those thoughts heavy in our heads, so dense we can't stop from saying to Our Mother, accidentally candid: *Do you know about the girl up the street, in that once empty house?* Our Mother's eyes sparkle. We blush. Like all mothers, she knows how to cave a boy's heart. The rain falls.

Once, we asked Our Mother about sex. We'd heard the word from some gaggle of girls on the playground. They'd giggled then pumped higher on the swings. We'd asked Our Mother about it that night. *What's sex?* She'd had the same sparkle behind her eyes. She'd said, *Sex?* Wind scuffed the shingles, limbed through the trees, levitated the spruce boughs in our yard. *Well*, she'd said, and the color washed from our faces as she labeled the parts, named the acts, told us what we never wanted to hear from Our Mother's mouth. She spoke until we couldn't take it anymore, until we stopped her with a pirate *Arrgh,* her smile going even wider when she'd said, *Don't ask unless you're ready to hear.*

Since then we've kept so many questions to ourselves. We haven't asked if we'll ever grow up, haven't asked if this township is all we'll ever know, haven't asked if the waves will ever bring back Our Father. We haven't asked if Our Father loves us. But tonight, when it comes to the ghost of a girl in the once empty house up the street, we can't help ourselves.

Twilight muddles through Our Mother's body. She bends to kiss our cheeks, her lips melting straight through, floating into our heads. The rain of ghostliness is closing in on her. For everything, all of it, there is hardly any time left.

There was once a boy in love with a girl, Our Mother begins, in answer, *in a township just like this. There were houses up and down the narrow streets. Spruce forests. There were stray cats in the alleyways. Some men were fishermen and some were pirates and mothers raised sons and daughters and the rain fell. Telephone poles leaned just like ours. Clouds gray, seagulls and bats in the sky. And there was this charming, rugged young boy, and he found this girl in a house up the street, where she radiated light.*

She shone and the boy swooned. He'd never known a girl who glowed, and he'd never felt what he was feeling then. He'd never been magnetized to anything so strongly before, and though he'd only seen her through the windows, he felt like his insides would explode. So he rode his bicycle to her house and knocked on the door. He stood waiting. He heard her hand on the handle then he saw her open the door and smile, and it lit the boy up too.

The only thing between them then was the door's threshold, that small plank separating one from the other, but the boy was scared. He didn't know if he was ready. He was so young, and maybe he wasn't ready to fall in love, to let those words burst from his mouth. But this boy, like so many boys, mistook lust for bravery, want for courage, and said what he shouldn't have. He exposed his heart to the world before it was ready.

This boy, he stood on the threshold of that girl's house, and he said he loved her. He said he'd never love anyone else and he'd never have any other heart but a heart for her. He swore, as the rain fell, that he'd never abandon her. And that was the day the girl truly became a ghost.

There is a difference we can't decode between truth and belief.

He said he loved her, and her heart went see-through. He said he'd never leave her, and she spent the rest of her life waiting for that truth to stop the world from falling down around her like rain.

We didn't know what to say.

Her name, Our Mother said, *is already in your hearts, and it's the same as mine.*

Mallory, we say aloud, unable to resist the name in our mouths.

o

They are a grungy lot, muddied and inked and scarred. Hair matted and clothes torn and soiled, loosely tied, cutlasses near to rusted. This new crew, they are like men uncovered from a wreckage, like corpses. But despite their creviced mouths and milky eyes, they have no shortage of want. Their hands are capable, their mouths inside frayed beards stuffed with pirate hymns. Our Father hopes this crew is the one he's been waiting for, the one to take him finally into that island of the moon, where eternity lies.

They take easily to their assignments, nails grim and knuckles corroded. They manipulate the sails and lines as automatically as water laps the sides. Our Father oversees the deck's expanse. They thrum like a machine, readying the ship for its next route.

Outside Port Honte, without map or compass, Our Father fingers the wheel. He raises his palm to the air, his chin to the sky. A rasp of clouds passes. The sun is a star come too close. Our Father closes his eyes and leans into the movement of the ship, trundling from the bay, gathering speed in the wideness of the sea. He stands, charting the surface until the pegs tilt, the smallest movement uttered from the deepest recesses of his heart, the crew bringing the sails full, curling the ship into position, eager in their new captain's silence.

We don't have any memories of Our Father mowing the lawn. Can't remember him painting the house, teaching us to swim, reading to us at night. Our Father has never hugged us so violently we can't breathe, telling us, *Someday, boys, you'll be pirates.* We only remember him gripping our hair and tilting our heads back, pretending to slit our throats before letting out a menacing laugh.

The crew's newness hardly shows as they anchor the ship offshore of a small island. They didn't even see its shores until Our Father called *Land ho*, and there it was. It feels both like they've just left and as if they've been sailing for weeks, this island unfolding strangely from a horizonless sea.

Our Father doesn't have a hooked hand, but the glint of his tooth is like a silver moon.

He stands at the head of his jolly boat, a second rowboat parallel, both gliding to the island. The water is clear, the sky one shade of blue, the sea another. Our Father's arms are deeply tanned, his face placid as the distance diminishes, as the prows slide up onto the beachhead, the sand ivory amid juts of volcanic rock and brush-covered dunes. Boots churn sand and the jolly boats are moored, this new crew eager to pilfer with their captain for the first time.

Our Father walks up the beach and they follow across the sand into the island's foliage. He leads them past outcroppings and over hills, through jungle and swamp and crags, stopping only intermittently to listen to his heart. They arrive at the center of the island sooner than any of them expect, their swords hardly greened, boots still fresh on their feet. There are no tribes to quell, no other pirates to defy, no doubt in Our Father's stride. Everything with him is compelling. He motions for the crew to stay put, and they watch him disappear into the dim jungle ahead, a figure cutting through branches and vines. The crew is left with the sun-spotted image of his body receding. They wait, shifting, listening for word or signal, for the sound of footsteps. It's moments like these that make his legend.

Our Father wasn't there when we learned to skip rocks or when we made our first treasure map. He wasn't around to see Our Mother's fingers go ghostly for the first time, or when the rain came so hard we thought the house would float away. He doesn't know how we longed to stuff Billy's bullying stories back into his mouth, or how good our buccaneer hymns are getting. Our Father wasn't there when we saw that ghost of a girl Mallory for the first time, and he wasn't there when Our Mother told us how devastating love can be, how the tide goes both ways.

When he finally returns from the jungle, it's his boots they hear first, tromping through the undergrowth. Beneath that it's the muted chime of roughhewn gold, the sounds of a chest being dragged. They see him split the foliage, a hull of leather and oak trailing his heels. He parks the chest in their midst, their eyes panting for its innards. It's decayed, held together only by a weathered shell, an ancient skin. Our Father dashes the lock with the butt of his cutlass, the metal falling to pieces, the lid lifted to reveal a mass of gems and gold shining in the sun. After a silence like a wordless prayer, Our Father picks a few gems from the lot. He places them in a leathern sack roped to his neck, which he tightens and tucks away again beneath his shirt. Then Our Father gestures with open hands and a humble nod, and the crewmen dive and horde. Each ragged, motherless pirate dedicated to him now more than ever. With so much treasure in hand, Our Father can ask them to sail into the moon, and they'll listen, and maybe they'll stay with him all the way onto its sands.

o

This morning's dawn is no different. Dense, ragged clouds. Sun begging through. A township wet with monsters. Water runs in the gutters. Water seeps into the lawns, the soil dark as tar. Birds cluster and dive, their blackened wings swooping, outlined against the sky.

We watch the waves in the bay, disappointed that Our Father's ship isn't there, rain cross-hatching the windowpane. Winds ripple the sea. The telephone poles aslant. The shore pebbled. If he did reappear, we'd bail down the stairs so fast we'd hardly be visible. We'd barrel into the garage, Our Mother at the jeep's helm and as fraught as us in the backseat, windshield wipers like our bursting hearts. She would strain to negotiate the curves where pavement turns to dirt then to the gravel shore. We'd rush, the three of us, joy plastered across our faces.

But Our Father's hasn't come, and outside is only rain and clouds and cliffs too low to suicide from.

Our Mother holds out our lunches while a kettle simmers.

When we're gone, she observes the jars and reads her tome, practices on vegetables and fruits. Our Mother is learning the cuts, the placement of the incisions, the shape of the organs and the structure of the cavities, the seams and stitches. She is beginning to understand the shrouding, how a heart can go on even beneath the canvas, even taken apart and put back together, if it is done with enough love.

Our Mother is rehearsing for the impending moment, for her boys who refuse to stop growing up.

On the playground, every time Billy opened his mouth, a ghost would fall out. Our Mother refuted his stories, each one, yet he persisted: *Everyone has a ghost in them. You'll probably marry a ghost. You're both probably half ghost already. Just wait until your mother abandons you. Imagine how alone you'll be then.*

Billy Schmilly, Our Mother said when we told her the latest, just before Billy disappeared.

The police found his bicycle at the corner store. They searched the shore where he sometimes went to throw rocks, the roads where he would ride his bicycle, the hillsides where Billy would stand in the spruce, looking over the houses shrouded in gray, saying to himself, *This township is all just one big ghost.* No one could find him. The police questioned us, Our Mother standing behind as we greeted them in the doorway. *Have you seen this boy?* they asked, and we shook our heads. *He's a friend of yours, right?* they went on, and we shook our heads. Meanwhile, no one moved his bicycle from its place against the corner store's siding, and the police went away, and the story with it, and Billy's existence too. We guessed he really didn't have any family, because no one else came looking for him. His bicycle began to rust and the tires went flat, defeated like a sunken ship.

What fascinates Our Mother about mummification is how calm the bodies look in the photographs. These earliest mummies, even a thousand years later, are as tranquil in their black and red and muddied forms as they ever were. They wear faint smiles, their eyes evenly composed. To Our Mother, these mummies are evidence that a body can be endlessly stilled, that children can be paused, held at bay from the rest of the world, captured before the sadness overwhelms them, kept in eager youth, hearts and arms forever open.

The last time Billy was alive, really alive, he'd been standing in the lawn across the street from our house. He'd ended up there chasing that same cat trailing muddy bandages. We were at the arcade. Stilled in the wet grass and rain, looking for the next glob of mud, Our Mother called Billy's name.

Billy, she said, and he'd looked to her in the doorway. *Billy?* she'd said again, and he'd crossed the wet street, sneakers treading water.

Yeah? he'd said, nearing the sidewalk in front of our house, only the porch left between them, not knowing Our Mother from any of the other widows in this township.

I'd like to talk to you about something, Our Mother said, and she'd opened the door wide, revealing the hardwood hallway, the kitchen table at the far end, the window and, through it, the sea and the tide and the cliffs.

Okay, he'd said, and walked into the house.

It seems impossible to hide anything from Our Mother. She sees the sadness in our eyes, across our faces at supper, the mournful power of it galvanizing in our bodies. She sees it branching no matter how we pretend, grief in the form of a yawing ship and a yearning for waves, crests like blood in the water.

If only Our Father would return. If only he was not a pirate. If only the sea carried him as a fisherman, his leather pouch a net of fish, the glint of his tooth a silver scale. If only his beard was wet with rain catching sunlight as he stood proudly in our yard, asking her to dance. But the fabric of her dress only billows like a sail now, like the sadness in us.

Billy, laid out on the kitchen table as rain hammers the roof, a bevy of tools at the ready.

His eyes closed, his brow lumped, unconscious, the world wet with blood.

o

Out of coins, we play marbles while the sunlight is still tangible through the clouds. But the arcade floorboards are worn, making our marbles curve and distend. We thumb the heaviest ones and they wander, running in waves, every game an ocean. Our thread circle strung on the arcade floor, we shoot and chase, marbles rolling into corners and under machines, the walls resounding with our voices as the sun descends.

Near dusk, one of us accidentally toes the whole mess of them, skidding marbles in every direction, small planets clinking against the floorboards and off the machine bases, bouncing from the walls. Amongst that sound we hear the slow patter of a few marbles falling overboard, a waterfall of slow-splashing over some unseen edge. It's coming from a corner we never play in, a spot where no marbles have ever wandered before. The marbles gravitate to a single warped board, one end raised to make a space for swallowing. As they spill into its dark crevice, we hear our boyhood slipping away.

We follow the raining of marbles to that low place in the floor and pry loose the board and the others around it. Some lift, some splinter, dampness soaked into them, molded and spored like the houses stacked in this township. Beneath them we find a rust-colored hole, an irregular tunnel of hardened clay leading into deep darkness, a bottomless mouth. The tunnel goes headlong, rugged on all sides with iron-rusted dirt and splints of wet-glazed rock. We peer into its child-sized opening.

We are intent on whatever is beyond the slick rim of its lips, but it's nearing dark, and we still have Mallory's name in our heads. *The tunnel can wait until morning,* one of us says.

The once empty house is on our way home, and we've been waiting all day to stand in front of it, to have courage and still ourselves there, bicycles captured between our legs, tires motionless, the rain falling.

We'd been saying her name the whole way. *Mallory*, the girl who appeared overnight, the girl we'd seen brightly through the veil of a parted curtain. *Mallory*, a ghost to fall in love with. *Mallory*. We thrive on its letters, running them over our teeth.

A silhouette swoons overhead, a seagull or a bat. The waves in the bay gather and soothe the sand, sculpting the shore anew. We close our eyes to imagine the spray across a ship's deck, to dream we are captains and Mallory is there, waving from the shore as we sail away, her heart radiant even at a distance.

We watch her house as we approach, the frames of the windows and the drapery resting. Rain slicks down its siding. The small porch has no welcome mat or rocking chairs, the yard is unkempt. There is no light emanating, but we have the weapon of her name. We shove off and circle, lopsided with slow speed, handlebars turning in jabs, bicycles balanced beneath our frames.

We unsheathe her name: *Mallory*.

The rush of her name makes us brave. We ride over the gutter and up onto her driveway, forearms resting on the handlebars. *Mallory*, we say louder. *Mallory*, our voices shout. The wind stirs. The rain goes hard and slant. There are no more silhouettes overhead, no cars driving down the wet streets. Spruce boughs jostle in the wind, the black soil holding so many secrets. We call to her and the distance closes until we are bellowing.

The rain subsides and we don't know how long her name has been echoing, how far the moon has risen behind the clouds. Before our throats can rupture again, a window lights. We perk up and are quiet, salivating, the letters of her name reverberating. The light grows until it is ghostly, and, in it, her shape, the unmistakable outline of a girl with pale skin and unbound hair, the light coming as if from within her. She pulls the drapery and shows her face, watches us astride our bicycles, looking straight into our hearts. She has beautiful eyes and perfect cheeks, lips to shape the world around us, in us. The curtains swing back then and she is gone, the light going with her. We stand, aghast, not sure what our next move should be, then the front door opens and she is there, radiating.

She steps onto our plane for the first time, her light ethereal, her breathing like the warmest wind on our faces, filling our sails. She burns, and it's as if we're seeing her heart through her skin. Walking in the rain, her steps are lithe and wonderful, her body pale, white dress transparent in the rain. She comes to us while her name hangs in the fabric of the air.

Hi, she says, her voice incredible and bright and daunting. We want to reach out, to put a finger to her sternum, to feel her heart beneath, to wipe the wet bangs from her forehead. We want to press our palms to her ribs, to see if our hands will cave through her skin. We want to say her name again, standing so close to us there. We want to put our lips on hers, make a new universe. We want to show her what kind of buccaneers we are. We want to take her down to the arcade's tunnel, into whatever that cave holds, to intertwine our hands there, Mallory cuffed between the darkness and us.

Hey, one of us says back, all we can muster, the rain falling.

o

Their pockets full, Our Father's new crew no longer cares about a map or compass, not if their captain is going to lead them to gems and coins where no X is marked. But Our Father needs more than their rough hands and rugged strength. He needs their hearts, so he heads back to Port Honte to uncage these men in the very place they first signed his parchment. He'll let them spend their spoils on drink and women, whatever they desire, let them spill stories of how easily he loaded them with treasure, how quickly he returned them home, all of it an exploit, a way of cementing their commitment.

At Port Honte, captain and crew walk the hard-packed ground.

Our Father shouldn't be there. He should be headed home, to the shore outside our wet township. He should be returning to his love. His anchor should be weighing the ship down in the bay. He should be there, attempting to be a husband, a father.

Instead he is at Port Honte, the moon hung in a sky full of stars, and all we know is how he left, and how the sadness returns, sharp and brutal as a pistol shot to the heart. The shape of his face swims in our heads, his image pillaged by so much time away.

And while the trip is made to lock in this crew's trust and faith, to bring their hearts to his mythologies, there is another reason Our Father is there instead of home. He is seeking something else: a woman who is not Our Mother. The one who'd leaned against the shack's wall, knee raised and ragged skirt loosely lifted, brow arched toward him as he passed. That woman in whom he'd spied the semblance of fangs, the secret of eternal life behind her lips.

Like us, he can't resist the chase.

For Our Father, though, this isn't the first time.

Long ago, at a tavern in Port Tristesse, he swore he saw winking fangs in the mouth of a barmaid, a woman with long arms and swirling hair. He ordered a drink, eyes cavernous with yearning. He ordered another. He drank and waited, until after so much eyeing across the room and lingered touches she finally unstrapped the apron from her middle, undone by Our Father's charm, and gestured to a staircase. He followed her. She unlocked a room using a key corded around her neck. Behind that door she disrobed, exposing the curves and capes of her body. *Citrazine,* she said, introducing herself. Our Father drank in her nakedness, the sheer openness of her there in front of him, until he too assumed a posture of want and took to devouring.

The room shook with their rampant rhythm, the lampshade covered in red silk, Our Father's cutlass and pistol unwound on the table. Our Mother was at home, hovering like a seagull in the mist, circling like a bat at dusk. The room spun and whirled, the sheets wrenched, wind curling through a half-open window. The moon shone, and when Citrazine began to writhe in Our Father's lap, he threw his head back, laid his neck wide as she trembled and rasped and groaned. Her whole body fumed, sweat running the length of her arms, beneath her breasts, skin flushing in patches, heart banging. Our Father's hands were latched, holding her, waiting for the inevitable, but nothing else happened. No teeth broke his skin. No fangs sank into his neck. No blood was traded for magic. Immortality did not charge through his veins. He'd been had.

From there, Port Tristesse dipped into violence.

He shook Citrazine and her eyes welled with surprise as he wretched a volley of curses down her throat. He asked where her teeth were, how she thought she could hide them. She shuddered. The curtains were limp beside the half-opened window, walls seething with Our Father's anger, with disbelief and shame. He pinned her body to the bed and pried her mouth open, and though she screamed and fought, wheeled with long limbs, Our Father easily pulled apart her jaw and unhinged it entirely, leaving it hanging loose from her face, only the tension of her skin holding it aloft. Her body slumped with pain while Our Father felt each tooth inside her mouth. There were no fangs. In rage, he wrenched her bicuspids from the gums, torturing the twin pair out with the brutal instruments of his hands, bloodied and bone slick. Her body pooled, two of her teeth palmed. Our Father left the door hanging open, the key resting against her naked, bloodied chest.

Our Father's pouch is tucked beneath layers of doublet and linen. Sometimes it's empty. Often, it's weighted with bounty. Other times, resting there near his heart, no one ever knowing, not even Our Mother, this pouch is filled with teeth. It shuffles with the subdued sound of those light bones tumbling together, the teeth of barmaids and wenches, the teeth of women who are not Our Mother, the teeth of those who turned out to be less than magical, the teeth Our Father pulled out in retribution, a penance to assuage the trickery, to mollify his wounded pride.

It is with this pouch near his heart that Our Father anchors at Port Honte, to interrogate another possible fanged mouth. This, in place of returning to land-sickness and Our Mother, instead of delivering the next palmful of rubies, instead of standing in the rain beside us, Our Father.

o

Billy is shirtless atop the kitchen table, his forehead swollen where Our Mother hammered his skull, a faint line showing the almost split skin. She used the smooth end of a meat hammer, knocking Billy flat onto the hallway floor.

The clock ticks, his breath a skinny rattle.

When Our Mother dragged Billy down the hallway, his heels trailed a rumpled staccato. Now, a mound seething above his brow, he is only the phantom of a boy, brimming with sad stories about false ghosts and the anxiety of growing up alone.

His body laid out, Billy's inhalations rasp from the shallowest recesses. The kitchen sings with the tides of their combined existence: his barely breathing and Our Mother rubbing her hands together, lips pursed, the sea draped beyond.

Billy scared us with his stories, frightened us with those monstrous tales. He made us so fearful we'd search anew for Our Mother whenever we came home, making sure she hadn't gone ghostly while we were away. *Billy*, Our Mother cooed, *if only you'd kept your big mouth shut.* Though really, she was lucky. Here was the experiment she sought in a boyish body. Here was the chance to test her mettle.

She started even-keeled, the stable of gleaming instruments set out beside her. She knew if it was done off-balance, with wrath instead of control, it would end in gore. She didn't want a bloodletting.

Our Mother can feel the hulls beneath our ribs, hear the sails in our lungs, see the vibrant red of our hearts. There is no time left. She needs a boy to experiment on, before it is too late, so that she'll be ready for us.

Houses worn and weathered, trimmed in white, stacked one on another with narrow side yards between, their rainy driveways leading out of garages. The shingles shed rain, gutters purge rivulets, everything gathering back to the sea, where the waves pounce and mewl. Porches reach out with empty swings.

Our Mother's tools: Meat hammer. Razor. Pliers and scissors. Saw. Lengths of twine. Burlap. Jars and tins, pans and kettles, towels and sheets. Needle and thread.

Rain falls on the roof.

With the first incision, Billy surges to consciousness, his brow crowding his eye socket. He sweeps at the razor, making a rough gash, blood spurting, a startled look in his eyes. Our Mother hammers him again and his eyes close halfway in forgetting, yet he won't submit. He bares his teeth, heaves. He tries to rise, forearm coated in blood, holding his hand atop the gouge, the red spitting between his fingers, skin too distended to clamp shut. Our Mother watches the confusion on his face, sees the terror in his eyes. She hits him a third time with the steely blunt of the hammer, blood skating over the surface of the kitchen, spraying up her hammering limbs.

Our Mother's book never gave any advice on this. She knows about the skin like a layer of fabric, the muscles beneath, the bones deeper still, how to clean and carve them from their tendons and ligaments, from the surrounding tissue. She knows how to repack and refill the opened cavities, how to form and shape and mold, how to cleanse the body for eternity. And she knows how to knit it back together, how to suture and thread, how to concoct the black or the red or the mud coatings. The only difference is that she isn't dealing with the dead. She is battling sadness, an infection of sorrow spreading across a live body, a boy who is lively and quick and strong.

When she'd slashed the cat's throat, the end was almost immediate, only a bit of clawing before the legs went limp. The seagull and the bat had been fast too, their faces muffled as she wrung their necks, wings held tightly to their sides.

Billy is a new kind of beast.

Half the streets in this township travel upward, curving over and around the hills like slick shadows. The slopes are covered in spruce and fern, roots pitching into the black dirt. Billy says the forests are overrun with ghosts, with the twilit figures of fathers lost at sea, of mothers faded in the midst of living. How purely that sadness is woven across his heart. He knows firsthand. He hasn't had a mother or a father for a decade.

The other half of the streets go downward, to the sea. There, the roads change from wet pavement to packed dirt to cobblestones. There, where the ocean exhales, the pebbled beach is velveteen in tide. There, the pirate ships and fishing boats anchor in the bay, fathers aboard jolly boats rowing to sea, see-through in the rain and tears. There, the apparition of bats and seagulls drift in the sky. There, everyone contemplates escape.

Our Mother is scarcely able to get one straight incision for all Billy's thrashing. With each new cut he wakes and she has to hold him down with only her ghostly weight, hammering him back to forced sleep. And even brow-hammered and cut, Billy springs back to consciousness over and again, until his head balloons, bubbled and misshapen, swelling completely over both eyes, dents and creases littering his head, until she can feel the skull caving into splinters, his blind hands groping for relief.

None of this follows through as she'd planned. Our Mother intended to knock Billy cold then open his skin, remove the muscles and sinews, drain the blood and pull out the bones. She intended to clean and brace and return each bone to a field of vegetable matter and fiber, animal fur and wet leaves, a shield against the disease of mounting sadness. She intended to sew Billy up and paint him manganese black or ochre red or muddy brown before waking him from a sleep of transformation and reanimating him into a newly contented body, set free from his grief. Our Mother intended to watch him take the first steps of the mummified, sadness no longer reigning.

Instead, she had to hammer and hammer, until Billy was grotesque. She hammered until it no longer had any effect, hammered until everything was smashed and purposeless, hammered until she knew Billy would be forever incapable of anything beyond blind compulsion. It wasn't what Our Mother wanted, so she severed Billy's head from his neck, the only way she could think to avoid his imminent, gruesome immortality.

She wouldn't be responsible for a boy lacking heart.

In this township, sadness weeps over the houses like a shroud. If the women aren't widows, they're waiting to become them. If the mothers aren't ghosts, they're only staving off the inevitable. If the sons aren't pirates, they will be soon, and then they'll sail from here, to fall in love with the hunt for buried treasure. But Our Mother believes she can cure all of this. Our Mother believes she can stop us before the terrible possibilities of growing up. Our Mother believes in mummification, where she can yield us in our boyish glimmers, hold our bodies eager and pristine in the perfect repose of youth.

Only now, with Billy headless on the kitchen table, lifeless beyond anything she intended, Our Mother's confidence is shaken, her beliefs scant, her heart throbbing in and out of existence.

o

In front of the bathroom mirror, we flex, observing our muscles, the stretch of our rib cages, the way our shoulder blades protrude like fledgling wings. We see the faint outline of previous tattoos drawn on one another, and how our hair does whatever it wants. Our reflection is a prophecy we have trouble believing in, the idea of ever growing old, of leaving Our Mother, of fulfilling our dreams of piracy.

On a ship like Our Father's, there are no mirrors. The only reflection is in the stilled water below the plank. Crewmates aren't encouraged to look inward.

With Mallory in our thoughts, we shoulder each other to make space in the mirror, roughing up our gruffest parts, finger-combing our hair, brushing our teeth and adjusting the angles of our shirtsleeves until they unveil peeks of bicep. We make faces, imagining beards blossoming on our jawlines. We stand with our hands in our pockets, posing, fingering coins and curling fists, looking for the charm behind our eyes, the oceans roiling there, sails blowing, hoping to see how buccaneer we are.

Sack lunches grabbed and coins pocketed, we ride through the rain and she meets us on her driveway, the morning light vibrating.

Hi, she says.

Hey, one of us says back.

The rain rains around us.

We want to say more but our thoughts go transparent. Last night, the first time she spoke to us, the first time she left her house to be with us there on her driveway, after a short hello we could only manage the awkward silence of three kids crushing one another with bodies too close, all eyes trending groundward. We left last night without anything except a lust for more.

This morning, when Mallory looks at us, it's as if she is looking into both of our twin hearts. Her gaze pries open the creases of our brains, where the synapses burst like cannons with tidal want. *Hey* is all we can manage at first, just like in the dusk of yesterday, and we are ashamed. Where is our courage? Where is our pirate charm? The rain soaks our clothes and hair as we sit straddling our bicycles, eyes flirting about the landscape, the wind swelling. About to be blown apart again, about to watch Mallory retreat to her house, her glow trailing, we gather and blurt: *Come with us to the arcade,* our voices weapons.

She smiles, her hair beautifully wet.

In this township, there has never been rain like the rain on Mallory's face and hair and hands and arms, on her glistening body. It's as if it's raining for the first time.

The games are good, we say, hoping she'll give us more of that beautiful smile. It isn't true. The games are nothing. Mallory toys with her hair and her fingers. We want her with us, pedaling into the sodden abyss of these streets. We want to see how strong her light glows beyond the confines of this driveway. We want to see her in the alleyways, under sagging telephone lines, in abandoned doorways and amidst the gloss of the arcade's buzzing machines. We want her to fall in love with us. We want her to see, under the battered bell of our solemn spaces, the piracy in us, how we are meant for so much more.

Mallory looks into our eyes. Wind ravages our faces. If she'd answered with any words, they'd have been carried off in the gust. One of us tucks his head down into his chest, the other closes his eyes, shielding them from the slanting rain. And when both of us look to her, moments later, she is still there, blazing in the rain and wind and the houses grimly nestled around us. We stand there, our three hearts, as the silence drifts.

We reposition, recover our breath again, and tell Mallory what we've never told anyone, not even Our Mother: *We found a cave.* Mallory looks deep into our eyes then, her face beaming with an even brighter glow. *We did,* the other of us says, encouraging, *a tunnel into the ground.* Mallory's smile widens, her light amplifying.

Show me, she says.

She steps to our bicycles and, rather than riding, walks between us, our legs like oars, rowing down the rain-slicked pavement. Two boys and a ghost of a girl, a new brightness in this gray.

Is your father a fisherman? one of us asks as we walk, the rain slim on our heads. *Is your father a pirate?* the other of us says, the township slowly passing. Her smile fades. She doesn't answer. We've never heard of any other possibilities for a father. *Then what is he?* we think but don't ask, the wind only a whisper.

Mallory has the loveliest shoulders. Her dress hangs wet nearly to her knees, revealing the paleness of her body. The rain doesn't dampen her like the rest of this world. It only makes her more beautiful. She doesn't say anything about her father.

When we reach the top of one hill, where the street wings over and down again, both of us ask if she'd like to sit on our bicycle while we coast toward the sea. Our voices are identical, so it's like the question echoes. Mallory, trapped inside thoughts of no father, is withdrawn and sullen, so we keep on as we have been, kicking our bicycles alongside her, legs rowing, sneakers scuffing the street, the sea aching over the hills.

At the arcade's grizzled door, Mallory's face remains grievous, and we regret how our mouths said anything other than *Avast* and *Arrgh*. We are trying to learn her heart, but we should have waited for the arcade and the cave to help ease her from her body.

We lean our bicycles against the arcade's siding. She looks up from the street to the grimed panes and weathered walls. We are sheepish, fearing she won't like what we've offered, scared she won't be able to love us back. In a blink, we imagine she'll be gone, running back across the side yards and the alleyways, through the veins of streets crosshatching this township, back to her once empty house.

But she doesn't disappear.

Mallory goes into the arcade with us, where the machines blink and chime, and she seems slightly uplifted by the noise. She steps to a machine and one of us drops a coin in. She pulls the joystick and giggles, her face breaking into a shatter of beauty and light. As the game careens, she abandons it and walks to the next one. We put a coin in there too. She presses a button and exhales a laugh through throat and teeth. In this way, Mallory wanders from machine to machine while we keep plunking in coins, the arcade buzzing, her not playing any of them, only delighting in the clamor, constantly birthing new rounds of tone and color.

When all the games are chattering, Mallory stands in the middle of the arcade, us flanking her as the sounds slowly drain away, retreating as one machine after another goes to *Game Over*, until at the very end the whole arcade stills, and there is only a ghostly girl and two pirate boys in the center of it all.

When the crest of the arcade's mechanical wave passes, Mallory asks about the cave, and we point to the lipped floorboards. She walks to it and watches us peel loose the boards from the cave's secret mouth. Mallory inhales the tunneled entrance. She stands at the brink of it, and we stare into the layers: the blackness of the hole, the rusted soil of its lips, the translucence of her skin, her dress still wet from the rain, her hair damp, and the floorboards leading back to us, gulping every part of this.

Shall we? she asks, looking down into the cave, and though we've never been down it before, we say *Yes*.

o

Port Honte is a collection of vagaries, a menagerie of buccaneers.

A pirate sits at a table facing a wall. His hair a tangle of red, beard raked. He leans into his ale, shoulders buried in his ears. Occasionally he wipes a strand of hair from his eyes or chews a fingernail. Mostly he looks into his mug, eyes pitted. There is nothing behind them. No waves, no unquenchable thirst. His eyes are only eyes. His muscles are bold and merciless. His face is framed in weariness. Despair and sorrow encroach on his heart.

Another pirate rests half his weight against a back wall near a dirty window. He wears a canvas hood pulled over his face, only his cheeks and jawline exposed to the tavern's low light. He raises his head and makes contact with someone across the room, a penetrating stare. He lingers there before his eyes come across Our Father. It's as if he's trying to look through him, to find the weapons packed beneath his layers, the jewels held against his skin, the gem of his insides. This is the sometimes kind of pirate surrounding Our Father, those who believe the world is out to get them, who want nothing other than survival.

There's a pirate wearing thin-rimmed spectacles on full and ruddy cheeks. A pirate binding a mange of ratty dreads into a headscarf, culling with callused hands, tying his hair into a thick mound. A pirate turning his chest toward the woman next to him, as if she's his, as if she's in love with him, as if he isn't about to slap a slew of coins on the table so she'll guide him to a back room. There is a pirate gesturing to another tucked in the darkness, a buccaneer lost in the shadows below the chandelier's withered candles. All around are sashed cutlasses and buried knives and sheathed pistols, skeleton keys and map fragments and secret mementos slung around throats and tucked in belts and hidden in hilted boots, memories and futures held by doublets.

In an arched window at the back of the tavern, a clutch of vines has grown through the pane, accumulating near a wall lamp, and three pirates beneath it are pounding each other's chests with the pointing fingers of a brewing fight. Our Father finds solace in those intruding vines, how they've moved steadily over the years to take their place along the wall, already reaching to the rafters, the other men of this tavern too busy mapping their riches to see the nature around them. Our Father sees it, though, the way the world goes on and on, even without him. He doesn't want to, but he sees it. An inkling of doubt at his buccaneer gambits.

This is the tavern at Port Honte, where he's released his crew for a night of indelicacies.

Our Father stands in the tavern's open space, removed enough to avoid hard scrutiny and the pestilence of their conversations, because he has no interest in what's being said. He's surveying, hunting for the real reason he brought the crew back to this place, the true aim for anchoring at Port Honte again instead of the bay at home, why he's staring into a gaggle of pirates and loose ladies instead of delivering the next handful of rubies to Our Mother. Our Father pans the faces of the candlelit rogues, searching for a woman with forever in her veins. He can't shake her image, how he saw her while he walked the hard-packed roads with that newly wrangled crew waddling like drunken ducks behind him. She was there, her back against a shanty siding, lips seared into him, and fangs, he desperately hopes, hidden behind them.

A pirate untucks an ivory comb from his sash and picks through his hair, fingering the grease. He combs his beard too then replaces the comb to his sash, tucked out of sight. The same pirate gargles a mouthful of drink and spits it on the floor. There is another standing at the bar, waiting for a drink. He's tall, dark stubble instead of a beard and a head shorn close to the skull, straggling veins stair-stepping along his temples. When his drink arrives, gradient and discolored, he drains the whole of it in one long swallow. All of it, all of them beneath their clothing and weapons, beneath the want for treasure and posturing, under the watchful eye of Our Father.

Two more pirates enter, one with a headscarf across his forehead, his long hair pulled behind it, silver coming in nearly as bright as Our Father's tooth. The other has a head of braided hair, pigtails cinched everywhere over his scalp, and it's only when Our Father is done taking in these newcomers that his eyes swing over the room and uncover the woman he's been looking for, appearing as if out of nowhere.

She wears a button-lined dress that curves as she walks, a rough knit sweater hung from her shoulders, a thin red tippet around her throat, its frayed ends smeared over the rise of her chest. Our Father is struck, instantly lost in her, in this woman he believes possesses the key to immortality, this woman he wants to violently unleash, trading piracy for magic. Our Father watches her cross to the bar where she whispers in the barkeep's ear, his rag spit-shining a glass. The barkeep leans as she talks to him then retreats to his former stance, talks to another buccaneer at the bar, pouring another ale for another peg leg. The woman stands a moment, making eye contact with everyone except Our Father, then exits through a door tucked in a shadowed corner.

Long ago, Our Father kissed Our Mother's neck, deep and longing, mixing his life with hers, their two hearts fusing into one. Nine months later it was twins birthed through that starry, dark canal. Between that kiss and the birth of his sons, there was only a single dance under the stars, one night in a thousand when the sky was visible, the clouds dissipating. What followed was talk of Our Father becoming a fisherman, then the bloody entry of children into the rain, and Our Father returning with treasure instead of scales.

What did she say? Our Father asks, having worked his way to the bar, the barkeep with a limp rag hung about his shoulders. His attention is barely on Our Father, paying no heed to the captain's plumage. *Hey,* Our Father bellows, his thirst for her ravenous.

Can I getcha? the barkeep says, not looking him in the eyes, not caring one bit for his feathered tricorne or his silver tooth, not worried about any leather pouch beneath Our Father's clothing.

Our Father's voice brays, *That woman, what did she say?*

The barkeep's eyes rise, and he scoffs. He spits on the rag and wipes another glass. *Wouldn't you like to know,* he says, nodding beyond Our Father to another pirate down the lacquered wood, the ale heads weeping.

Our Father, when he wants our attention, he grabs us by the shirts as if grappling for our hearts, pulling us into his beard. His breath smells of smoke and brine, seabed and pistol shot. He wrestles us into his chest and we wriggle like caught fish. Then he either speaks the words directly down our throats or turns our bodies to his and whispers the command into our ears, syllables like blade strokes.

Our Father extends the length of his brackish and brutal arm to the barkeep's shirt, tangling the chest hair beneath into his fingers and yanking him close. Through clenched teeth and a head packed with fanged dreams, he seethes into the barkeep's ear, *Either you tell me what she said or I'll split you on my ship's prow. You'll be our new decoration, blood and guts hanging in the wind.* The words hover between them and the swaying chandelier, the pirates of the room cavorting, gagging one another on tales of fist-sized gems. Our Father releases his grip and the barkeep eases back into his body. The tavern hums with the constant threat of violence. The chandelier shifts. The barkeep leans an elbow on the bar: *She said to tell you nothing. Tell you nothing unless you threatened me, unless you laid a hand on me, like you done just now, then she said I could tell you that door there, it leads to a hall filled with more doors, and she's behind the last one, way in back, a red one, at the end.*

Cheers, Our Father says to the barkeep, and with a fingertip he places a sliver of treasure on the bar, revealing it beneath his fingerprint as the clouds would uncurtain a crescent of moon.

o

Despite Our Mother's intentions to open him like the cat, like the bat and seagull, to gently flay his skin, to remove muscle and tissue from the furrows of his body, to snap the sinew, to sever the joints and remove the bones and scour them, to scrub their surfaces to a stark, broiled landscape, to return Billy's bones to Billy's cavities, splinting them with sticks and twine, packing them with animal fur and vegetable fiber, mounting them with leaves and spruce and rain and soil, to cut and pry and wrench and saw beneath the sternum to the organs warm inside, alive with the will of youth, to see the blood mostly drained, the heart stilled, the lungs paused, the body no longer assured in its ark, Billy wouldn't stand for it. This was meant to be her final study, the last lesson in refitting a body for immortality. This was supposed to give her the last tools necessary to attempt the work on her own sons. She'd intended on stitching and sewing, masking the slits and openings, making neat incisions, coating him in red or black or mud to mark Billy as a boy purged of grief, stopped before the sadness could spread, returned to the rain as a forever-boy. But he'd woken so many times.

The cat had been blood-let first, its throat cut wide, a rampant red grin added below its mouth, and she'd learned from its feline body, its skin and bones and organs. When it was done, she'd shrouded it, ragged chevrons bleeding through the fabric, and buried it beneath the arms of a wet spruce, its body painted muddy and its whiskers wet with rain. Loading the last shovelfuls atop the mound, Our Mother didn't know the cat would rise again. She was hopeful, but it seemed the cat was just another practice. Then it appeared, unearthed, tangling through the side yards and alleyways trailing segments of its battered shroud, scuttling through lawns with a head as if floating inches above its neck, limbs working against themselves. Seeing the cat, Our Mother knew she was brewing a different kind of forgiveness, knew then that everything was possible, if only she could dig her hands deeper. Then the cat peeled around a corner and there was Billy, watching its fleeting tail. Our Mother had invited him into this, and now here she was.

The fight in the boy was the problem. And if there was this much in Billy, she couldn't begin to imagine how much would be in her own boys. Billy kept waking, flailing, begging new knots onto his forehead, swelling from the flogging, until his skull was wreckage and spite.

Wresting Billy's head from his body was the only way she could find forward, the only way to quell his fitful waking. She'd placed his head beside the sink, a red puddle slowly forming beneath it, his face still facing her. And though his eyelids were drawn, his head canted because of the panicked angle she'd cut, Our Mother sensed him watching her. But she couldn't bring herself to move his head again, to face the sop and suck it had made when she'd set it there, trailing bindles of endings and blood and remnants, a soaking sound nothing like the rain. Rather than move it again, rather than even chance the drag and stick of rotating Billy's face toward the wall, Our Mother turned herself, addressing his headless body from a new direction, putting Billy's head behind her, doing her best to forget it even existed.

Temporarily spelled, Our Mother returns to his body with promise, to learn as much as she can from it. Recalling the book's pages, she breathes and steadies herself. Even headless, hammer-knocked into extinction, Billy is her skeleton key. What she will learn from him will make the process clearer, cleaner, neater, better. What she will learn will leave the heads on her sons' necks, will make their blood stronger inside their red or black or mud mummy bodies.

Our Mother sees the sadness of us expanding, creeping like vines through a shattered window, magnetized to our hearts. She knows she can't pretend it away, can't simply play at forgetting. It is already almost too late. Our Mother is perpetually ghosting, her sons becoming pirates, their masts as if anticipating the bay, rain sounding on the roof. Our Mother knows the truth of it, and she knows too what kind of magic it will take to undo this. Billy is the key. Billy will teach her how to stop this sadness, how to free her boys of grief, how to capture their youth. Billy will show her how to distill them, how to maintain them in forever.

As Our Mother works, as Billy's body comes undone, her memories weep open.

When she removes the bones of Billy's arms, she remembers holding her sons, newborns nested in the crook of her arms. It was raining, and her infant sons tilted their heads back to look into the rain. They opened their mouths, letting the rain accumulate, her sons suckling from the sky.

When she removes the bones from Billy's legs, Our Mother remembers showing her sons a pomegranate for the first time, its bulky and ominous shape on the kitchen table, their jackets dripping on hooks and the clock ticking between them, the boys drawn to the bruise red of its leathery skin. Our Mother had split it open, her fingertips stained, a smattering of loosed seeds spilling onto the tabletop. Her boys leaned in, stretching toward the red gloss. Our Mother plucked a seed from the table and placed it in each of their mouths. They crunched the seeds like tiny bones, blood red juice on their tongues. How she'd pried open the rest, releasing a torrent of red, a gush of ruin.

When Our Mother wrenches Billy's ribcage wide to remove his organs, she remembers climbing the steps toward a thud in the room, a sound too loud followed by sounds too quiet. She'd known the postures of her boys' pirating by then, the buccaneer presence so ingrained that erasure seemed impossible, yet still she sought ways to suppress it, to lessen the sadness of Our Father forever sailing away. How she opened the door that day to find one son atop the other, holding a knife to the other's neck, the blade drawing a line, and both laughing at the thinly streaming blood.

Our Mother knows the resilience of a boy's body. She knows the pull of a boy's muscles. And now, thanks to Billy, she knows how many cuts it will take, how deep she needs to press into the hollows, how fragile a boy's head is and how quickly a brow can balloon. She is learning to move swiftly, to act with purpose, to work with solid hands, and to cut with all her heart.

In this way, Billy isn't a total loss.

o

We don't want to dive straight down the cave's mouth, skyfall beneath the buzzing and machine-lit arcade, under those loosed floorboards, but Mallory is here, and she wants us to. We'd left our exploration of the tunnel for the next time we came, only we didn't know the next time we'd be flanked by Mallory, eager to see what's beyond the darkness under the arcade's floor. We didn't know she'd be standing above the tunnel, beaming, begging us into it, brightening at the prospect of caving, this ghost of a girl. We are scared. We have no rope and no plan, only the pried boards and nothing to fashion into a ladder, nothing to keep us from spiraling into the void. The cave's mouth is as long and dark as any dream we've ever had, and in our sidelong vision we see how disappointed she is at our stalling. She doesn't say a word, doesn't have to, there is the beginning of a grimace in her eyes, the coming look of impatience. Mallory had brightened at the revelation of our cave, this tunneled mouth yet to be explored, this darkness awaiting our young buccaneering, but standing here now, realizing we may not be up to the task, she has faded, and we wonder if maybe we're not ready to begin a kind of life with her in it.

Though we may have already failed in her estimation, we can't dare show Mallory how overwhelmed we are by the possibility of dropping into those stony shadows without rope or ladder, without a lantern and some form of weaponry. Instead we let our fright and shame propel us, one of us wedging his way into the cave's mouth, legs propped on the sides, back against the rim, bracing himself in a crouch between mud-packed walls and wet sneakers. Every muscle is pressured, holding him to the sides, abdomen clenched. We are losing her, this ghost of a girl who needs buccaneer boys, and it moves us on, further into the separation. From the moment she came glowing down the driveway, we'd known she was what each of us wanted, and if we couldn't tap into the mouth of this cave with triumph on our faces, we were no prize, no boys to fall in love with.

Against better judgment and sweltering fright, the one of us continues downward, fingers gnawing the walls, legs crabbing, feet inching down its soaked sides. Mud and rusted iron are all there is to scrabble against for control, a pit of darkness welling beneath. The other of us kneels over the cave's entrance, heart exploding, willing his brother to hold strong, to move slowly into the darkness. There is a world growing between us, a moment unlike any we've ever experienced. But Mallory's body regains some of its glow, even as one us is only halfway down the cave's mouth, the other standing by the tunnel's rim, barely breathing, gripping the floorboards.

Love seems impossible like this, dangling above an abyss, between the two of us.

The brother inside the cave's mouth shimmies down as far as he can, down to the cusp of the shadows, where his body is engulfed and his head threatens to dip black if he makes one more downward move. No matter how he strains his legs, reaching, there is no visible floor, no bottom to touch. If he lets go, he'll become a part of the cave's absence, lost to forever. We've brought Mallory here to show her we are buccaneers, that we have piracy in our hearts, except now, trapped between darkness and light, we are frightened. We're like little boys clinging to damp hopes. We want to make Mallory smile, to excite her with our exploits, with our willingness to spelunk instead of growing pale.

He can't, the brother atop the cave's entrance says.

I can't, the brother inside the tunnel's mouth echoes.

All right, Mallory gives in, folding her arms across her chest.

There is no pretending our way out of this.

The rain slants down the arcade roof.

The brother in the hole struggles his way back up, pawing at the rusted soil, legs pinwheeling. The boy atop the cave's mouth grapples his brother out, reaching as if for stars buried behind clouds, to keep his brother from falling away. There is a scramble, an embarrassing shuffle out of the darkness, a winnowing from the cave's entrance, then the three of us standing among the dirty light through grimed windows.

We're sorry, one of us says.

Yeah, the other adds.

It's okay, Mallory says quietly, unable to tell the truth.

When we leave, the sun isn't setting, dusk not yet eating at the horizon. Still Mallory seems about to disappear. Disappointment is draped over her like the thickest fabric. We walk our bicycles up the streets, the rain on the hillsides swirling as we imagine ghosts would.

We see the mangled and muddied cat breach an alleyway, trailing bandages sodden with soil and crescents of stain, its head nearly separated from its body, a gap winking at us between jaw and shoulders. It recedes through a side yard, and though we want to tell Mallory about the specter of it, her eyes are locked on the pavement, and we no longer have the hearts to wade through this.

So your father, he's dead? one of us asks, commandeering the silence, steering it altogether wrongly, desperate to regain the setting.

Mallory doesn't say anything.

Do you think he's a ghost? the other of us adds, desperately clinging, hopeful for some engagement, for anything. There is only the rain. We shouldn't have asked, but we hardly know what else to say. Mallory has been quiet for so long. We pull any words back into our mouths.

Sorry, one of us finally says.

Yeah, the other admits.

It's fine, she says.

We walk Mallory to her house, and there is hardly any glow in the window as she moves behind the curtains. The house has never been less radiant. Rain falls. We walk our bicycles home, so much less buccaneers than we'd been that morning, dusk finally coming on, a bat or a seagull looping above. The moon is a fragment behind shifting clouds. We've never felt such kinship with its ruptured body.

Our Mother isn't home, and we worry she's gone ghostly, only we don't have enough energy left to trace the possibilities. Instead, we gather supper and bathe, pitiful, faces downtrodden, bodies wracked with failure, afraid the mouth of the cave will always be too much for us, afraid we aren't pirates at heart. There is never a fin or a gill in our dreams, and what does a boy become if he isn't a pirate or a fisherman? There is too much rain tonight to know. Since birth, we've dreamt of jeweled seas and masts and sails, though right now Mallory is our brightest worry. If we aren't boys to fall in love with, we are nothing.

We rest, lost in our beds, watching the glow of the moon behind a skein of clouds. The night drifts. We drift. Then: far into the night, restless under the sheets, each of us awakes to the same possibility, the same potential for remedy. The rain gushes. Rhythmic waves shed across the shingles, slivered moon buried beyond, and this sudden spark of redemption, an idea we cradle.

Quietly, we creep into the garage. The jeep is there, parked where it has been since the last time we went to shore. Hung on the wall are Our Father's rarely used tools, outlined on a pegboard. We find two pairs of pliers, knowing Mallory will settle for nothing less than pure buccaneering. We imagine Our Father's silver tooth catching sunlight, its glint visible even as he sails away. Pliers in hand, we lift each pair to the other's mouth and clamp down on a tooth.

Inside one another's eyes we see a ship sailing, a captain on deck, a crew lashing and jibbing, the rigs tucked and tied, prow slinging through the sea. The waves crash, the water goes red. Suddenly, there is a tooth in each of our palms, gleaming, and it isn't until Our Mother opens the garage door that we realize we're laughing, the blood running from our mouths.

o

Our Father walks past the pirates slogging drinks, their tattooed biceps and hairy knuckles, the women hugging their own waists, conglomerates of ill-gotten treasure smelted onto their bodies. The barkeep's voice fades into the ale, the tavern distending behind as he walks into its dim corner, the door closing behind him, sounds hushing. The corridor is long and narrow, Our Father's shoulders touch the sides as he walks, tricorne in hand. He walks determinedly down the corridor, doors appearing on either side, keeping his hands on his hat, feather brushing the walls. He passes door after door, his footsteps falling into a rhythm, the length of the corridor exceeding what seems possible, some trick of the architecture. When Our Father reaches the end, where the barkeep instructed, he finds a slim door flush with red, a blood-colored entry.

Our Father has faced so many mutinies, all of them whole-hearted, and all of them ending with him alone, raising the sails, heading to the nearest port to cull a new crew to his weathered deck. Every mutiny has been instigated somehow by Our Father's belief in immortality, his lust for forever, the want for a legacy beyond the body. All the blades and pistols have stemmed from some thread of this revelation, not the island in the moon but Our Father's search for vampires, for blood to exchange with his own, a key to forever. One mutiny came when he told a crewman in confidence, a mate Our Father confused for a friend. Another time it was because he'd left his crew to their own ends in the taverns and shanties of a port while he chased down a fanged possibility, never thinking they'd hear of his exploits and carry that knowledge back to the ship. Another time it was because he'd said it as plainly as calling *All hands on deck*, hoping he'd finally found a crew to wield myths like truths, hoping the conviction of his heart would empower theirs. This last time, he'd been caught speaking to himself on deck, presuming the crew asleep below.

As he walks the length of the corridor, the pouch of rubies and teeth thuds against his chest, whanging below the small hollow where, if a thumb is pressed hard enough, it will burst the airway, final sighs grimly burbling out.

The door at the end of this corridor is the color of a mutiny.

Our Father should be returning to us, should be delivering his latest reaping to Our Mother's hands, and his excuse is the way the shore spins, the way he goes parched and pale, the way his skin turns sallow and his vision blurs, his arms incapable of even undoing the sash at his waist. Yet here, on this or any other port, he is able to stand, feeling bright as the sun, sturdy as a sail. Land-sickness doesn't seem to reach him here, where he's searching for everlasting life, where everything is hidden, far away from home. Land-sickness is only another story he tells.

When we came tunneling out of Our Mother, he was there, at home, rain pattering the roof. Our Mother was at the clinic, nurses shaking the water from umbrellas, robed in white beneath blots of wet. They checked her vitals and she waited. Then the rain came harder and she pushed and we were birthed along with the blood and carnage of one life giving way to another. She wept in joy. This is how we were born, one then the other, Our Mother's body exhaling the placenta before they stitched her back together, leaving her to dream about what all of this would become.

At the same time, Our Father was in the house, listening to the rain, looking out the window, wishing he was on his ship, all the other fathers already out to sea. He didn't want to leave us or Our Mother, didn't want to be elsewhere while we grew up, but he knew he couldn't be the kind of father we deserved. He knew his cutlass was a religion, his pistol an absolution, his lust for rubies an affair he couldn't shed. He knew he'd only be a pretend father, terrible and sickening. If he was a pirate, Our Father wouldn't be there to taint our hearts. If he sailed into the distance, his sons would get to imagine their father, remember him however they saw fit, piece him together, make him stronger and clearer and better than he ever could have been on his own.

When Our Mother called from the clinic with the news of twin boys, the phone just rang and rang, Our Father back at his jolly boat, rowing to sea, a crew prepping the deck as their captain bloomed from the shore.

Eventually Our Mother took us home, placed us on the sheets and cradled herself to sleep. She hadn't expected Our Father to be there. She hadn't been surprised when he'd stayed there in the doorway as she left for the clinic, her belly round as the moon, sons ready to fire like pistol shots. He'd kissed her when she left, but she'd seen the waves in his eyes, knew he wouldn't be there when she returned, no matter what his heart wanted. Rubies were the first excuse, the talk of glimmering. Land-sickness would be the second. She'd only phoned because the empty ringing was better than not knowing. She needed to know for sure. He claimed to breathe easier at sea, stand taller, feel stronger. On the water, he said he felt invincible. In this township, he sags like wet paper.

When Our Father reaches the red door at the end of the narrow corridor, it opens without his hand on the knob, a wafer of candlelight inside like a waning moon. He steps across the threshold and there she is, on the bed, fingers tangled in lovely locks, body splayed and sprawled, legs kinked in the shape of willingness, thighs open. In her sheer nightgown, this woman looks ghostly, ribbons in tides at her hips. Our Father takes in every horizon of her body, stares into the paleness, her lips covering any reality of fangs.

At Port Honte, it is not raining. The stars shine, a breeze fingering the curtains, every object between them poised in some state of inclination. Our Father closes the door, disappearing into the moment, while Our Mother returns a newly muddied shovel to the garage and finds her boys pulling teeth from their own heads.

o

Each of us stands with a pair of pliers in one hand and a bloody tooth in the other, laughing, red streaming from our mouths. The jeep is crusted dirty with dried flecks of mud from the last family trek to the shore, beneath the cliffs too low to suicide from, where we'd dropped him off again, Our Father sailing away into a sonless world. The mud on the jeep is a tattoo of his departure, the pegboard showing the empty black outlines of the pliers and of a shovel too, the one in Our Mother's hands as she opens the garage door. We smile, nothing else to do, each with a tooth missing, the black gaps resonant, the rain forever falling.

We were very little when Our Father's silver tooth appeared. We weren't talking or walking, only babbling in a mimic of waves, only toddling perpetually off planks. It was so long ago, Our Father still pretended to fish, packing gear and lines, netting and bait buckets. It wasn't a charade but a plea, a desperate clinging to what could never be.

Back then, Our Mother would watch his jolly boat go, scattered with billows of nets. Coils of lines. Pails of chum. He would row to the ship anchored in the bay, a crew then like now, the same strain of muscled and inked men. Our Mother would watch him leave, his smile bone white as he rowed. She would say *I love you* and he would grin. She would say *Have at them* and his face would broaden. She was never fooled after that first palmful of rubies. It was only pretend. He would return days or weeks later, his back to her as he rowed ashore, skiff emptied of coils and pails and nets, Our Father's beautiful stroke of oars, Our Mother's hands falling through one another, the sun catching on the glint of Our Father's silver tooth for the first time then, winking at her like an uncovered star.

It had taken all day to finish Billy. She'd worked so late into the afternoon she'd grown afraid she'd be discovered, her boys back from the arcade while Billy was strewn in pieces around the kitchen. Quickly, Our Mother cleaned the counters, hid the tools, and sacked up the smithereens of him under makeshift shrouds, canvas bandages for his hurried burial far across this township. She'd left just before dusk with the heavy sack of him, blending into the twilight of spruce and rain, shoveling in the darkness.

With the slivered moon resting on her back, Our Mother punched Billy down in the soil on the hillsides beneath ferns, near the escaping highway, beside empty lots where houses were supposed to arrive but never did. She buried pieces of him in the alleyways between wet streets, near the depths of our own backyard, and in the pitch black beneath a neighbor's lawn. She intended to stop his reanimation, burying Billy in a hundred pieces in a hundred places. Unlike the cat, Billy wouldn't be able to simply heft his head back onto his shoulders to muddle back through these streets. Our Mother didn't want to turn a corner and find him there, wet and muddied and awful, betraying the mire she'd made, showing the world how she'd wrecked him to save her own sons.

The cat had been nearly headless, its neck almost shorn from its whiskered face. She'd flayed its body open and sutured it shut, wrapped it in muddy paint and burial shrouds. She'd entombed it in the soil of the spruce hillsides, yet it had risen again, trailing bandages. Its head seemed to float, its limbs hiccupping, its body a wreckage. She'd buried it in a quiet plot but it had taken to the streets anyway, parading its shabbily mummified body through the rain. But the cat was a marker of success, the way she knew she was making magic. Billy was otherwise. So she'd cut him into a hundred pieces, wrapping and dividing every part from the next, every bit buried in a puzzlement throughout the township, buried at different depths and under different landscapes. In this way, Our Mother was sure he'd never rise again, would never haunt her with the evidence of her treachery. And he'd never haunt her sons again either. Billy would never tell another ghost story.

But Billy was right: everyone dies, and before that some become pirates and some fishermen and some widows and some ghosts, only she didn't want her sons thinking about that. She didn't want them to have those nightmares on top of Our Father sailing away, on top of her impending ghostliness, the arcade their only consolation. Our Mother knew the sadness was in her boys from the start, in the rain they'd swallowed as infants in her arms. Our Mother didn't need Billy hastening the rot, unearthing what she was constantly trying to bury.

Rubbing her shoulders and forearms, the knots re-doubling, she was glad to have severed Billy so completely, already thinking to the next, which body would provide her with a chance to ply her new skills with better results. One last instance and she'd be ready to mummify her own brood. Sore from the hacking and sawing and cutting of Billy's limbs, from shoveling him beneath stones and mud and dirt, Our Mother almost smiled thinking how, even in death, Billy's resolve had been unexpected. Her muscles ached, but another lifetime was swelling near her fingertips. Then she found us standing in the garage, blood running from our mouths.

Over the years, Our Mother had marked our height on the bedroom doorframe. She'd witnessed the words multiplying on our lips, the perception of our sight expanding. It wasn't a surprise when she found the oceans behind our eyes or heard the waves in our hearts. She'd known that treasure maps filled our dreams. We never said the word *apprenticeship* out loud, but Our Mother could see it when we pedaled our bicycles up the wet pavement, heard it in our pocketed coins, felt it in the curses we slew quietly at one another over the kitchen table, future cannons budding. It was no shock.

As newborns, even our babble had been tidal. As toddlers, every object in our hands became a pistol. As boys, our bicycles turned to ships, our bodies to masts, the rain to spray against the rails. We tried to be boys. But the posters we hung on our walls were meaningless, any music prone to becoming pirate hymns. The *Avast* in our mouths refused to be hung. We spilled our longing and sadness like blood, accidentally, and this time, it strung across the garage floor, our pulled teeth only another slick, bone-rendered reminder of how quickly we were becoming what Our Mother feared most.

Since her fingering of those pages, the tome worn and weighted, she'd known what was coming. She'd scoured each illustration and photograph. Memorized every cut and bone and organ and layer of tissue, every stitch and bandage and smearing of homemade ink, all in preparation for this, to make red or black or mud mummies, to keep her boys as boys forever, children who will never leave her side, sons who won't swell with any new sadness, who won't need to become pirates, who won't make their mother a ghost. Sons to be sons forever.

We stop laughing, stunned to find her revealed by the slow upending of the garage door, in the middle of the night, a muddy shovel in her hand and the blood at our lips beginning to dry.

Our Mother has no other choice. It is time.

One of us wipes the blood from his mouth while the other spits red. One of us closes his fist around the pried tooth while the other rests his quietly in a half-opened palm, held out for her to see. One of us looks Our Mother straight in the eye while the other stares into the jeep's flecked tattoos. One of us swallows back every noise while the other tempts his mouth toward the shape of buccaneer curses. Even we too are changing, becoming something separate.

o

We spend the slim remainder of the night in our beds, listening to Our Mother move about the kitchen. When she found us in the garage, pliers in hand and teeth pulled, we thought she might leave our heads there beside the muddy jeep, but she didn't lop our faces from our bodies, didn't saw at our soft throats, didn't slit us ear to ear. She only looked at us with a heavy heart, with a disappointment in how we'd mutinied against our bodies. She stood there, quietly agape, then walked past us as a ship divides a wave, placing the shovel she was carrying into its outline on the pegboard and leaving us alone again.

Our Mother is becoming ghostly. We've watched the veil fall over her body for as long as she's watched us looming into piracy. Some nights she is translucent and some nights we walk the plank amid imagined pistol shots. Some mornings she is see-through and some mornings we wake with masts beneath our sheets. We watch the lamplight stream through her skin and she hears us bellowing pirate curses above the ticking of the hallway clock. Our futures are coming for us. In this township, among the buildings boarded up and the arcade and the hillsides covered in spruce, among the drizzled streets and the painted houses tucked together, among the curtained windows of hollow rooms and the land soaked black, is our inescapable living.

Our mouths throb as the sun rises behind clouds, the pits in our gums bleating. We tongue them, astonished at our own resolve. And yet, all the while, we fear Our Mother's impending wrath. But we can't wait to share our new lunatic faces with Mallory, to show her how buccaneer we've become. We picture her standing in the driveway, our bicycles keeled, rain falling. We picture her arms crossed over her ghostly body, a look of disillusionment carried over from the arcade. Then we'll smile—we'll smile the widest smiles, and the bloody gums will mark our determination, the black gaps will make her understand our brutality. We picture the idea of piracy breaking over her like roiling waves, and how she'll glow, astounded to witness who we truly are becoming.

Breakfast is on the table, but Our Mother is missing. She was gone last night when we came home. She was gone while we made our own supper and took our baths. And she was gone when we tried to sleep and instead snuck to the garage to mangle our smiles. Now she's gone this morning, and we are sure her wrath is only biding its time.

We slog through breakfast, gums niggled by pain, thinking of Our Mother missing, her absence different than ghosting. We can still see her in the straightened chairs and the clean counters, in the neatened rugs and the carefully placed breakfast settings. We can still see her in the perfect tilt of the curtains against the wet windows, in the way the house exudes purpose and being. She isn't gone forever, we know that much at least. If she was, the house would be keening, littered and dusty and sad. She isn't a ghost yet. There is still time before it happens, time to make our lives count, time to go before Our Mother does, before we are left in an empty house beside the sea.

Our lives are moving so fast.

Comforted in the knowledge that Our Mother hasn't gone forever, that she is only missing for the moment, we turn our thoughts to Mallory, our hearts pounding, the impending awe of our buccaneer show-and-tell bursting inside each of us.

Breakfast finished, we dash out of the house. The front door closes behind us and rain lands on our cheeks. We raise our bicycles from their resting place against the siding and ride up the street, pedaling our gap-toothed smiles through the wind. Mallory's house is dark in the distance and it remains dark as we come closer, no glow within, no light brightening as we ride over the curb. It is a sorry sight, when this house doesn't burn with Mallory's insistence, and we stand astride our bicycles, in her driveway, calling her name, our faces lowered to hide the surprise of these new mouths. Still, there is no light.

The longer it takes the more we start to worry that our failure at the arcade was too much for her. Maybe she'd only given us that one chance, a single instance to see us as we were, and we'd failed. Maybe Mallory was only here for a breath, a day, and we'd betrayed our innocence, our weakness, and she'd disappeared. Maybe Mallory isn't the kind of girl who stays to suss out possibilities. Maybe Mallory is a girl built on facts and rhythm, on absolutes instead of chance. We want her to take a chance. We want one more moment. We want to show her the spaces in our mouths. We want Mallory to see that despite our our bumbling hesitation at the cave's mouth, we can be the kind of boys she could fall in love with.

We stare hard into her windows, through the curtains, searching for any glimpse of her beautiful silhouette. There is no movement, no sign, and we can do nothing but waver in the rain and continue calling.

Unable to wait any longer, we go to the front door. We knock faint at first then heavily, not worried anymore about the surprise of our teeth. The door handle doesn't give under our hands. We hear no floorboards creaking, no footsteps coming down the stairs, no hallway clock to mark the intervals between living and dying, to chalk the seconds until we see her heart radiating again. There is nothing.

We make our way around the house, putting our faces up to each window, squinting through the layers of rain and glass and drapery. She can't escape us, not that easily. We look in one window then the next, rounding the house, finding only our own pale reflections and the dusky shadows of empty insides, the spill of vacant rooms.

Coming around the corner, near the kitchen's bay window, the mudded cat darts over the lawn, head appearing to balloon upward. It's a ghost dodging into the bushes, and we want to careen after it, to pin it to the ground, to explore its devastations, but we can't stop our search for Mallory. We long to feel the cat's trailing bandages, to see if our hands sink through its muddy body, but we let it disappear. Instead, we take positions at the bay window, our hands blinding the peripheries, finding inside only too much open space, unadorned and vacuous, stark walls and empty countertops. From this window, we can also see the bottom of the stairs, and there, the faintest light threads down, like the creep of an angel appearing.

We want to break the window and climb in, to shoulder the door or demolish the walls. We would destroy this house to get to Mallory. We would climb the sky. We would burrow under the world and rise up where she stands, all to trace her ankles with our fingers, to hold our hands against her calves, to show her who we really are. We want to feel her lightness on our skin. We want the truth of everything. We want to know what she holds inside her light, every curve and detail, every fact and facet from birth until this very second. We want to know what happened to her father, if he disappeared entirely or if she watched as his body boarded a vessel. We want to know if there was a ship he went down with or a day when he still loved her. We want to know where her mother is, if she ever had one. We want to know how she was birthed, and where. We want to know what she's seen outside this township, outside these spruce hillsides, beyond this rain-soaked living. We want to carry her heart in ours. We want to know what it would sound like to hear her lips making the shape of our names. We want to know what it would feel like to have her hands wrapped around our bodies. We want to know every actuality buried in her ghostly heart.

But we don't shoulder open the door or demolish the walls. Instead, we backpedal into the lawn and down the side yard, to the front window, this house wearing the rain like a weathered dress. We step onto the driveway again and look up to see the curtain slightly peeled. She hasn't abandoned us, not yet. There is hope. She is maybe only playing it cautiously, careful for whatever is coming, the potential we have to either sink or sail in this tenuous life. She is there, in that window, which means we still have the chance to show her our real hearts. Watching us, her gaze of disappointment greater than we could have imagined, we dig deep and smile, showing the gaps we've made in our mouths, the bloody stump of gums where silver teeth will one day reside, and Mallory blazes. In that moment, she knows exactly how pirate we can be, and her skin bursts.

o

The red door closes behind Our Father, the threshold crossed to this woman set before him on a bed, her angles unashamed and the luster of her skin inviting, infectious. She says his name and Our Father doesn't understand how she knows it. His name is well-buried, secreted beneath the routes and ciphers of the most complex maps. Even though his exploits are easily known, whispered about from port to port, Our Father is usually referred to as *Captain*, and nothing more, yet here is this woman, her body open wide, using his other name, the real one, unfurling it like a sail. Wind blows through the partially open window. The curtains sway. There is a lamp lit by the bedside, dancing shadows and silhouettes.

Her voice slides to him. She says his name again, and he is too astounded to react. She begs him forward. Our Father hears the stars in her throat, the gem of her drone, the jeweled lilt running in waves around the fangs he almost believes he can see. She is a treasure. Our Father takes a dazed step forward. She says his name again and *Yes* is the only memory his lips can recall. She rises from the bed, her hair following, kneeling near Our Father's sash, her gown draped and woven sheer around her body, her skin exposed as candlelight.

Our Father stands looking into her eyes, her lips closed against any true glimpse of teeth.

So many women end up in front of Our Father, their bodies open to his magnetism, to his charm. He never forces his way into their arms, never rails for their hearts. Women spread before him like sand on a shore. This woman, though, she is more curved and luscious than most he's encountered. Her skin is radiant, as if lit from within, a glow bursting from her heart, and when she opens her mouth, down on her knees in front of him, her eyes coo. She holds his attention on her tongue, the wet there glittering like stars.

Our Father believes this woman could be the one. This woman could pray against the altar of his neck and murmur magic into him, plunge forever beneath his skin, replace the whole of him with endlessness. Our Father plays his fingers through her hair, sees the flush of her cheek and the flutter of her lashes. He exhales and his breath is sails and wind, hers like vines grown through cracked panes. Our Father grips her hair and wrenches her head backward, stretching her throat, pulling a grinning gasp, his fingers tracing the veins of her neck, her breath spinning out endlessly.

Our Father has never shown us how to make pirate maps, or how a compass works. Our Father has never looked us in the eye and told us how to be men. Our Father has never kissed our wounds. Our Father has never explained the importance of tides. Our Father has never wrangled a ship for us to apprentice, and he has never shared with us what it really feels like to fall in love. Our Father has never parted the clouds or calmed the ocean or roped the moon for us, to bring it closer to where we are, to let us step aboard. Our Father has never caught the sun in his hands for us to see, or to burn away our ghosts. Our Father has only done what little he can.

He drops the gown from her shoulders to marvel, to caress a woman who is not Our Mother, whose name he'll never know, who called his own in a throated quiet, and who still hasn't let a smile be coaxed enough to part her lips. She has opened every other port though, wide and wet and ready. Their limbs tangle and his clothes go strewn about the room, pirate gear and tricorne buried under doublet and breeches, wind threading through the opened window.

Our Father kisses her toes, kisses her feet, kisses her ankles and her shins and her knees. Our Father kisses her thighs. Our Father kisses her hips and her abdomen and her ribs and her breasts. Our Father kisses her fingertips and her palms, her wrists and her forearms and her elbows. Our Father kisses her shoulders and her neck. Our Father kisses her cheeks and her eyelids and her lips, every swatch and swath as she writhes on the bedscape, their moans heaped. He is seeking immortality, and the lust for it overtakes him, candlelight breathing for them both.

With forever, Our Father could be whatever he wants, no matter anything else.

Before he reaps the treasure warm between her legs, their nakedness under the curtains fluttering, before he spills, this woman raises up and presses Our Father out to arm's length. She says his name again, calls it like a gust diminishing fertile soil. He clings to the bed, on the edge and holding there, grasping, gasping, a place Our Father isn't put very often.

She covers herself with the dingy sheets, curdled as spoilt milk. Our Father goes up on an elbow, trying to hide his unease. She waits as if recalling an entire past life, a catch in her voice like a hook in a fish's mouth, realizing what he's really come for, beyond these bodies. She stalls, her nakedness retreating, his motives suddenly suspect. When Our Father looks into her eyes, there is a ship with masts ready to break, enormous sails razed, water pouring over the sides, lashings severed and the lumber splitting. He would say anything to right the vessel, to get back to where they just were, him about to explode and her about to dance immortal fangs into his skin, but her face is leagues away. She rises and approaches the window, brushing the curtains aside, trailing worry and sheets behind. Our Father waits as patiently as he can, hoping she is only soaking in this momentous occasion and not, as is more likely, balancing his worthiness against what she has to offer.

She puts her hand on the sill, wind sighing into the room, the candlelight shimmering, their shadows exhausted. Our Father cranes his neck to watch her standing in the faint moonlight, evening colors fragmented on her skin, her mouth closed. Fragile and vulnerable and naked he rests there atop the bed, a baby grown to unfamiliar and weak heights.

In the past, these trysts have always ended the same way: At the moment of climax Our Father opens his neck to the woman's mouth, to her jaw and exposed teeth, and he waits for the sink of fangs, for the moment of immortality. When it doesn't happen, Our Father becomes incensed. He snaps the woman's neck or thumbs her eyes into her skull or cinches the breath from her throat as quickly as he can. He pulls the teeth from her mouth, bloody proof that she housed no fangs or magic, dropping them into that leather pouch beneath his pirate layers, and walks back to the dock, to his ship and crew.

This time, Our Father is left waiting, naked in the breeze of an open window. Momentarily dizzy, wanting to leap at this woman who is not Our Mother, to wrack her about the room, to pry her mouth and confirm her fangs, to find the evidence of magic in her blood. But every bit of Our Father's momentum is sapped. He can't leap or wreck. He stands slowly, methodically, attempting strength and virility while his body feels instantly aged, taking his breeches from the floor and gradually stepping into them, another small plague of headspin making the moment last too long. And when he looks up again, she is gone. Where she'd been at the window is only night color and the noise of taverns, her figure vanished into the roads bordered by dirty hovels and tiresome pirates, drunken men and abandoned women stumbling into each other's beds or out to sea.

Our Father stands in that breeze, in that port, in that room behind a red door at the end of a narrow corridor, sure he's finally found what he's been looking for. Why else would she run? Why else would she shake herself from the moment of impact? She has what he is looking for, what he must have, and now, he only has to draw her teeth to his skin.

o

When we were younger, we'd make cards for Our Mother. We'd construct them in our bedroom with scissors and glue and markers, carefully cutting and folding and writing and drawing, inking messages from our hearts, words of love, a map of our desire to make her proud or to forgive us our trespasses. We'd write *Your heart is wide* or *We love Our Mother* or *No one rivals you.*

When we'd descend the stairs to deliver them, Our Mother was sometimes seated in the tiny light of her sewing machine, her hands ghostly as she shifted to see us, the sun straggling through the clouds. She would be sewing a dress to wear on Our Father's next return to shore, a dress to make him love her again, to dance beneath another sky of parted clouds, bright bulbs strung across the lawn, her hopes poured into the fabric like rain cascading off the eaves. We'd appear, card in hand, our mouths bulging with a message of love, using the least pirate voices we could, and she'd beam.

Our Mother is stronger than this township. She will never become a widow yawning at the rainy sky. Our Mother will embrace her ghost. She is not afraid to haunt. Our Mother tackles loneliness with needle and thread.

But this morning, when we go with card in hand to deliver Our Mother from the piracy of our tooth-pulling, it is different. We've grown, that much is clear, but also, she has changed. She's seated in the tiny circle of light at her sewing machine, though she isn't sewing. The machine isn't humming and her hands aren't threading fabric, her foot isn't pressing with the rhythm of the rain. She is silent, one hand held over her heart, her eyes closed, solemn and sullen. We call her name, first a whisper then bigger, scared she's gone invisible inside. Her name in our mouth brings her back. She turns to us, gently taking the card, just like we used to make. *At least my heart hasn't given up yet*, she says.

At some point, Our Mother stopped making dresses. We have been so beset with dreams of Mallory and our own piratical longings that we've missed the change, how her sewing machine rarely hums anymore, the halo of light no longer spread about her in the dusky wash of the hallway clock. We see her seated there sometimes, though it's without purpose. It's become an illusion, a tableau of normalcy, a truth none of us can believe in. And she is missing more and more mornings now too, and many nights when we go to bed. Meanwhile we can't stop dreaming of planks and sails and cutlasses and pistols, of ghostly love, can't stop lusting after treasure, no longer have as much naivety to protect us against our piracy.

Instead of sewing, most often we find Our Mother reading *Chinchorro*, exercising its words over and again, its accounts of the oldest mummies, the first of which was a child, preserved for seven thousand years. Our Mother consumes the photographs, ingests the descriptions. How that child's body was excavated, tissue and muscles hefted out, skin splayed. How that child's bones were removed and washed and baptismally charred, how the blood was let, how the organs were cradled and rubbed and rinsed and returned to the cavity in stunning rearrangement. How that child's insides were lined with vegetable matter and fur, the leavings of the land, and then the child was coated in ink, washed in a thick paint of black or red or mud. How Our Mother swoons at this new world, reads it through and again, nights on nights while we slumber, the rain on the roof. The book tells how they made the bandages, how they wrapped the bodies, how they sutured and stitched and pressed the puzzled pieces into forever. She sees in the child's face the calm and stillness of immortality, a body living on and on without ever growing up, without ever abandoning its family, without any new sadness ever creeping in.

This morning she is bookless, and not sewing, seated with our card in her hands, saying *At least my heart hasn't given up yet.* We tangle in her meaning. This card we've made came with regret, in apology, a pirate ship drawn on the front just like Our Father's, waves lapping its sides, wind almost visible in the sails. Ghosts of tears immediately set in her eyes, rain whispering on the shingles as she reads. Tears fall and there is no hiding them, no holding back, no way to pretend otherwise.

On the inside we've written, *We are sorry for the piracy of our hearts.*

That night, when Our Mother goes back to *Chinchorro*, using our card as a bookmark, she stares into the photograph of that one particular child, the oldest example of mummification, the thousands and thousands of years heaped on its body, and she imagines how smooth its face would feel against her palm. She dreams of traveling to where this child resides, to look directly into its ceaseless face. Our Mother imagines herself holding it like a newborn, the airiness of its concave stomach and the ease of its pallid cheeks, the velvet of its inked skin. She imagines placing her hand on its chest, warm to the touch, and she imagines how she would be able to feel the still-beating heart within, a child made for forever.

o

When we were very young, we remember Our Father in the open arms of a kitchen chair, listening to the rain on the roof. We remember trying to see him as a buccaneer, not yet understanding what piracy meant, imagining him with an eye patch or a hooked hand or rum on his breath, with a parrot on his shoulder or a peg leg limping down shanty roads. We remember trying to picture Our Father commanding a crew on a ship's deck, cutlass sashed and pistol sheathed, bats looping erratically above our heads. Our Father, in our eyes, unafraid of everything. We remember him humming pirate shanties, hymns that were both lullaby and prayer, all of this when we were very young, when we still believed he would apprentice us, ask us one day to pillage and plunder beside him, take us on as crewmates then captains, our chests swelling with pride.

Those days, Our Mother would call us to the table and we'd burn down the stairs, jousting with one another, our feet thunderous on the steps, the thudding resonant throughout the house. She'd have a kettle burbling on the stove, a wooden spoon resting between the burners, her apron atop a dress she'd recently crafted. Like us, she'd already waited so long for Our Father to return, even when he was there with us, even when we were very young and he was on land, even then.

She'd wipe her hands on her apron and tell us to sit, that he'd be in any minute, and we wouldn't have to ask where he was. We could hear the chink of his shovel in the black dirt of the yard, where he was digging a hole as deep and long as himself.

Back then, in our backyard, Our Father would dig and re-dig holes, laboring, his shoulders slick with sweat and rain, hair matted beneath a headscarf, beard beaded with wet. The shovel was a heartbeat, pulsing in the rain. We would listen to it, like a landscape all its own, hearing it as the sun wrapped in clouds and the bats, dipped black, came in with the night. We wondered if he was digging his own grave, if he'd been sick for years and we just didn't know. As if he'd only been at sea not to pirate or pretend fish but seeking some undiscovered remedy, a restoration for what was ailing him. He did look brighter and fuller whenever he returned from the water, more alive after a bout of ocean. His skin would seem thicker, his muscles stronger, his words sharper. And sometimes, in those long-ago days, when he'd return from a short trip seeming rejuvenated and refreshed, he almost looked like he could love us. But even back then, the longer he stayed in our house, the more colorless he became, the paler his skin and the duller his words. He'd spend that time digging and re-digging, burying and re-burying, so much weight on his thin shoulders.

We tried to keep count, secretly penning marks that quickly outgrew our wall and, by then, we hoped if he was making his own grave, he would stay forever dissatisfied, never ready to lie inside its length. We didn't want him buried in our lawn like some ill treasure rotting, so we stopped counting, stopped ticking off the possibilities, turning instead to admire his strength, one pit after another. We loved him then more than anything else.

We remember Our Mother wringing her hands, and we'd lose sight of her fingers. She was threatening translucency, worrying herself into ghostliness, and we wondered if it was maybe not his grave, but hers, Our Father setting aside all the stones he'd unburied because he knew her disappearing body would need to be weighed down, to stop Our Mother from floating upward to be with the moon and the clouds and the stars, to hover with the rain and the bats and the seagulls.

We remember wondering too that, if it wasn't either of theirs, maybe it was ours. Maybe Our Father was planning to bury us head to toe in a single plot in the rainy backyard. We knew we weren't the pirate boys he wanted, otherwise why was he perpetually sailing away? Every time he looked at us or asked us a question we couldn't answer about the sea, he seemed sadder, embarrassed by the pitiful swing of our pretend swords, the weak firing of our pretend pistols. We remember preparing for a life under dirt then, imagining what it would be like to breathe soil, to be skinned in mud, our arms and legs trapped under the heaviness of lawn and disappointment.

Later, we thought maybe these weren't graves at all. Maye they were guesses. Maybe Our Father had buried some vast treasure in the spruce-bordered dark of our yard and because of his land-sickness, he was having trouble recalling the exact placement. Maybe he'd lost the map or had forgotten how to decipher it, and these holes were his attempts to locate that stake he'd set aside for us. Maybe a ripe treasure was waiting for us there, somewhere underground, and he only had to stay on his feet long enough to find it, to start us on our own buccaneering.

We'd wait those nights at the dinner table while the soup simmered, until finally Our Mother would turn from the window and tell us, *Go on and eat.* We listened to the slink and cut of his shovel, those grave sounds through the rain, everything in our lives equally elusive.

Dishing our bowls full, we knew Our Mother and Our Father were on the rim of something steep. We sat back at the table and ate, spoons mimicking his rhythm, clinking against our dishes as he carried on, Our Mother watching him while we ate, occasionally wiping tears from her eyes. We couldn't see his face through the window and the weather, but in this township, it is hard to tell the difference between rain and belief.

We would finish our dinner and wash our bowls and go to bed without Our Mother's say-so, brushing our teeth and putting water to our faces, scrubbing them as she would have, her thoughts wrapped in the rain trestling Our Father's back.

In bed, we would listen for his digging, the sound never abating, never slowing. We would listen to the slide of the shovel's head into the ground, the chink and clunk where rocks and roots gathered, the scuttling as he lifted dirt up and out, a pile of stones and soil building beside another grave-sized plot welting in the rain, looming larger with each bodily motion.

When we were very young, we still believed Our Father would see us for what we truly were, what we were meant to be.

Finally, late into the night, we heard the shoveling stop, and the universe went quiet. We listened, straining to hear Our Father entering the house, removing his boots by the back door and spooning up soup from the kettle, talking to Our Mother in quiet tones. The silence was so profound and our bodies so tense we jumped when the bedroom door opened, Our Father backlit in the doorway. His boots were still on, a smeared mud trail on the threshold of our room. We didn't pretend to be asleep. *Why do you dig in the yard?* one of us said, and Our Father's eyes drifted like an unmoored ship. *Sometimes, a man just needs to find his footing again, and if it isn't under him, he digs to find it.* The rain went on. *Did you find it?* the other of us asked. *No,* Our Father said, *not yet,* softly closing the door on us.

Under the spruce trees, their boughs softly sighing in the wind and rain, the seams of Our Father's digging have all healed over. No one can tell where they were, except us. We can still spot the places where he used to unbury and rebury his fatherhood, his husbandhood, his longing, his anchoring to the land beneath our feet. We can still see the marks he left in the yard, the ones that showed his fear of being tethered to the three of us.

o

The first time we'd taken her to the arcade, Mallory walked beside us on our bicycles. Even before the embarrassment at the mouth of the cave, she was a hard sell. Maybe she could sense the fear in our chests, the weight of sadness in our hearts. But when Mallory saw our newly gapped smiles in the rain, she beamed and agreed to join us again at the arcade. She is no doubt still waiting to see how we negotiate the tunnel mouth, but she's willing enough to hop on the back of one of our bicycles. She can't ride on both of our bicycles, and her choice brings a flash of jealousy, but then there is the air whistling through the holes in our grins as we ride, and our competition ebbs, even with her ghostly forearms wrap around the waist of one of us.

This could be the forever we've been waiting for, and we won't let it split us.

Round a bend and down a hill, water tracking up our backs, the rain is more like a mist today. We feel so complete with Mallory there. The spruce trees dripping, cascading from their branches, coating everything in a sheen. We pass the corner store where Billy used to thieve nickel candy, pass the clinic where we were born, mapping Mallory through this township as we ride, hollering to her about this and that, pointing out whatever she might not know, light surrounding her like the emblazoned possibility of love. We raise our arms toward the ocean, to the waves, listening to the sea in its tidal cadence, Mallory aglow. The rain is like the spray over the bow of a ship, rubies in our eyes and coins in our pockets and a love ripening, everything we've ever wanted.

Mallory's smile remains as we arrive at the arcade, leaning our bicycles on the sidewalk. *ARCADE* is embossed above the pitted window, decades of residue diminishing its light. One of us opens the door and the bell chimes, Mallory giggles, the lights flicker, and our hearts rush forward. We wend through the field of machines, the colors fluorescing from their mechanical bodies, one of us dropping a quarter in a slot, a habit too strong to ignore, a reflex even in passing. The machine blinks to life, the triumphant noise of beginning as we continue toward the tunnel-mouth with Mallory between us, guarded by our strengthened pirate hearts. We tongue the gummy holes where our teeth are missing, the slightly raised floorboards pried and lifted to reveal the iron-colored dark of the cave's entrance, our bravery bright as the remaining teeth in our smiles.

The first time we were here with her, Mallory almost stopped believing in us, and we didn't trust ourselves in that moment either. No plan, no rope, no gumption. But now, with holes in our mouths and the exposed cave under our feet, we have the courage of a thousand pirates. We don't need ropes or ladders. We don't need a plan. We only need our arms, thin and sinewy like Our Father's. We only need Mallory by our side and we'll spelunk this cave as far down as she wants, past the threshold of any reason, piracy smeared on our skin.

Mallory's face burns as one of us leans over the hole and spits down into it, listening for the soft landing below. A machine calls from the arcade. The coins in our pockets shift. Mallory's breathing is so close between us. Our cheeks blush. The rain on the roof has picked up. A wind stirs. We don't hear the spit land, though right now we don't care if the cave is endless. We'd drop down its throat ceaselessly if that is what it takes to get Mallory on our side, to make her love us, to keep her radiance there beside us forever.

One of us brothers belays the other, hand in hand, helping him into the mouth of the cave. Once he is a body-length down, he puts his palms on the opposing walls, back braced against the tunnel's side, two feet beneath, worming his way, grinning while his brother and Mallory sit topside, watching him disappear smugly into the darkness. There is no hesitation. He goes down as steadily as the moon behind clouds. He climbs down until he is only a shadow in another shadow, machines humming in the background, the rain on the roof and Mallory's breathing, our hearts in a tangle. He descends until there are no shadows anymore, only the darkness itself and the scuffling sound of shoes and hands on the tunneled wall, wind atop the arcade's electronic pulse.

When he reaches the bottom, he calls up to us from the black: *Land ho*. The depth makes his voice resound. It is impossible to tell how far down he is. The rain drops in sheets outside. *Dark*, he says from below, *like, dark dark. Pitch black*.

The other of us thinks about that phrase, how dark pitch is, tar black, then that same one of us up there on the rim calls *Girl ahoy*, scooting Mallory to the lip of the moment, wasting no time keeping her body between ours.

The brother on the topside of the cave's mouth holds Mallory's hand and the touch sends a warmth radiating through his body like an electrical current, the spark of a dawning fire. Her hand isn't ghostly, though he can feel the inherent transparency of it, just as he can feel the blood beating there, those quick pulses of energy within her, shifting and running, pummeling the shores of her beautiful organs, the wide sea of red she contains. *Thank you*, she says, looking into the ocean of one brother's eyes as he helps her down the first inches of the tunnel. Her voice shakes him, a touch of something surreal. Love. She places her feet on the cave's rounded sides and, with his help, moves slowly down the tunnel's length, her feet slick on the walls. The topside brother doesn't know what else to say. He watches Mallory creep into the dark, his mouth an anchor as the brother below braces to receive her.

Though neither can see the other brother in the darkness, in the thick of the blind tunnel, the arms of the brother at the bottom are stretched as high as they can reach, waiting for his turn to hold her, to touch her, to feel that electricity ripple across his skin. *She's in your hands now*, the topside brother calls, finding his voice again as he reluctantly relinquishes his grip on Mallory's hand, their fingers un-twinning, their hearts as if threatening to do the same. *Aye*, he hears from his brother below, her body disappearing in a final tide, the darkness enveloping her. With his empty hands, the topside brother remains at the cave's mouth, stomach down on the floorboards, head dipped toward the darkness, listening to Mallory's descent, feeling for the first time what it is truly like to be alone, to be without a brother, to have love fall out of his grasp, to tumble into the unknown.

For a long moment, it is just him and the arcade's machines and the rain.

He listens for his brother to call out something more, or Mallory to land, or the world to shift in a way that means he can fit too, alongside his brother below and that ghost of a girl who is there with him, down in the silence. Nothing happens. There is no word, no sound, unless the rain on the roof is telling him something, unless the wind is actually sighing the reasons for all of this and he just hasn't been listening. He listens. He listens harder. Still nothing.

Finally he can't wait any longer. Without a word from them down in the depths, he enters the tunnel on his own, his palms and back and feet working quickly down its depth, calling, *Look out below*, before the darkness swallows him. He is not as swift as his brother, not quite as strong either, or as self-assured, so his feet slip and his hands slag and before he knows it, he has slid precariously and without grace down the length of the rutted, ore-stained tunnel, landing hard on the ground, his entire body encased in black, the only sound that of his breathing in the slim cave.

His brother and Mallory are not there.

He trails his hands along the wet walls, ducking into its low ceiling, searching for any candle width of light to lead his way. All is black on black. He stops to listen and hears only his own breathing. It's as if he's shrouded. He nearly calls to them. But if he calls, it shows fear, embarrassment, trepidation. If he calls to them, to Mallory and his brother somewhere here in this cave, it'll mean he can't stand on his own, without his twin by his side, without Mallory's light. They couldn't have gone far he thinks, so he waits, stills himself until his breathing calms, until his heart eases back into itself. Tiny step after tiny step he edges forward, so dark he can't see his hands groping down the cave's narrow pathway, barely raising his feet, worried about a drop-off or some other unexpected malignancy rising up.

Then a faint twist of breathing and the scuff of a shoe. A rustle of clothing. A pinpoint of light emitting, the guidance of Mallory's heart.

He rushes toward it.

He assumes the three of them will link together, run as a band of adventurers playing through this cave, arm in arm with Mallory between them, each twin equally in love. Instead he sees the unmistakable melding of their faces, the resonant slick of lips meeting, neither's hands on the other's body but their faces leaned in and their mouths touching. At a distance, he watches the kiss ignite Mallory's skin, every bit of her shining, the cave abuzz with their energy. In the burning light, he watches Mallory raise her hands to embrace his brother's cheeks, to hold his face to hers, the kiss elongating, the severing of their twinship emphasized. He watches them, his brother and Mallory, their eyes closed, their lips coupled, unaware of him there, unaware he is bearing witness to any of this, unaware that the end has begun.

He steadies himself against the wall, vision so blurred he loses his brother in front of him. He wants to faint, never having felt this before, not knowing this sensation of solitude, this tightness in his chest, the way his blood feels unbalanced, sloshing like water on the deck, uneven and loose. For a moment, it's as if his heart doesn't exist at all.

Here, Mallory says, when their lips finally part and she sees the other brother stumbling toward them, lurching as if he's ready to collapse, not sure what has happened to him, not understanding how her kiss on his brother's lips is so much like a dagger to the heart.

She reaches out to him as her light whispers down, a candle sputtering.

His heart is dark as the walls, Mallory's glow dampened, his brother encompassed in shadows, his skin made nearly black.

This is the first real mutiny either has ever known, and there is no answer for it.

The cave winds long and dark into the distance, so much left to explore, but for today, this one mutiny is enough.

Back down the confines of the tunnel, the three of them move silently and without touching, the walls cold and wet, their footsteps quick. The cave's entrance waits for them like the rain, the meat of their brotherhood quietly cleaved, heaped and bloodied.

The three of them clamor out of the tunnel mouth and return Mallory to her house, the only sound between them the bicycle tires and the rain. When they are back at their own home, nestled amongst the neighborhood of others, they eat supper at the table in the kitchen, breathless and sullen, knowing this is the last day of them, *we* no longer an apt word to describe what is coming.

o

Our Father, doublet and breech re-suited to his body, tricorne on his head and pistol in his hand, rumbles through the rooms of this port, searching for this woman who is not Our Mother, the one who escaped him just before revealing her fangs, the woman who vanished into the wind.

In one room he finds a couple coupling in a corner. They startle like mice under disrupted hay. In another he finds a young girl being dressed in white by an ancient man, scraggly beard and cataract eyes, his hands in all the reaches of her body, her face draped in fear. In one room he finds a woman stroking a man's hair as he weeps. In another he finds a pair of girls with a buccaneer between, a mountain of want scenting the air, the window closed and the heat accumulated. In one room he finds cards strewn about a table and two men pointing pistols, panting, neither turning an eye toward the door when it opens, both too occupied to deal any sidelong glances. In another he finds an empty table near the window, set with a steaming bowl.

Room after room Our Father takes in scenes of debauchery and treason, the want and its dregs. Some doors are unlocked, others he pries open, the locks nothing more than rusted bolts or latches too tired to believe in themselves. And when a lock refuses, he kicks the door in, boot smashing wood, hinges breaking from their frame. In this way, Our Father tends to every room in the narrow corridor, desperate to find her, this woman who holds forever in her heart.

As the sun rises, Our Father's crew reassembles on deck. Some were back in the early hours and others arrived nearer morning. Most had come to inside the guts of Porte Honte, heaving up their evening of distractions and pulling on their breeches, tying their sashes as they rose from the brothel floors like drunken phoenixes. Now, on the ship, they are all bustling, readying for a captain who hasn't shown. Last they saw he'd disappeared at the cusp of twilight, slinking into the back room of a tavern, and last they'd heard in the rumors abounding on these shanty streets, the room was empty when the barman went to reset the rotten sheets. Every other door had been opened or booted in, but not one person would bear witness. *The wind done it* they said. They'd seen the look on Our Father's face. They knew Our Father's heart wasn't like their own.

Our Father is still miles deep in port, exhausting the last rooms of the last shanties and shacks. But he finds nothing. There is no sign of the woman, not a slip or a whisper. He has never felt so close to a life without end. He could almost taste it on his tongue as their bodies coiled, was ready and waiting for immortality, could feel it racing in his heart, his blood spinning with its impending magic. But she is gone.

The last place Our Father checks is a humble shack with a single dirty window far out on the shoreline, holding its own on the distant reaches of the island, where the path gives out and the sea rumbles. He opens the door without knocking, without even looking into its thin, greased window.

The room is sparse and quiet, a small bed on one side and a chair set at a table, a candle stunted halfway, sunlight mixing through the open doorway. He's ready to leave, to call it a bust and head back to man his crew, when a scrap of light catches on the table, a fragment glinting like a cryptogram. Our Father moves slowly to the table, touching his fingertip to the glint: a finite hair of slivered ruby. He lifts it like a drop of blood. He gazes into it, seeing there another world, one where he lives forever, one where he lives long enough to right all his wrongs. A life so massive and undaunted that he can become everything he ever wanted. Inside that red glow he imagines how his blood would be exchanged and another man revealed. In that sliver he finds the sea, and all the boats upon it, himself forever sailing. He sees the unlimited and weightless expanse of a life like that, there in its deep red recesses, magic to wash away the guilt and regret and self-loathing, time enough for it all, to raise a family and plunder the seas, to sail the world and be in love.

Our Father puts the fragment on his tongue and swallows, the act both an answer and a prayer. The gem of it courses through his veins, recommitting him to the search, to the hope of fangs, to finding a life without death. It recommits him to the journey too, to the golden promises of the moon, to setting foot on its radiant shores, where he can finally become whatever he wants, over and again, for as long as it takes.

Fishermen have hands less gnarled and backs less bent than pirates, shoulders proud with sun char. Their scars are lovelier too. And most importantly, fishermen return, shrugging off their voyages like seawater. They are a greater species of men than pirates, though Our Father will forever say that he had no choice. He drew from his heart, and he came back with a bright red future.

What happened when Our Father first went to sea is a story no one believes, the versions so fantastic none can unbury the truth. He told us the fish jumped off every line. He told us the mouths came free from the hooks at every last moment. He told us the fish found holes in his net faster than he could repair them, never allowing him to touch a single one of their silvered scales. *Rubies can't swim away*, Our Father would say. Or he'd tell us, *I went out in that little boat, and I called to the fish, and they came aboard, one after another. I didn't even use a rod or reel. I didn't use nets. I only called and they came, floundering onto the deck. But when I set to gut them, when I put my finger in their mouths and wrenched, meaning to rip out their innards, their insides were covered in bright clusters of gems.* Or he would say, *The rod was a cutlass, the reel a pistol. My heart pulls to treasure. My belief is a compass. That's all there's ever been.*

Outside the empty shack, a slivered gem ingested, Our Father stands on the far shore of Port Honte, the last vestige of humanity for hundreds of miles, the place where this woman has escaped his confirmation of fangs, the reality of a vampiress. He plants his feet in the yellow strands of grass lining the pebble walk, the sea crashing as it does, calling to him. He closes his eyes and listens to his heart.

New visions stack in his head: a ghostly ship with no crew, an island of crags, a crew halved as they sail into forever. Another mutiny, bodies left to the deep while the ship runs aground, broken on shoals. He sees himself rowing toward a golden shore, beams bursting from the sand, and a march to the island's dark inside, through a jungle, the light diminishing with each step until the foliage is only shadows. He sees himself scrambling over a mountain of rock there at the center of the darkness, finding a deep cave pocked with the dimmest red. There, he sees everything he's ever wanted, a better version of the world, a pitch-colored cave like a womb giving birth to ruby-red immortality.

On the last dirt road of this port, where a woman who is not Our Mother has disappeared, he listens to his heart, and it tells him to seek these answers on the water, to follow these visions. At sea, his heart tells him, the darkness of the moon will turn golden, and he'll find exactly what he's been seeking, exactly what he needs, exactly what his heart wants. He only has to find the cave of the moon, holding forever in its mouth.

Until then, Our Father says out loud to no one, a wind stirring, walking slowly back past the brothels and taverns and shanties, returning to the bay where his ship is anchored, where the crew is poised to sail, where another story is set to unfurl.

o

Sadness is a disease.

In this township, women are abandoned, their partners becoming fishermen or pirates, lost to the sea. The ocean collects their drowned bones, ships perpetually leaving. The widows trample the walks, soaking in the rain, unable to purge the memories. They moan from the houses jigsawed together on these wet streets, opening their mouths wide enough to drown, their children wrapping them in blankets and walking them back inside quiet homes to sit by a fireside, to dry off and try to forget that there was ever another life to be lived, a life with someone who never came back, someone who was lost chasing down the ends of the earth, someone sailing away with a loose heart.

The women like Our Mother, those mothers and wives who are not yet widowed, they watch themselves becoming ghosts. It happens first in their fingers and toes, in their ankles and wrists, noticeable only to those who still love them. For the rest of the world, the transparency seems only a momentary lapse, as if the body has mistaken its purpose, going accidentally see-through. But if their fishermen or pirates are lost at sea, if their love leaves this township forever, if their children become mired in sadness, they turn ghostly. It creeps upward from the feet, inward from the palms, overtaking the forearms and the legs, spiraling toward the chest, rampant, an invisible conflagration transforming their hearts.

There are daughters here too, exceptional girls born into this catechism of clouds, born to walk over spruce hillsides where rain meets boughs, where family means pirates and fishermen and ghosts, soil-soaked treasure and wet memories, the sky a constancy of covered stars. There is the bay and the fish and the anchored ships on the horizon, the cliffs too low to suicide from, the mothers going see-through. These sacred, lost daughters.

The sons here are too young to apprentice their fathers, too boyish to be fishermen or pirates, too naïve or frightened to begin their own gilled or buccaneer routes. They are boys caught in this township just like the rest, caught in the rain and a yearning for fathers who don't return, lamplight shining through their mothers. They are boys who fall in love with girls who haven't yet come to know the widowing or the ghostliness, who radiate with impossible possibilities.

The rain on the rooftop echoes the sea, sadness steeping in everyone, in the sons and daughters, the widows and mothers, the whole of this township.

Our Mother wants salvation. She's studied *Chinchorro* first page to last, digested its diagrams and its illustrations and its descriptions. She's made a muddied cat rise with weary limbs to trail bandages around the corners of houses, and she's painted a bat and a seagull back into the sky, their organs cradled and cleansed, bones charred and reset, bodies packed tight with the leavings of the landscape. She believes the world is still capable of forgiveness, those animal silhouettes hovering in the sky and loping through lawns.

Her sons have very little left to hold to. Our Mother can see the finite border between living and sadness diminish in them with each passing day, with every misted sunrise and rainy dusk. It is a sliver as thin and red as a fractured ruby, as her broken heart.

She knows what has to be done.

This is the only way.

Our Mother buys belts and rope. She buys a scalpel and a set of needles, thick thread and forceps and hemostats and forked scissors and a heavy hammer. Our Mother sterilizes the kitchen, boils kettles of water, exhausts her arms wiping down every surface then dresses the table in white, the better to see the blood spitting, the better to find the culprit veins and put them to rest. She drapes the counters in towels and puts the instruments in order. It is a divination, a litany for the future. She lines the table with pans, where the blood will ease and run. The moon isn't visible through the clouds, but she can feel it there, resting in its half shape among the stars, watching her prepare to expel the sadness from her brood.

She walks the stairs like a plank to the soft snoring within their room. The son she came for, the one who seems the strongest, the one who over the last few days appears to have brightened, to have found some new handhold on the world, he shifts awake when she enters, framed in the light from the hallway. She puts a hand to her mouth, indicating silence, then places her other hand on his shoulder, a signal to not disturb his sleeping brother below. The stronger twin's eyes are half open, groggy in the twilight yet somehow seeming ready for this, for Our Mother there, bathed in hallway light and nervous for this foray into the actual. His skin is warm beneath her palm. He rises to her beckoning, soft and silent and powerful. She encourages him forward, motioning for quiet, then walking down the stairs without looking back. On the way, her fingers go momentarily invisible on the handrail.

In the kitchen, surrounded by sheets and towels, by pans and tools and belts, Our Mother watches one twin descend. The hallway clock sounds. He has followed her there, obedient to the last, more awake now, his eyes a little more open, taking in the implements and their gleam, Our Mother's intent clearer as he comes to in the middle of this tableau. She gestures for him to lay down on the kitchen table draped in white. There are saws and pliers and knives. Her son surrenders, laying full out on the table, his face showing only the barest cusp of fear, hardly noticeable even in Our Mother's eyes. She doesn't know it, but this son's heart is shored up by Mallory, by burgeoning love, making him perfectly ready for what she is about to begin. Mallory kissed him, and that has made him different, stronger, better. He can do whatever is needed.

Our Mother brings the hammer to his head.

o

Our Father stands aboard his ship, the crew working around him, night drawing on as they render the sails, swab the decks, store the provisions and shore up their hammocks below. The crew hefted throughout the morning, regaining their strength after a night of carousing, waiting through the sunlight for Our Father to return. Now, with their captain finally back on deck, the tall feather in his tricorne, they move twice as fast. They are a blur of tattoos and teeth, headscarves and sashed cutlasses. Our Father is ready to set sail, to wind away from this island, to travel into the island of the moon. This is his direction, one he doesn't share with the crew.

The moon has been thin for weeks, nights only barely brushed with it, the color of the sky tempered mostly by the glow of townships and ports, of candlelight in the windows and stars beaming. Tonight, Port Honte soon to be left behind, scant clouds absorb and refocus the moon's partial glow, ransacking the stars as it rises in twilight. Our Father has no doubt about the moon. Even if clouds came in thick as paint, even if a brazen storm loaded with lightning covered the entire horizon, he'll still know when the moon is ripe, when the golden shore of its island is ready for boarding. It will pulse in him like a tide, bleating against his bones. When it's time, Our Father won't even have to look to the sky. He'll only need the sheer magnetism of his heart.

Ship's ready, the first mate tells Our Father, the fraction of moon blurred above, as if viewed from beneath the water, as if seen through a rain-filled glass. The first mate views Our Father as a captain with a hooked hand and a parrot on his shoulder, a peg leg and a voice of charcoal and blood. He is none of those, but his silver tooth shimmers, and a sword is tucked to his waist, a pistol sheathed, sash red as blood. It doesn't matter to Our Father. They see what they want to see. They see what they are willing to understand, to follow, to be a part of.

Ship's ready, Captain, the first mate says again, because Our Father hasn't responded. A winged apparition hovers in the sky, near the hangnail of moon. A seagull out late or a bat readily diving. A wind ripples the water. The crewmen idle near their posts, awaiting the legend to take hold.

Aye, Our Father says, the first mate relinquishing the tension in his shoulders, stepping down from the helm and back into the huddle of waiting men.

Our Father is quiet because he's listening to his heart. His reactions are slow for the same reason. He's calculating. There are so many factors at play. The wind stirs, billows the sails without direction, a rustling of raw potential.

Aye, Our Father says again, even quieter, his face widening as he inhales the last remnants of Port Honte. They are awaiting his orders. *Aye* will not be enough, every crew always needing more than that to direct the vessel, to limb out into the wide-open sea. Our Father though is not thinking of routes or paths. He is thinking of the tavern's narrow corridor, the red door at its end, the open window and the breeze blowing through. Our Father is thinking of the shack at the end of the road, where he swallowed a renewed belief in his future, the whole of it compressed into a vision of an island's dark center, a slice of eternity burning down his throat.

The wind gusts. Our Father comes to. He calls his orders. The crew snaps into position. He clears his throat, a wrenching back into real life, eager for what is to come, eager for the ship to move out of the bay, the port's dim light receding, stars mingling on the waves, torn clouds covering and uncovering the whisper of moon, a new bout of venture at hand.

Out on the open sea, the island finally fading from view, the water goes gentle, and the charms of the night are irresistible. They sail. The men work the lines, guiding the ship. They see no compass and no map in Our Father's keep. They've looked through the porthole of his quarters, his wheelhouse where a hammock is hung. There's a bundle of clothes where his head rests, a table near the wall, a chair tucked in. There's an empty stein. There's a half-diminished candle. It's a dare the crewmen took all morning, awaiting his arrival, to sneak to the porthole of Our Father's quarters and duck their heads to the glass, to scan the captain's cabin with their own eyes. They don't doubt him. Our Father led them to an unknown island, to buried treasure, to a grand share of coins and jewels. He even brought them back to Port Honte to spend their earnings before they were asked to set sail again. They have no cause to doubt him. He is already legendary in their esteem.

They've heard the rumors about his want to sail into the moon, to board its golden shore, but to them, the gossip is a marker of genius, a predilection for the strange. They signed the parchment, marking their buccaneer bond, knowing Our Father was branded on the tilted side of things, where crews and ships go awry. The dare to view his captain's quarters is only pirate play, not accusation, and the residue of Our Father's true beliefs aren't visible there anyway. The crew doesn't find Our Father's belief in magic or his love for the unimaginable tucked into his quarters, nor do they find his soft guilt at leaving home or his hard hope of transforming into something immortal.

Our Father breathes deeply as they sail, the small portion of moon eventually dropping below the other side of the world, the night lit now by the lingering shine tucked beyond the water. Soon, they will sail to where the moon fully kisses the sea. Soon, they will sail onto its golden sands, where Our Father will find the dark center of everything, a blooded magic to finally hold in his own veins, his last will and testament: to be made for all eternity.

Late into that first night, far from port, far from the last glimpses of any shore or rocky shoal or beach or volcanic silhouette, when the crew has dropped to sleep in the holds below, when it is only Our Father left awake, another ship appears in the distance. The crew's hammocks sway as the stranger ship presses forward, chasing them like a horizon, a thick, hellbent speed toward where Our Father's ship rests fat on the water.

He withholds his judgment, any leap to weaponizing. Our Father can be a rational captain.

At first it is like an island or a dark heap of boulders, then the masts become visible, the jut of its hull, the definition of its wooden shell and the scoop of its bow, though no mates appear. It comes nearer. Our Father can see the details of the sails, the lashings, no colors raised, no light scooping the darkness from any of its portholes.

The ship looks empty, set adrift.

Our Father is not surprised.

Tonight, one sail into the darkness, his crew idling below, thoughts of immortality unspooling in his head, he is not surprised by this seemingly empty ship floating closer. It is all part of the vision, the journey.

He lets the crew sleep on, sprawled in the holds, the prow looming steadily closer. Closer still and there is no visible crew on its deck, no captain at its helm, no sign of anyone aboard it as the hull slags nearer, as if the ship is simply gravitating toward his own.

Tying and positioning and mounting and rigging, Our Father suddenly becomes dozens of men on deck, slowing his ship to a crawl before he wrenches into the other, the sea stilled in compliance, allowing each to nestle gently toward the other, leaving only a small gap between, a space over which Our Father rests a quiet gangplank, an ominous connection between spirits, a threshold meant to be crossed.

Slowly he boards the ship, guardedly examining it, pistol drawn, cutlass at the ready. Even with the vision in mind, he won't throw out his caution, knowing a leery crew could leap from a corner or out of a shadowy pocket, could assail him with weapons and plunder his own ship. In every hold and area, Our Father finds the vessel empty, truly and wholly empty. He checks and double-checks every corner, every hiding space, all the catches and dark notches. There is no one, only a ragged Jolly Roger pooled on the deck like black blood, only slack hammocks hung in the holds, barely shifting on the glassed sea, only provisions stowed and untouched, as if for a long voyage. There's not even a whiff of rot, only tools and riggings pinned to the walls, stowed and latched for travel, accumulating dust.

Our Father walks again through the captain's quarters, gathering the details. There's a table with a chair tucked in, an empty stein and a half-stunted candle. There is no map or compass, only dawn tempting to rise, the crew of his own ship soon to wake. This cabin is his cabin. This table his table. This chair his chair. This empty stein, this half-stunted candle, this lack of map or compass, his.

Our Father already has two lives, one at sea and one in our rainy township. What would it mean to diverge again, to dilute himself once more? A panic overtakes him, knowing there will never be enough of him for another life, for the route this could possibly take.

Swirling, buzzing with a nervous energy he hardly ever experiences, Our Father hurriedly finishes his walkthrough of the empty ship, unnerved by its hollow mirroring, and as he steps onto the gangplank between the two vessels, he closes his eyes for an instant too long, a deep breath to reset himself, and it is just long enough for the world to slip away.

When he opens his eyes, the night is perfectly ending, and Our Father, straddling the two ships, finds it impossible to tell which is his. It's as if his heart has been accidentally exchanged, one captain's tricorne traded for another. It's as if he's been lost between transformations, stuck amidst the end of night and dawn, when the moon changes into the sun, when the bat becomes the seagull again.

He closes his eyes, desperate to hear the faint snarls of crewmen asleep beneath, those small snores and defiant snatches of breathing that will help him decipher which ship is the right one, which path is best, which life is his. When he opens his eyes, he is back at the helm, hands on the wheel, only one ship in the water, no other anywhere.

o

Our Mother tightens the straps across his hips and thighs, across his ankles and his chest and his arms. She tightens another over his forehead, circling the strap around the table where this son has eaten every meal of his life. The tools are set where she wants them, arranged while the boys slept. The setup is meticulous, but the night is already more than half gone, waves lapping at the shore, rain shifting to mist in the bay. Deep in her heart, she wishes Our Father would just appear, return out of nowhere, rowing his jolly boat to shore, eager to fall in love with them all over again, to hand out the last palm of rubies he'd ever need to chase. If only he appeared, all of this would be unnecessary. She could stop tightening the belts, put down the scalpel and concentrate on a different way to love. If Our Father returned, made a pact to stay, her sons would quit their grieving, their sadness would dissipate like a cloud in sunlight, and she could rest, focus on staying solid. If only.

In the folds of her heart, she still believes in Our Father.

The clock whispers in the hallway. The sun will soon be up, and his boat still hasn't arrived.

She hammered this son just once, a blow right above the eyes, and after knocking him out, she worked the belts tight, knowing the strength of his muscles, the power of his persistence. Our Mother, bursting with the hope of forever. Done restraining him, each belt taut as a stringed instrument, Our Mother cleans his left forearm, his palm pointed to the roof, the skin easy to puncture, the incision a tremendous first step.

Our Mother doesn't know how long she's stood at the table with the scalpel hovering millimeters above his arm. She is a statue of possibilities, time stilled everywhere except for the clock continuing against everything, until the scalpel is cutting the skin of his forearm, making the blood run. The pans catch each droplet. Beneath the skin is a layer of wet tissue, the slow build of new skin and the wrap of fat, the veins and arteries undone and clamped with hemostats, a temporary closing off. His muscles are resilient, stunning in their architecture, in the way they cling to their boyhood armature. She puts her whole strength behind the teeth of a small saw, working on a portion of muscle near the elbow, sweat beading on her forehead and on her upper lip. Then it's ligaments and tendons unburied, snapped from their holds, revealing the bones.

Later, it's Our Mother at the table, the night bleary with clouds, rain falling. She is seated instead of standing. There is a cup of tea in her weary hands, a saucer beneath the dainty white cup. It was the bones that exhausted her. She needs rest, a momentary respite. They are delicate institutions, the structures around wrists and elbows, beautifully evolved in their complications, and Our Mother had a difficult time finding the emotional fortitude to undo them. Until then it seemed possible to just forget everything. Until then it seemed she could just re-seam the arteries and suture the veins, let the muscles retract to their housings and pin them there, stitch the whole of it and pretend she hadn't done anything invasive. His arm would still function. His wrist would turn. His elbow would bend and he'd be back to riding his bicycle. But Our Mother knows how the sadness would return too like falling rain, impossible to quell. If she doesn't do this now, the grief will overtake him. Without this, her son will be lost to the world just like his father, becoming nothing more than a fleeing pirate, a heart obliterated by sadness and treasure lust, and she'll be a ghost of a woman widowed three times over.

She must go on.

Leaving her tea unfinished, she picks up the scalpel and returns. She makes the next cuts, severing the tendons and pulling free the ligaments, exposing the joints, sending spittle across the draped sheet. It makes an enormous noise, a sound she fears is so loud it will wake his sleeping brother, bring him to the bottom of the stairs to witness the wrack and ruin of this twin. The blood runs heavier now too, pooling. Other fluids run as well, the night filled with impending sun. Our Mother's nerves are tenuous against the nag of the brittle clock, but she goes on, she must. She removes the bones, the two curved forearm segments like brothers nestled, disconnected from his bodily wiring and leaving a bright red cavity. Each bone has its own distinct weight and texture, variations in coloring, and though she's seen plenty of others in the cat and the seagull, in the bat and Billy, she is temporarily caught in the realization that these are not simply bones. These bones are her son. One of her boys here on this table. This is no longer some animal but her own brood, and she is changing his architecture.

She sets the twin bones in a pan, dried and cleaned, worked over and scraped close, a smooth gleam of yellow white. A gathering of sweat reconfigures on her forehead, clouds shifting slowly to daybreak. She sets the pan in the oven, the heat blaring.

Billy had awoken so many times, slapping and punching at Our Mother. Her son has been completely different. Even without knowing her intentions, he laid himself willingly on the table, took the hammer blow without a word. Since then he's rested prostrate and silent, hasn't twitched a muscle or made a sound as she's cut and snapped and sawed. His pulse has been an even, steady beat as she's worked, continuing even now, while Our Mother watches the oven's light across the floor, waiting to return the burnished, changed pieces of him.

Our Mother boils water in the teakettle, dips another sachet into her cup. She sits back in her chair. Rain picks up on the roof, the wind curling, the clock ticking. Our Mother rests again, fingers pinched on the cup's small handle. Her son is unconscious on the table, his forearm bones braising in the oven, the rain rattling against the windows. She raises the cup to her lips.

She has to keep working even as the sun begins to rise. Her other son might come down the steps at any moment, and if he does, she'll have to look him in the eyes as he sees his brother bound to the kitchen table, forearm pinned open, slick red insides showing, the instruments of her surgery protruding. She has to keep working because when the bones are finished she still has to prep and tie them, bind them, splint them with sticks and twine and place them back where they belong, carefully reattaching every joint and ligament and tendon and muscle, repacking the arm's cavity with tissue and veins and arteries, with vegetable fiber and animal matter, with leaves and spruce needles and the black soil of this township. She still has to wash it all in rain, suture and stitch, seam the skin atop, bind it in a row of Xs as if to flag a treasure neither of her boys could have ever dreamt. She still has to ink this son's forearm permanently black, just as the first mummies were, imprinting the darkness of night on flesh no longer limited by life, unbound from this living.

Our Mother works, and the sun spills over the horizon.

o

He stretches and yawns, exhales seaward dreams and extends his arms as far as they can go, groaning. He makes two fists, relaxes back into bed, sheets woven through his legs, chest warm. Rain hits the roof. He rubs his eyes in the cloud-filtered light and calls to his brother on the bunk above. There is no response. He calls again and still nothing. He listens for the shallow rustle of blankets but hears only rain. Working his feet quietly against the underside of the mattress, he gives it a swift boot, bouncing the empty mattress almost out of the frame. It moves with the weight of no brother in it. He calls again, continuing to jostle the room with his voice, finally sitting up then standing, turning to the top bunk and pulling himself level with the rail to find the covers laid back, the bed empty.

It feels, inexplicably, like a heart cut open.

He stretches again, ribcage pulling and calves tightening, standing on his toes in a half yawn, brushing the corners of his mouth with sleepy hands. He scratches the small of his back and looks through the gauzy curtains to clouds pinned in the sky. He rests his head against the top rail, listening to the rain, closing his eyes to reinvent the world. He takes his time dressing, putting on a shirt and a pair of weathered jeans, socks, hair ruffled into some usual shape before heading downstairs, ready to eat and load his pocket with coins, to pretend like yesterday hadn't happened, like his brother hadn't received so much from Mallory and him nothing at all, like he wasn't left in the dark. Each step down the stairs he thinks of her, of Mallory, and how maybe today will be his day, his turn to be the twin she kisses, there in the darkness of the cave, beneath the arcade's worn flooring.

Mallory.

When he'd held her hand while lowering her into the tunnel, he'd never felt so simultaneously sparked by someone and separated from another. For the first time, it wasn't two brothers against the world. For the first time, it felt like two other people. And after finding Mallory's lips latched to his brother's, her heart radiating, it was obvious that another kind of future threatened. Downstairs, he can hear the clock stuttering in rhythm with the rain, the floor creaking as the sun's warmth pushes through the clouds, the womb of the house stirring.

Mallory.

Yesterday, at the topside of the cave's mouth, when he'd helped her down and she'd said, *Thank you*, his heart had fluttered. Then she'd disappeared, and though he'd waited for her voice or his brother's to beckon him, to bring him into their light, there was only the rain on the arcade roof and his own pulse. He'd dropped into that rust-colored tunnel on his own, partially falling, the space vacant below, the glow used up, his breath dark against dark walls, her ghostly heart at a distance he couldn't find. When he'd come upon them kissing, how lonely it had been to see their lips like that. Shame and disappointment stacking together in his heart.

Mallory.

There was nothing else. Her only other touch had been a brush of the shoulder as she passed. His brother felt severed from him like a tendon from bone. They'd not gone any farther. They'd come back up the cave's mouth, ignoring any other possibilities buried there. After covering the cave's opening with floorboards, after walking their bicycles back to her house, after the silence of their parting, he knew the three of them had been changed in a way none could properly voice, a heartbreak he hadn't anticipated, a rogue wave that blindsided him.

Mallory.

Dressed and ready, he hits the last stair, his hand on the newel post, and there is his brother belted to the kitchen table, his forearm flayed, the wound grim and bright, the horrid and deep interior of his brother opened amid slick blood gathered in pans and the shining metal stalks of tools protruding. He smells burning in the oven's orange glow and for a moment the world stops existing. Everywhere is stillness. Then the rain picks up on the roof and he comes back to himself. Our Mother is seated there but she doesn't say a word. Outside, the clouds are hanging over the bay where Our Father hasn't returned. Our Mother looks exhausted, her face an ancient treasure hefted through the centuries, the dark hurt of keeping so much so far down. Our Mother finally has absolutely nothing left to hide.

He stands there, seeing through her. He doesn't know what else to do. At the bottom of the stairs, between the front door and the kitchen table, one hand on the newel post and the other limp at his side, it's as if there is no living left for him. Yet his heart continues to beat. His breath comes and goes. The air is rife with beginnings. He puts his feet absently into his shoes. The space between himself and Our Mother and his prone brother belted to the kitchen table is saturated with the unsaid. He pauses just beyond the threshold of the front door, rain pelting the porch. He vomits on their doormat, braided with the word *Ahoy*.

He closes the door, cutting off what has just happened from whatever is coming next.

It feels so strange to pedal along on his bicycle, strange to feel the rain on his face and neck and shoulders and not have his brother beside him, strange to pull into Mallory's driveway and find her skin with only the faintest glow, as if she already knows something is wrong. He doesn't know where else to go.

Hey, she says, so many questions bursting out with it, her eyes searching for the other brother, the brother she kissed, the brother she has found herself longing for.

This brother, the one who is here, he is forgotten.

Hi, he says back, which isn't any answer at all.

He was on the table, opened, and Our Mother readying tools is what he should say, but he doesn't. Instead he offers Mallory a seat on his bicycle and she takes it and holds lightly to his sides, hoping he's taking her to see him. He pedals them up and over the wet streets, along the spruce-covered hills, the houses stacked and the rain falling, weaving not to him but to the arcade, where the floorboards hide the tunneled-mouth. Everything around them silent. There is only rain and the dim ARCADE sign.

He pulls board after board, steadily revealing more and more of the rutted hole beneath the floor. Mallory wants to smile, as if this one brother is enough, but it is unconvincing. One brother is not enough, if it is this brother. She wants the other. Her mind is already made up. The machines call out, remind him that he's worth something too, but his coins feel lightweight, false. Maybe he isn't worth anything.

Does this mean they aren't twins anymore? Up until this morning, they'd been identical, only he hadn't woken to instruments sticking up out of his arm, blood all around, a strange unidentifiable smell growing from the oven. Is it him or his brother who is different now, and why?

Mallory is here, but she is not an answer either.

When the cave's mouth is uncovered, he realizes that without his brother, without another pair of arms to hand Mallory down, they can't spelunk any of this. Before, his brother had been below, waiting in the darkness with upstretched arms. They had been pieces of one another. Mallory sits on the floor near the cave's mouth, floorboards billowed around her, her body barely ignited.

What was it Our Mother was doing, and why wasn't she doing it to him too?

Can I kiss you? he asks out of nowhere, pleading as if there is nothing left but this one chance. Mallory's eyes are downcast. Mallory's smile isn't real. The rain goes on. The machines sing. A small tug of breeze rises from the cave's mouth, darkness chilled by its walls. A few strands of Mallory's hair rustle.

I guess, she says, surprising herself. He knows he isn't the pirate she wants, but she leans in, kissing him on the lips. He doesn't linger, because he can feel the forced nature of it, and when he closes his eyes, hoping his heart will skip and dance, it only gives back images of Our Mother hunched over the kitchen table like some mad surgeon, blood spray on her clothes.

Mallory doesn't radiate at all now, only rests still and lifeless against him.

He'll be okay, he tells her, their breath mingled.

Okay, she says, tipping her hand to the inflexibility of love.

The cave's mouth whispers to them again before he puts the boards over it, the machines humming, the rain falling. So much is inevitable here, yet all of this feels unexpected. He didn't know that yesterday would be the last day of living. He didn't know he'd woken up dead.

Mallory invents a new smile, sadder than any he's ever seen. She feels for him, this pitiful brother who seems to be dying right in front of her.

The boards rest over the cave's secret mouth. The kiss didn't change anything. Rain paws at the windows. He checks his heart for something buccaneer, something pirate, even something buried deep in a hidden complex of caves. There is nothing left, like the sun obscured by clouds, like the rain going on.

o

Do you want to be legendary?

Our Father asks it of every new pirate. When he's signing another crew in the wake of another mutiny, he asks each man, and they imagine their names immortalized on the seas. They want it all. They want to be a part of an illustrious pirate crew, part of a lore that never stops haunting the water. But no one ever answers the question. They smile or nod or offer some faraway look, but they don't answer. They can't. It's like a dream, that question. It's a route only Our Father can identify. Even so, they place their mark on his parchment, ready and willing to believe, to follow him onto the sea.

When Our Father was a boy, and when Our Father's Father was home from pirating one night in every thousand, instead of stories about seagulls or bats or suns changing into moons, Our Father's Father told tales of the everlasting. Our Father's Father would say, *Out there is a kind of woman who never dies. A kind of woman who never grows old and never loses her beauty and never wants for anything other than exactly what you've got.* He'd unlock his jaw, realign his teeth. *This kind of woman looks like any other woman, no difference in her skin or her hair or her eyes.* Our Father's Father would cough and look past the rain of this township, the houses then precursors to the houses now, the rain the same. *These women, they don't have pale skin or blood-red lips, don't have a look in their eyes like they've lived forever. You can't tell it from a glance, from some easy look. Fangs is the only thing. Sharp, pointed teeth made to deliver their magic. Fangs are the only difference between the kind of woman I'm talking about and any other one. These two right here,* and he'd tap the bicuspids in his gumline, curved and smooth. *If you can get them to smile, you'll see, because they hide them. They don't want anyone to know, because it's a treasure, a gem like no one else has. Can you imagine, living forever?*

Our Father could, even way back then.

If you can find one of them with those fangs, if you can coax them into sinking those points into your neck, then you'll know. You'll be stilled by the magic too. You'll live forever. You'll be endless. No oceans would stop you and no shores would exhaust you and no treasure would escape you. You could right every wrong you'd ever committed. You could become whatever you wanted: pirate, husband, father, king.

In those old houses tucked across the hills, when Our Father's Father told that story, the rain fell in the same unmistakable semblance of a heartbeat.

Our Father is following the moon, watching it grow one sliver fatter each night, his ship chasing the horizons where it rises and sinks. The crewmates do as they've been directed, their skin paling as the ship stays longer and longer at sea, enough weeks now that they've lost track. They watch the widening of the moon because it's the only indicator between one day and the next. Our Father doesn't tell them about the ghostly ship that first night from port, the soulless vessel he boarded, the one he found identical to their own except for the crew asleep in the holds below. He doesn't tell them how he could feel the weight of its years, its eternity, and how the broadside of it vanished with the dawn. At the helm, Our Father keeps a hand on the wheel, his mind wandering across the generations of stories he's been told, the crew no recourse but to keep on, to continue this chase without land in sight, the suspicion of Our Father's brazen obsession distending with the moon, one slow fraction at a time.

The wind changes direction and the crew adjusts, keeping the ship on the path Our Father demands, their captain with a faraway look in his eyes. In front of them is only a vast expanse. They've sailed and sailed and all that is ever between them and the moon is a great distance of water. The provisions run lower each day, the flag on their mast ragged with every storm, the horizon less and less definitive in their eyes. Stars hang like taunts in the curtains of the sky. These are the kinds of voyages that change pirates into savages, make beasts of men, the kinds of journeys that bring about hard mutiny, swords and pistols billowing like storm clouds in the distance.

They sail and sail until, one day, a darkness appears on the watery plane, a spot of black hope. It is a mound birthed out of an otherwise unbroken sea. It looks like a tiny island, or a whale's broad back, and regardless of which it is, this crew will gladly set upon it, for though the men haven't the full look of mutiny, the word is gathering. Land is the only out for any captain who faces this moment, land no matter how thin or unbelievable it may be, land to set their feet upon, to ease their mounting grievances. Our Father isn't oblivious to this. He can feel the treachery of no map and no compass idling in them, can see the hope washing out of their faces day after day, how they are beginning to believe there is no end to this voyage, that he has brought them not to treasure but to the brink of loneliness, to whatever is the opposite of salvation.

Our Father sets a course for this lump of darkness rising in the middle of a vast and endless sea. As they sail nearer the island, it clarifies into a rock shore with no outline of trees or jungle, a shadow they seethe toward. It is tiny and black and cragged. It is barely land.

Our Father calls *Land ho* and *Anchors out*, the loudest he's been in a great many days. The crew is mesmerized by the semblance of anything that isn't water, though Our Father's inflection says this isn't an expected island, that there's a danger to it. There are never enough stars to illuminate the truth.

The crew heaves anchors just beyond the black mass, Our Father on the prow looking to the island, scouring it with his gaze. It has no vegetation or sand, no palms or cover, no beach of any sort. Every inch of the island's surface is volcanic rock burbled from some monstrous ache below, hardened into pocks and jagged dents in which the waves catch, creating miniature pools, each with their own small, mirrored reflection of the dark sky above.

Search it, if you like, Our Father says, without looking to the crewmates who are desperate to abandon ship, to walk the gangplank and set soles on any land, no matter how menacing it is, no matter how many warnings sing on the breeze. The air chants through the riggings. A sash rustles. A cutlass wavers. *Have at it*, he says, and they do.

Our Father knows what this is, the island of crags.

They lower jolly boats and row the short distance from ship to stony isle. The underside of the boats mournfully scrape on its unforgiving shore as Our Father watches from the deck. He can see what omen this is, knows too that there is no stopping them. The men disperse across the island's stony hide, moving over the shallow pitches, the pools of water trapped in the creases, reflecting them. They trudge over the pits until, as Our Father suspected, each mate is eventually stilled, stopped or stooped as if made of stone themselves, locked peering into a pool of caught water. Some crouch, others stand. Some lean with their hands on their knees as if they are about to be sick. All these postures yet the same ghostly pallor on every face. Our Father is sure of what they are finding in the watery crags: they are seeing their greatest treasures unfolding, as if anything were possible. They stare, and the longer they look into those small pools, the more realistic their dreams become, mirrored in the reflection there, bright and beautiful and entrancing.

Wind ruffles the tops of their heads and the bottoms of the sails. Anchors hold the ship.

Our Father watches them gaze into forever, into this pretend immortality, these myths. These are not truths reflected, only dreams of treasure as if they'll come true, the crew's most heartfelt desires playing out in purest form, a siren song in a stupor of water.

Our Father doesn't leave the ship, and he doesn't call to them. He only stands, letting it unfurl. The men will stare into these pools until they collapse, and even then, they will only claw their way back to the same watery reflections. Our Father won't wait. When he's ready, he'll take the pistol from his waist, hold it to the sky, cock the hammer, and fire a single shot into the air. Whichever men are startled back into existence, those are the crew who will continue on with him. The rest, those who don't flinch or move, they will be left there, locked forever in the lusts of their hearts. Those men will stare until they grow weak, until they are ruined by hunger and thirst, and even then, they won't look away. They will die gazing into their dreams.

Our Father doesn't need a siren song. He only has to look to the horizon, where the moon will rise one day full and ripe.

o

The last stitch goes into his arm at midday. It happens while the other son is out on his bicycle, attempting to erase the image of Our Mother with hands gloved in red and that forearm sickly opened. The house is slick with rain, and the ink she paints is cannon black, running effortlessly over his skin, seeping into the stitches and the seams, across the ripples of his boyhood. It soaks from elbow to wrist, a black block wrapped around his forearm. The stitches are doubled against the strain of his muscles, against the pull of his re-tightened skin, vegetable matter and mineral fiber packed inside his mummified arm. This forearm will never age, will never decay, and if Our Mother extends the process across his whole body, he'll never accumulate even one more ounce of sadness. He'll cease his mourning for a pirate father and a ghostly mother, he'll stop grieving in this township's rain. Instead, he'll be a Black Mummy.

She removes the belts. He is unconscious, unstirring. She shifts his body as she works, rubbing at the indentations of the straps, soothing him until he half wakes. In his exhaustion, she gets him to his feet, her arm around his middle. He clings to her and they limp up the stairs, his new black arm dangling loosely at his side. The clock goes on. Our Mother knows how much more there is to come, how this is only a beginning, how every drop of rain is another second washed away, but she's pleased with the progress she's made.

Upstairs she wrangles him to rest in the top bunk, his legs climbing the bedframe as if he's asleep, as if she is only tucking him in. He uses his boy arm to pull himself up, holding the mummified one to his chest like it's splinted. He hasn't seen the sutures or the seams, the taut skin, its black paint like a bold tattoo. He hasn't opened his eyes wide enough yet to understand.

Shhh, she says.

She brings the covers over his legs, his abdomen, his ribs. Rain soaks the lawn. She rests his mummified forearm neatly next to the other, his body recalling sleep. He doesn't move or flinch, doesn't call out to her. He only sighs back into bed, yawning as he's done a thousand times before. Our Mother's heart fills with thankfulness, the sun doing its best to sever the clouds. She places her own tired hands on top of his, feeling the stitches and inspecting the incisions, checking for the warmth of blood beneath. He closes his eyes, unable to raise his head from the pillow. He doesn't yet know his new charm, the strength Our Mother has woven into him, the gleam of a black forearm.

The rain presses.

Shhh, she says again.

Rain runs down the roof.

Shhh, she sounds out as he drifts to sleep. Our Mother listens to his lungs, to the pummeling of his heart, to the rise and fall of his insides. She glides her fingers over the stitches, studying the diligently painted black, how deep it has already gone. She watches for a bit then leaves him there, nested above the empty bunk where her other son will sleep tonight, leaving the door open as she exits, the sun and clouds and rain begging toward dusk.

The Black Mummy sleeps, dreaming of masts jutting farther into the sky than he's ever known, dreams of the sharpest cutlass, of pistol shots smearing the air. He dreams of seagulls becoming bats, their white feathers shedding to leathery black skin.

Downstairs, Our Mother cleans. She washes her tools and recounts the procedure, start to finish. How she positioned her wrists, how she held the instruments, how she breathed. How taut she made the straps, how deep the incisions, how quick the moves when she came to a new layer of tissue or arteries or veins or muscles. How she held the bones and what temperature in the oven, how the clock whispered from the hallway. She recalls how long it was between each movement of the remolding, of the tacked stitches, the painting of his skin. She is making notes for the rest, so much more boy still to take care of. Soon, she will dive into his body and wrangle the last possibilities of sadness from his chest, from every organ and bone, from every crease and fold, from every drop of blood sailing through his heart.

The longer her sons are alive in this township, the more sadness they accrue. The longer Our Father is gone, the stronger Our Mother's need for salvation. The more rain that comes, the greater the disease of grief washes over them. Our Mother has to mummify these boys as they are, to still their bodies and their hearts before they become otherwise. In this way, she will keep her brood young and yearning forever, nestled in her arms, beside her heart.

She tucks her tools into a canvas bag, making mental notes about little tricks and hints she'll incorporate next time, to make the process even better, smoother, more efficient and with greater ease. Her confidence is only hiccupped by the coming transparency. When every tool is tucked, she removes the bloodied fabric from the table and the pans from the floor. She cleans them and places them in the drying rack. She puts the sheets in the wash, to scrub away their gore.

Moving down the hallway from the washing machine, she catches a shadow in the window and stops to look, finding only clouds and rain. She continues down the hall into the kitchen and glimpses again a dark shape in another window. She looks out to the yard and finds something there. It moves through the grass like dark ruin, the rain and clouds and coming dusk making it hard to fully distinguish. Our Mother slides open the back door and steps under the eave, the coming night bristling her skin. She sees the crumpled mass straggle past the corner of the house, and though she wants it to be the cat, this figure is much larger, the unmistakable stature of a boy. She stands waiting, watching, her hand still on the door handle.

Then the figure is gone, and nothing else happens.

Upstairs the Black Mummy stirs, staring into the stitches of his forearm, a new luminescence on his face. Hearing him him rustling above, Our Mother rushes upstairs to take stock. His inked forearm is moving as he grips the sheets, lifting his body to a seated position. Our Mother blazes, ecstatic in what she's accomplished, already imagining how she'll mummify his other arm then his legs and lungs and heart, how she'll stop the entirety of his body in forever, how she'll combat the sadness pouring down on him like rain. For Our Mother, it's as if every dream is suddenly possible.

Her eyes well and she turns to shield the Black Mummy from it, not wanting him to see the tears fall through her skin. But as she turns, she catches out the window that same snatch of lumpish boy, that childish figure near the lowest spruce boughs in the yard, its shape moving through the trees, the branches wavering. What arrives from underneath the spruce, spilled onto the grass, is a grimacing and mangled mass, a horror of bruising, of running seams, of limbs hardly held together, of bone grinding against bone, each part hung to another in a hulking wound, devastated by amateurish stitches, skin raw and bleeding. Our Mother watches in disbelief. Its motions are haggard and menacing, its legs dragging. It hobbles from the spruce into the rain, gravitating toward the house as Our Mother helplessly watches from the upstairs window.

Billy.

The Black Mummy sits farther forward, seeing Our Mother tense as she watches out the window, hearing her inhale as if she has just witnessed the most terrible eventuality. *Only the rain*, she says, turning back to her son, attempting reassurance, and though she wants to smile to convince him, she can't. This moment, like everything in this township, is drenched in rain, buried in a brutal tide, limping toward ruinous grief.

o

He didn't know how his brother had changed.

He'd never been separated from him before, had never gone to the arcade without him, had never talked with Mallory by himself or ridden his bicycle up these streets without a pirate brother at his side, water racing their twin spines. He'd never been treated differently either, Our

Mother always portioning identical plates, precise and symmetrical routines: the same number of arcade coins, an equally transparent hug, so when he found his brother strapped to the table by a series of belts, the tang of blood in the air, he couldn't understand why he wasn't there too. He didn't want to be cut open, but he didn't want to be held at bay either. He couldn't understand why his brother was getting something he wasn't, even horrendous and violent as it appeared. He didn't know how Our Mother could have chosen one son over another.

That afternoon he left Mallory at her once empty house up the street, but when he arrived home, he couldn't bring himself to cross the threshold of the front door. Instead he sat on the steps, tears streaming. He waited there through dusk and into the darkness, afraid to see his brother maybe still belted as he'd been, bleeding into the kitchen, Our Mother vile with surgical scents and metallic instruments. So he waited, watching the sun wash down through the rain, the night coming on and the clouds building and no stars to wish on. When it was dark enough, he re-entered the house, finding a clean, quiet kitchen, no brother or surgeon there, only the shine of cleanliness and Our Mother reading and the loneliness as if he were caught in a dream built for one.

The rain was light, barely pelting the roof. He went to bed without any supper, and she didn't even attempt a word of explanation to him.

The stairs creaked on his way up. The hallway light bright and their bedroom door half shut. The shape of his brother covered in the top bunk, the quiet sounds of his breath like a tiny, humble accordion.

His brother's shoulder blades peeked from beneath the blanket, the back of his head visible in the hall light, the partially closed door letting in the same swath it always had.

He lay noiselessly in the bottom bunk for a long time, hands clasped on the pale white of his forearms. He tried to imagine rubies and ships and tricornes but all that came were splashed red decks and betrayal. He thought of Mallory but only thought of how her kiss with him was steeped in pity, her glow beyond dim, as if she wasn't really there. He tried to remember Our Father, the look and sound and smell and feel of him, but his thoughts only ran like rain.

The clock went on.

Unable to stand it any longer, he rose and stood on the bedrail, toes stretching up to see his brother, watching his back billow and recede in those quiet breaths beneath the covers. He waited, listening. There was the light rain and the stillness of night, the darkness mixed with the light across the floor. Nothing seemed changed. He went back to his bunk below and fought for sleep.

He woke to the sun poking through mist, yawned and heard his brother stirring in the bunk above.

Morning, he said, trying to avoid the questioning or fear in his voice, the jealousy and anger bound in him still, surrounding his heart even in the morning light. There was no answer, only a yawn and sigh so much like his own. Our Mother appeared in the doorway, arms folded, undisguised hope on her face.

The Black Mummy dropped his head over the side, arms hanging toward his brother, the length of them in full view. The tattooed block of the Black Mummy's forearm was stretched, his skin reshaped in new muscle, in expanded hills of tilled landscape, a row of perfectly aligned stitches and long sutures running its painted length. The Black Mummy smiled at him, and he mustered a smile back, though it was enormously small. Our Mother flushed from the threshold, cheeks genuinely reddening in a joy neither boy really understood, before she disappeared through the doorway.

The Black Mummy jumped out of bed with a hammer of feet, hustling on a T-shirt and jeans, his new black forearm resolute, absolute, the paint and stitches and new muscle combining into some buzzing, buccaneer potential, a morning of bright, towering possibilities.

The other son rose and followed, but with no bounce in his step, and no smile on his face.

At breakfast, it was difficult to avoid the Black Mummy's forearm.

The haunt of it was mesmerizing, tattooed and stitched, commanding attention. It was so changed from his own moon-pale skin, and when the hand below that black tattooed forearm grabbed a spoon for the first time, the metal folded like wet paper, the extra strength unexpected and uncontrolled. Our Mother took the bent one from the Black Mummy's hand and placed another in front of him. Likewise, when he lifted his glass, it shattered, as a dream bursting. Our Mother gave him a new glass, easy, as if this was expected, the Black Mummy unable to hide the way he felt, enamored with this change, with what he was becoming. He could snap a sword in two with this new strength, could break a neck with only his grip, could splinter a prow with only the slightest clutching. The Black Mummy knows it now, and his brother knows it too, and this only a fraction of the change monstrously washing over them in the morning light.

Then there are the usual coins placed in their palms and the lunches in their hands, as if this were a day like any other. The boys put on their shoes at the rug, the clock murmuring with the rain. They close the front door and take up their bicycles, their shoulders already wet, their hair and the Black Mummy's tattooed forearm shining. He watches to see if the rain will cause his Black Mummy brother to wince, if the newly painted skin will run into the gutter, but the ink stays and the Black Mummy goes on beaming. He looks almost refreshed in the rain, grinning, pedaling, sack lunch pinned between palm and handlebars.

There is a hearty glow in the window of the once empty house, Mallory's heart shining already behind the curtains as they ride onto her driveway, the curtains swaying as she comes bouncing out the front door and down the porch steps, her hair and limbs splaying, her energy ecstatic because today there are both brothers instead of only one.

The Black Mummy stands astride his bicycle, his brother feeling more irrelevant with each gust of wind. It is four forearms across two sets of handlebars, and the tattooed arm of the Black Mummy glistens in shades of triumph, Mallory entranced. She strides straight to the

Black Mummy and asks if she can touch it, her hand already there. He nods and she runs her palm the length of it, fingers the black skin while her body radiates, as if the whole of the township is lit entirely by her light, lightning trapped in a jar, as if she was caressing the spindle of a captain's pegged leg.

She doesn't need to say anything.

Watch, the Black Mummy says, and with only the smallest motion of his mummified forearm, he bends his handlebar ninety degrees then straightens it back. It leaves a crease in the metal, a divot, and no one is looking at the brother with two moon-white forearms. Mallory's heartbeat is audible from every distance. Her skin burns, her fingers unwilling to let go of the Black Mummy's inked forearm. No one is paying attention to anything else.

The other brother stands beside the two of them like a lawn ornament. His mouth hangs open, the gap in his teeth no longer momentous. There has never been a wider expanse between them. If he tilted his head upward, it would fill with rain. Mallory luminesces and the Black Mummy falls headlong into her warmth. The other brother can't even look at her.

They ride their bicycles down her driveway, Mallory taking a seat on the back of the Black Mummy's bicycle, her arms laced around his waist, one of her hands stroking the tattooed block, the streets puddled, the sun muddled behind clouds, Mallory having found her pirate.

o

The rock mass is barely visible now, even in silhouette. The outlines of the men left standing or crouching there dissipate into the distance, the ship running smoothly over the water, the wind hearty. The only crew who remain are those who came to when Our Father fired his pistol, the men who could let go of their dreams for the promise of Our Father's golden moonlit shore, or those who were at least smart enough to see the reality of the pooled creases of rock, their blunt, empty offerings. Those who are left are the buccaneers Our Father wants, less than half of the crew ready to sail toward the sands of the moon, to work the riggings while their captain stands at the helm, hands brushing the ship's wheel, water lapping the hull.

Why couldn't we save them? a crewman asks later, wrenching his headscarf in his hands as he speaks, his hair a mess, his hands all knuckles, his chest shrunken beneath a neck of dingy layers.

Our Father stares into the horizon, the volcanic crags gone, the pools of water left behind. The night is rounding on them but Our Father is the only one who notices, these rugged leftover crewmen temporarily blinded by the siren song of those cragged reflections, of their own lustful dreaming gifted up through seawater. It will be many days before these men have gathered back their full vision.

This mate before him though, the one asking, the one with the caved teeth and gaunt face, half-blinded as he is, mangy and racked with exhaustion, he wants answers. *We could have snapped them out of it,* he says, bravely wielding his tired lungs, hands constantly wringing as he blindly eyes the horizon. Our Father has seen this same guise many times before, pretend bravery atop a shaken soul, and how a simple blow to the head would drop this crewman drooling to the ship's planks. Instead, he chooses a cutlass of words.

It will rain soon, Our Father begins. The wind blows. The clouds building gray, not a storm purpled with gales but the coming of a steady, unholstered soak. The crew is managing the ship, keeping it on Our Father's course, lines sliding through their hands.

I have two boys at home, Our Father continues, *and they were in bed one night. They were asleep and I was on the front porch. It was raining and the clouds were dark, much darker than these now, and the moon was nowhere to be found. It was a black night and I was sitting in a rocking chair, listening to the rain.* Our Father looks into the mate's cold eyes, his face expectant though confused. But this mate is hopeful even in

Our Father's meandering. Only wanting to know how he could leave behind so many of their crew, abandon them there on that cragged island to die of thirst or starvation, to fade clinging to hopeless dreams.

I was there, listening to the rain, and then the lightning started. There was rain on the roof, rain on the lawn, rain in the streets. It ran down the gutters and out to sea, carving paths to the shore that the tide had to get busy erasing. And when the lightning began, I was happy because for all the rain we see, lightning is rare. In our township, lightning is still a spectacle, and that night, sitting on the porch, the wind shifted and the clouds built and the lightning let loose.

A line swings overhead and thuds against the mast. Men move to re-rig and maneuver as the sun continues setting, as the tiny island made now of men and rock becomes a dusky memory.

And because there was lightning, I went to get my boys. I shook each of them awake and slung them over my shoulders, wrapped in blankets. I took them to the front porch and sat them on my lap. They were rubbing their eyes and leaning into my chest. I said to them, This is lightning. They watched, awed, and I sat there with them for a long time, my boys, until, do you know what they asked? The mate shook his head. *They asked if they could catch the lightning. They asked if they could get jars from the kitchen and climb up our spruce tree and reach out and catch it, hold it forever. I laughed, and I told them, Yes, by all means, go ahead.*

So they went inside and got jars from the cupboard, then they screwed the lids off and crossed into the yard, the lightning bashing all around, the hairs on my arms standing up. I could see their faces every time the air cracked, the lightning heavier than I'd ever seen. Those boys, though, they weren't scared in the least, didn't even flinch. Then Our Mother came running out and I grabbed her arm before she could make it into the yard, her nightgown glowing her up like some kind of ghost. She cursed me, asking what I thought I was doing letting our sons out of bed this late, letting them run like fools in the lawn with lightning crackling. And though I know I shouldn't have, I laughed. I laughed and I kept hold of her arm until the fight in her died out, like it does when we have some buccaneer skewered and we're only waiting for his blood to let. Eventually, she asked: what are they holding? I told her, Jars, and she said, Why, and I said, They're going to catch some lightning. She laughed a little then too, in a panicked and fitful way, and I kept my hand on her arm, until it became more like an embrace, watching our boys climb.

Our Father pauses, standing at the helm, his hand tilting the wheel fractionally, the wind picking up, the sun cresting downward, the rest of the crew still running and rigging but with an ear to this story, this long answer to one mate's question.

Those boys climbed that spruce tree, each disappearing underneath. Then pretty soon, in the flashes, we saw them scrambling over the branches, toward the sky, way up high, higher even than I thought they'd get, all spindly legs and arms. We watched them, and I kept my hand on Our Mother's arm because I wanted to see how it would play out. We stood together there, the two of us, on the same swatch of land, mesmerized by what was happening. For a moment, I think both of us wanted to run into the rain and the lightning too. For a moment, we could pretend that nothing was too far gone, the whole lot of it, and us especially.

Our Father's eyes swell imperceptibly.

Those boys, they climbed way up onto the top of the tree, trunk slick under their bare feet, the lightning lighting up their faces, shocking across their hair, each of them holding an empty jar to the sky, believing they could catch that lightning, hold it to their chests, take it to their rooms like a nightlight, crackling and alive, a match for their boyhood.

The wind pulls the sails toward the rising moon.

And then, in that moment, just when I was starting to see that maybe they weren't really boys anymore, that maybe they had some pirate in them after all, that maybe they were ready for swords and pistols, riggings and the plank, ready to face an island of their own hopeless dreams, the next lightning hit, and it was like they were swallowed by its light. Our Mother gasped and we heard the fragile mist of broken jars raining down.

The mate stands in silence. Our Father looks out to sea, the story done rolling from his mouth.

In the silence that followed, she said to me, Why couldn't we save them?

Every crewman on the boat is stopped, paused in the workings of the ship. There is nothing else to say.

I'm sorry about your boys, the mate finally manages, unsure what to offer their captain.

Don't be, Our Father says, *it was only a kind of dream I had once, a very long time ago.*

o

Some nights later, Our Mother wakes the Black Mummy from the top bunk again, his forearm nearly healed, the stitches settled, the swelling finite, the ink beautifully embedded in its permanent block. He can control the strength now too, its bright new energy spreading throughout his body, encasing him in courage and muscle and might. A newfound spark has brightened Our Mother as well, her hopes seeming suddenly attainable, as if this whole scheme is one she can actually achieve before her body mutinies.

The Black Mummy rises with eagerness when she appears again at the bedrail, walking quickly and quietly downstairs, the kitchen table set with her same tools, the tabletop draped, the pans placed and the straps ready. There are pliers and forceps, hemostats and scissors, needles and thread and scalpel and knives. There is the hammer. The Black Mummy goes willingly, thinking not of the pain but of his black forearm and its endless grip, its gigantic strength, its power, the tattooed darkness of the piracy thrumming in his veins, and how Mallory looks at him when he rides onto her driveway, the electricity that runs through him when she touches his forearm, when she wraps her arms around his waist, the two of them beginning to meld into something greater, on the cusp of it.

But her other son isn't asleep in the bottom bunk below. He witnesses the whole of it through fake-sleeping eyes, watches as she wakes the Black Mummy and rustles him across the bedroom floor, leaving only dim light bathing the boards. He is awake, listening to the rain plead on the roof, listening to their paired footsteps down the stairs, past the clock, through the hallway and into the kitchen. Then it is only rain on the roof again. He wants to open his eyes, to speak out, to tell her that he's ready too, to show Our Mother how the sadness is overwhelming and how strong he can be, how quiet and still and obedient if that's what Our Mother needs. He wants to hold his moon-white forearms up to her, to show her how each could be cut open. Instead, he pretends sleep, listening to a lifetime recede, no dreams to be had, alone.

But he can't let Our Mother see how weak he feels, exhausted for the lack of painted skin. He can't let her see the ocean swollen behind his eyes, the infection of Our Father sailing away. He can't let her see how laden his heart is, the weight of imagined seas steadily burying him. If he guts himself that way, if he lays bare his feelings, it will break Our Mother, it will be the last thing she hears before going see-through. So he only rests there, eyes closed, hearing snags of Our Mother and the Black Mummy below.

He hears a muffled blow, like a hammer on dense bone, then the leathery strain of belts being strapped, the metallic latch of buckles. He hears an exhale or a cinch of breath. He hears the faint ping of metal instruments one against the other, of pans being lifted, of tins sliding across a sheet and water running. He hears Our Mother's footsteps and the moan of a chair on the floor, rain and blood pooling, the moon rising behind ragged clouds.

This unmummified brother strains toward the sounds, muscles tense beneath the sheets, frustrated with his own inaction. He doesn't rise. He doesn't speak. He doesn't join them. He remains in bed, tethered to weakness, telling himself to have patience, to trust in Our

Mother, to breathe, to soak in the sound of the rain. It is difficult to do any of this. It is difficult to keep from pitching himself off the roof.

Downstairs, Our Mother is far into the cutting and severing, to the closing off of arteries. She is working swiftly and efficiently, working without sweat beading, keeping a firm grip on every aspect, a careful drawing of pans, instruments polished, each detail as it is meant to be. When the blood runs, she catches it. When the fluids spatter, she cordons the leaks. The clock chants as she works, her heart rhythmic beside it, the night presiding over the two of them, each doing the best they can to alter this future.

She moves forcefully, even aggressively, as the night goes on, knowing that behind this there is a singular pressing thought: Billy. She can't stop thinking of Billy. She can't loose those thoughts from the shadowy corners of her mind. It was Billy in the yard that day, when she'd finished the Black Mummy's forearm, when she'd been tucking him into bed to rest and recuperate. It was Billy in some monstrously reassembled body ducking under the spruce in their yard. She didn't understand how he'd unearthed himself from so many pieces, how he'd sutured himself back together, cobbled into a boyish amalgamation. But she knows it was Billy, hobbling through the rain in some horrendous reconstruction. A body grotesque and blank, lumbering without composure, dumbed and vapid, arms crooked, head barely held to his neck.

Our Mother believed she'd quelled him, thought she'd rent him into enough scraps, buried him deep enough that he'd never reappear, never bring the guilt or the loss back to her, like some mad dog returning a murderous bone. She didn't want to be reminded of her betrayal, of her failure, of the botched job she'd done on Billy, the way his body had come undone. And if Billy was able to assemble a new and horrible body from the pieces she'd scattered, from the tiny renderings she'd buried in the black soil and rain across this whole township, then there was so much more she wouldn't be able to control.

These were the thoughts that looped as she worked on the Black Mummy's second forearm, desperate to work quickly, to remain effective. She can't go back. Billy was what Billy was. There is no forgiveness for that. And this son, his skin is already knifed open. She can't afford to stick on some recurring nightmare of Billy in a muddy body.

She breathes, settles her head, tries to tell herself that Billy is an anomaly, is irrelevant, unimportant. People make mistakes. She's made mistakes. And that figure she saw, looming outside, it was only a figment, a leap her mind made out of guilt or fear. Billy is only another ghost roaming this township.

But as she pulls the bones from the Black Mummy's second forearm, readying them for the oven, they fall through her hands onto the sheeted table, clattering. It's a short drop and no harm is done, except that she feels the disappearance of her heart in the same instance too, the whole of her going blank, unblooded. Only a few days ago, while the Black Mummy was healing, she'd held a piece of fabric to the sewing machine, and, as her mind wandered, her hand walked beneath the needle, fully up past the fingers, but it left no puncture wound at all. She'd sewn halfway up her hand and the needle had met nothing but air. Her ghostliness is building. The world is beginning to melt through her grip, slipping through her fingers.

The constant drain of it, this impending ghostliness and Billy's unexpected monstrosity, it is wringing the newfound confidence from Our Mother. Once she gets the Black Mummy's bones in the oven, only the repacking and replacing left to task, only the reshaping and the sutures and the stitches, only the black ink to paint onto his skin, Our Mother looks to the future, her self-assurance waning. She is panicked about how the organs will be sustained, how the heart will continue. It isn't time yet, but she has trouble avoiding the thoughts. How will she keep her boys from becoming a mass of decay, a slow rot anchored to them? She listens to the rain, but there is no pressing the thoughts away. The hallway is empty except for the clock watching her, mimicking the pulse of her heart.

She finishes before the sun comes up, coating the right forearm as beautifully as she had the left, a black tattoo blocked from wrist to elbow. She only has to get him into bed, to let him heal a second time, then she'll feel better. She only has to regain these confidences, to feel again like anything is possible, like Billy is a freak, her sons so much better at listening and doing, such greater bodies for excavating.

With the last stitches in place and the ink soaking, Our Mother rouses the Black Mummy, unbelts him and helps him up the stairs to his bunk bed, her other son still asleep beneath, the sun nearly risen. She returns to the kitchen and boils the pans, cleans the instruments, scours until she can no longer remember the red pools in Billy's eyes or the whisper of what she imagines are his broken arms dragging down the siding. She puts her tools away with her doubts, stowed though not erased, and as the sunlight breaks, she watches the rays strike through her transparent arms, knowing that these are the last days dawning.

o

In the upper bunk, the Black Mummy wakes anew, his right arm matching his left now, black ink and sutures, new muscle in the shape of Our Mother's mummification. In the lower bunk his brother wakes from barely any sleep, skin paler than moonlight, exhaustion in oceans beneath both eyes. The brothers yawn, stretch, rise to put on T-shirts and weathered jeans, sneaking glances at one another, one's pallid skin and the other's blackened piracy. They head downstairs, coins jangling, breakfast on the table, sunlight peering through the clouds.

The pale son eats with his head bowed, his neck thinned, face drained. Our Mother sees his sadness deeper than ever before, sees the jealousy burgeoning in his heart. *Soon*, she wants to say to him, *before you know it*. She wants to put her hand on his head, his hair strewn like a broken hull, to touch his wrist and align herself with the faint beat of his heart, the tissues and tendons and bones. She wants to tell him how close she is, how he isn't going to be left behind. But she only asks, *More?* He doesn't reply, doesn't lift his head, doesn't sound one vowel into the dead space between them. His skin is so pale and his heart beats almost without purpose, while the Black Mummy's seems to be drowning in future buccaneering.

The township around them this morning is wet with desperation.

They clear their dishes, take their lunches from the counter. They ride their bicycles to Mallory's where it isn't a glow anymore but like a sun trapped inside the once empty house up the street, intensely burning. Her heart punches even brighter when she sees the Black Mummy's second inked forearm, Mallory ablaze with want.

Can I? she asks, though she doesn't need to, and is touching him before there's an answer, their contact each day more and more like something older, something forbidden, something that looms.

The arcade? the pale brother says, speaking up from astride his bicycle, standing in the phantom fathoms. He uses his words as a blade between them, meant to interrupt, though his voice croaks and he's forced to clear his throat. Mallory nods, the Black Mummy never looking away from her and she the same. It's as if the rain isn't falling on their shoulders, as if it isn't matting their clothes, as if the sun is shining on his blackened forearms and their blooming love.

Another bicycle ride, another round of torture as one brother watches the other with Mallory hugging his waist.

When they walk across the arcade's floorboards, the Black Mummy drops a coin in the slot of a machine, inviting a chorus of blips. Mallory is as smitten as any ghost of a girl can be. The pale brother walks behind them, a witness to every glance and glow, every bit of flirt and desire, watching them pull together at the corner of the arcade where the lifted boards expose the cave's mouth, gently raising the planks like unswaddling some dark newborn, and by the time the black of the tunnel is revealed, this brother with moon-white limbs is more drawn to its gaping throat than he's ever been.

He gives in with his entire heart, unsure of what else to do.

He storms between them, through their connection, charging down the ore-colored walls of the mudded opening. They are startled by his disappearance down the tunnel, hearing his voice calling up from the dark, angered and sullen, *Land ho*. They follow, the Black Mummy strong enough now to lower himself and Mallory down together, smoothly descending, an embrace inside the cave's gullet.

On the cave floor, Mallory and the Black Mummy stand in the circumference of her light, her radiance swelling around them, yet they can't see the other brother, can only hear his steps in the dark distance ahead. They keep pace with his ebbing sounds, his savage steps, until they reach the place where they first kissed, not far down this cave's trajectory. The Black Mummy and Mallory, their hearts beginning again to tangle, they stop, and kiss, and dance, brothers learning that the world won't always be theirs together.

As Mallory and the Black Mummy let the pale brother's footsteps fade into the dark, their hands roam over one another's bodies, the Black Mummy's indelible arms, forever inked, sailing over her like a ship across the water, and Mallory's ghostly fingers running over his shoulders like rain. They feel every ripple and curve of their collective ligature, reveling in the sinews of their bodies, in his darkness and her transparency, in adolescent lust pounding out of them.

A scream deep in the cave ahead breaks the moment, the tone frightened and awful, the guttural sound of a brother lost.

Breaking their kiss, the Black Mummy calls to his brother.

There is no response, only long echoes of his voice down the tunnel.

The scream of his brother dies out pure and pale and sad, sending Mallory and the Black Mummy headlong, racing the cave's length, spearing ahead until they catch his sniffling in the pitch around a bend of the tunnel walls, where this becomes not just a cave but a complex of caves, a multitude of paths branching into separate darknesses, each its own possibility, and the other brother's whimpers issuing from one branch.

Down the path, the Black Mummy and Mallory come upon toothsome spikes attached to a rusted pipe arm swung into the tunnel's space, a crude trap left for a meddlesome pirate or a prying boy, placed at a height to alleviate blood from the head and abdomen and groin. This is where they find him, the lost and pale brother cowering on the ground beneath the spikes, his courage and anger equally cauterized, his defeat obvious and awful.

They kneel.

It was a long-ago adventurer who'd sprung the trap, whose head is now only a jawbone and a chunk of skulled forehead posted on the spike, the body disintegrated into ragged bones and pooled clothing. The lost brother is crumpled at its feet, a stream of blood running from his hand where a spike pricked him as he stomped forward, tantrumming through this dark complex of caves. The wound is a stigmata, his pants wetted. He collapsed when the jawbone with its lurid teeth lashed out at him from the darkness, when the spike licked his palm and his courage poured out. He is still balled, weak and moaning and fetal, ashamed at the noises he can't stop making, even as Mallory's nears, even as his Black Mummy brother arrives.

Mallory and the Black Mummy take in the age-old sprung trap, the small blood rivering from the brother's palm, the bone spiked and how it must have looked so ghostly, hovering in the darkness as he ran dead into it, a brother whose strength now is only wiry adolescence and awkward solitude. These are no longer twins. They are something else, and the Black Mummy has a hard time believing they'll ever captain together after this.

They lift his fragile, worn-out body from the ground, careful to turn him away from the desiccated half head clinging to the topmost point of the trap. This leftover brother is nearly weightless in his grief, in his loneliness, in his longing for what used to be.

On his feet, Mallory and the Black Mummy lead this sad brother back down the path, worming their way through the complex of caves, the weakened body supported between the two of them, the Black Mummy's strength easily carrying his weight and Mallory's touch keeping his exhausted feet moving, nothing for any of them to say. All that is left is to ascend the tunnel's wet ironed walls, coated in these new, unknown darknesses, to go back to the world and see what else it holds.

o

When someone asks Our Father a question, he tells deep and complicated stories, and it takes a certain kind of listener to hear what he intends, a particular breed to understand or decipher, his stories so much more intricate than the directive to sail or a call to arms.

The crew who remain after the crags still don't know why Our Father wouldn't row himself to that rocky island and grab those men by the necks, tote them back to the ship like baby chicks. He could have saved them all. He could have taken them by force. He could have a full crew still, even if they were maimed by their own dreams of everything so close at hand. The remaining crew assumes it was fear that kept Our Father on deck, how he might have been afraid to see his own treasured wants reflected in those pools, afraid he'd get mired in that forever alongside those mates. But this is only an assumption, because no one is brave enough to ask Our Father any more questions, not after the last answer of lightning and sons, that story which seems impossible to unload.

There are as many assumptions about Our Father as there are stars in the sky.

He is said to have sunken an entire buccaneer fleet by himself, cannoning one ship after another, their bodies sagging to the sea, the boats collapsing, and his own ship with not a mark on it. He is said to have shot the feather from a rival's tricorne at a thousand yards, like firing into a speck on the horizon, no way he could have seen the target, and yet the feather was torn asunder from his pistol shot. He is said to have burned every building in Port Vide, setting them ablaze against the night sky, burning all the people too, each one of them torching, screaming, the doors barred and the rooms lit up one after another after another. Our Father is said to have snatched countless women from taverns and brothels, from shanties and shacks. He is said to have wrenched the teeth from their mouths, to have kept them as tokens in a pouch strung around his neck, the sinister rattle the only piece of evidence.

But this crew, like every other Our Father has led, they want answers where there are only rumors, legends, stories infinitely unfolding, making the truth impossible to decipher. Every tale Our Father tells seems as implausible as the last, his crew no longer confident in the realities of his words, or of their voyage, shaken first by the loss of so many mates on a rock island of dreams.

When they signed his parchment, Our Father asked if they wanted to be legendary, and they'd marked their names, wanting to live forever alongside him, not knowing this kind of future was what he meant.

Days and days go by without guidance, without direction, only ever gossip and rumors floating between the mates, stories they sling in whispers along with the lines and the netting and the sails. There is no land in sight, Our Father only changing slight direction with each passing of the moon, continually eyeing its lunar surface far above the water and not uttering a word of real information, only more stories. He sails with a steady heart while the crew only sees water and half-moons, trying to wash the lost crewmen from their heads, the images of them stooped and knelt over cragged reflections on a desolate island where they will perish, the crew wondering which fate is better.

For now, it is only ever water and more water, the moon not yet full.

They keep the deck clean. They check and re-check the riggings. They do whatever they can to stay busy, to avoid the swelling ideations of mutiny, to avoid asking Our Father anything further, to await the moon rising full and shining on the brim of the ocean.

When it does begin to happen, the moon landing on the cusp of the ocean, almost ready for boarding, Our Father is telling the crew of his sons, how they'd once taken everything from the house and buried it around the township, drawing an incomprehensible map and him too dizzy to chase down his belongings. The crew was trying to smile at the storied antics of those twin boys, how many they'd heard, Our Father using them to pretend everything else away. The hammocks swayed, the boat creaked. Then mid-sentence Our Father rose, slow as the tide, his voice muted among the crewmen in the half-empty hold, each trying to see or hear what Our Father sees with his heart. There is the jostling of rigging and the shuffle of a hammock under a buccaneer as Our Father leaps up the laddered steps, fondling the handle of his cutlass as he goes. The men follow in a stupor, their captain's sudden silence and departure so unlike their own movements, soggy with the sea, exhausted from the endless pursuit of golden shores.

Topside, the moon is luminous on the water.

Our Father's face warms, his eyes welling.

There it is, he says, *our golden shore.*

Among them a mate scoffs as the sails shift. The small sea of crewmen weaken and part to reveal the culprit, a burly mate with a white headscarf, a tail of hair escaping, eyes wild and golden hoops in each ear. His collar is ringed with dirt. He is tall, a furred chest showing out the top of his doublet, muscled arms and legs thick as cannon barrels. Our Father listens to the water against the hull, the wind on the sails, moonlight reflected in his eyes. He and the mate both have blades sashed to their waists, pistols tucked in sheaths, dagger hilts protruding from boot tops. There is no parrot between them though Our Father's silver tooth winks like a star. The water sways and the near-full moon shines, the sea composed of all the rain that has ever come before.

The men give Our Father a broad aisle as he approaches, stepping to this mate who scoffed, who let out into the open his lack of belief.

What was that, my friend? Our Father says, his voice eloquent but grave.

Nothing, Captain, the crewman says, trying to look strong with tremors of fear beneath so many muscles.

When we scoff at the beliefs of others, Our Father says, reaching up and holding tight to one of the man's ears, the golden hoop and the lobe it's threaded through, *do you know what we're doing?*

No, the crewman says, nerves breaking across his face, the deck awash with tension.

We are anchoring ourselves to the world. We are forgetting that there are always other possibilities.

The rumors of Our Father are running holes in the mate's courage. He's become too jumpy to respond, too anxious to properly handle any of the weapons around his waist. Even his muscles, big as they are, provide little comfort to the moment. Our Father's hand stays locked on the mate's ear, the waves lapping, the ship lifting on small swells. The crew clings with weary legs to the deck, boards salted in moonlight, sweat ringing the air. A loose rigging clangs. Our Father winks at the backdrop of crewmen, to ease their collective breath, the mate's ear still in his grasp. Then, in a single swift motion, he lifts the dagger from his boot and cuts the man's ear clean from his head. Blood runs and the mate's shoulder goes dark red.

Don't cling to the wreckage, Our Father says under the man's shrieking, the man cowering on the deck in a wetted doublet. *Don't count out the impossible*, he adds, tossing the ear and its golden hoop into the sea. The mate holds his hands to the opening, the blood gushing. He can't quiet his weeping, even as other crewmen move to hold rags to the wound, to staunch the bleeding. Otherwise, the night is silent, the sails beautifully winded.

We are headed into that moon, Our Father says. *You've never known such treasure. The dreams you thought you saw, the ones I pistol shot you from, they're pitiful next to what we'll find on that golden shore. All you have to do is believe.*

o

There is no choice in love.

When Our Mother came down the dim, morning-lit hallway, she was humming a song of sun and stars, practically glowing. Days before, the Black Mummy had risen with both forearms healing and his pale brother in tow, riding away to the arcade. The Black Mummy's strength and resilience is unmistakable now, unavoidable. He is bold, courageous, and the grief he'd shown, what is mounting still in his brother, has settled so low she would have trouble finding it. This is it. She has the answer. So she hums in the morning light, knowing soon she'll be able to mummify the rest of the Black Mummy, down to his very heart, turning his sadness invisible, gutting it like a tumor, and setting him back into a revised future. Then she can start on her other son, and before the ghostliness sets in, she'll have rectified both of their paths.

The rain falls lightly, sun tendriling through cloud banks, the clock softly issuing.

But as she rounds the hallway to the kitchen, Our Mother is halted, her enthusiasm disintegrating as she finds that pale twin laid out on the table. His skin is moonlight in the morning's strangled sun, eyes as if he hasn't slept in days, bagged and bruised. He's draped the table in white, found her instruments and set them in a perfect mimicry of her surgical litany, all the tins and pans and tools, all the blades, and he is resting in the middle of it, ankles and thighs and forehead strapped, the belts only needing her final cinch.

Our Mother hasn't properly soaked in the Black Mummy's triumphs yet, the flawlessness of his forearms, the sleek ink and power of him. She hasn't had time to fully rejoice in the results, to give thoughts of Billy enough time to dissipate. She isn't ready for the heart, not today, and not on this son who seems ill-prepared, sunken into sadness rivering deeper with each day. Yet here he is, pale and partially strapped to the table, waiting, desperate for the scalpel's touch, even if she isn't ready. He's been waiting so long. He's been so patient. He is so desperate.

She wants to tell him it isn't his time, how there is more for her to digest, how the Black Mummy is only piece by piece and she has to finish the act, carefully, and with restraint. She has to do this right. She only has the one chance. She wants to drape promises like rain across his body, though she knows those words would only be like Our Father sailing away again, sentences like another ship slipping over the horizon.

He is so broken, so devastated. All that is young in him, all that is innocent, all that is unyielding to the world, it is slipping, day by day, and now minute by minute.

So she chases the logic away and follows her heart.

Our Mother looks to him and his shirtless sternum, limbs like leafless branches, veins visible through the skin. He closes his eyes, ready, ripe with destiny.

Our Mother checks the tightness of the straps he's placed over his own ankles and thighs and forehead, pulls taut the belts and adds one across his shoulders and collarbones, where Billy rose each and every time, ballooning his head, careening the experiment.

She lifts the hammer.

No, the pale son says, Our Mother's arm raised. His voice is a sail snapping in the wind. He exhales, the hammer held aloft. He says he wants to feel it, asks her to put the hammer down, begs the scalpel forward instead, motions it not to one forearm or another but to his chest, a gentle command at Our Mother's elbow. He has to take it all. All the pain. All the suffering. All the momentous change. It's the only way he'll catch up to his Black Mummy brother. It's the only way he'll recuperate from whimpering on the cave's floor, from Mallory's pitiful kiss on his weak lips, from the loss of so much piracy. The rain falls. She hovers the scalpel above his heart, quietly detonating in this son's belief.

I need it, he says, and her will is gone.

The sadness in this son is more than she can withstand. She sees the hurt, the pain, the loss in his eyes, the ships once dreamt now tossed on raging seas, incessant with suffering. She sees his jealousy too, something she has created by letting one son transform while the other is forced to watch from the outskirts.

I am so sad, he says, the most honest words he's ever spoken.

Make it stop, he says.

It is the sadness of Our Father not returning, of Mallory's unrequited love, of brother jealousy, of her own growing ghostliness. It is a sadness in the canyons of his heart, in this township's rain, deep in the complex of caves, and he's begging her to cut it out.

Our Mother touches the scalpel to his sternum, gently, without cutting.

She'll have to crack the breastplate. She'll have to open the ribs, the gush of blood like a tide, running from the heart. She has to forget about Billy. She has to forget about the Black Mummy. She has to focus on only this one son right now. It is a rescue. He is drowning.

As she makes the first incision, a tear runs down her cheek. The blood exits his chest but he doesn't stir. The blade pushes through one layer then the next, the tissues, the veins, the muscles. Her son closes his eyes. His chest, his organs, they'll be a thousand times more complicated than the Black Mummy's forearms, but she'll endure, she'll beat back the doubt. She'll conquer this moment.

There are long, stretching muscles, the vital organs tightly packed, blood spitting and pooling in places the pans don't reach, bones Our

Mother has to break and pry. There is snapping and spurting, organs she fumbles with transparent hands, slicked spots and scarring redness, dangling strings of inner holds she hasn't planned for, her hands shaken, her instruments slipping, no place to rest her mind.

He is open now. There is no turning back.

She pulls his chest wider with each run of the scalpel, with each next tool and the force of her ghostly forearms. She blunders another organ out of the cavity and it flounces on the table. Her son's eyelids flinch. When his lungs are uncovered, she watches them shallowly compress and expand. She unpacks the rest, and then he isn't moving anymore at all, everything pulled out of his body. She has never been this far in, not even with Billy, and it's as if she's lost at sea. Up past her elbows in blood and fluids, the heart of her boy is beating its slow sadness out in the open, slowing amidst the splayed complexities of his split body. His eyelids flex and jog with the pressure of her hands and the instruments, his heart struggling.

She works on, desperate to right his ship, to make him what she knows he should be, but the work is daunting and unknown, the complexities too much for her, the distance between everything distending until she can hardly see, the world a blur.

Then his heart stops. It is there on the table, thieved from his body, Our Mother's hands gruesome, her forearms coated in blood, the table awash in the procedure, her son's presence like the still frame of a rupturing.

It was too soon. She should have waited. She should have listened to her head instead of her heart. She needed one more bout with the book, one more run of experience with the Black Mummy. She needed more time, or the world to slow, or Billy to disappear. She needed what she couldn't have. She needed everything.

She will not lose him. She cannot lose him.

No longer concerned with his mummification, Our Mother seeks absolution, salvation, this pale son's chest an endless smash of red and wetness. She has to unbury him from death's shore.

Beginning anew, Our Mother works in reverse, returning all of him as quickly and soundly as she can, with as much adeptness as her see-through fingers will allow, putting the organs where she found them, cleaning them as best she can, correcting any slights, mending as much damage as possible, patching and restringing the miscellany of veins like the threads of a soured dress. She scours the surfaces of each passage, the organs and tissues and muscles and arteries, the casings soaked in blood and tears. She reattaches veins to veins, sutures arteries to flow again into the mouths of one another, sending the blood back into the rivers of the body, reconnecting the loosed holdings of his sad and failing flesh.

And while she'd like to pack him with vegetable fiber and animal fur, with the leavings of this landscape, with spruce boughs and rain, there isn't time. His heart is stopped, broken. So she stitches and sutures, the body reassembled and packed as best she remembers, her hands going ghostly over and again as she hurries to finish. A needle drops into his chest, her fingers bloodily scrounging to recover it, to re-thread him. His ribs push against the skin as she sews, unable to return his sternum to its original curve, the thin muscles stretched out of shape, pulling awkwardly against the seams. The end result is her boy put back together, only with a chest sunken at its center and billowed at its extremities, varied and harried stitches running the length, no balance or symmetry or beauty, only madcap rescue, hope pitted against loss.

With the last stitch, his breath comes back, though it is devastatingly shallow, and his heartbeat too, except in tentative rhythm, so little blood left to circulate. He is a crushed fragment of what he used to be, laid on this unforgiving shore, where the tide is only ever a violent whisper. Our Mother has failed him, and she can do nothing but concoct a hasty batch of red ink to paint and repaint his torso, to cover the mess of blood spackled haphazardly everywhere, the already welting seams. She coats from his shoulders to his abdomen, the red seeping in, blood and ink blending on her hands as the Black Mummy appears on the stairs, looking down the hallway to his brother's maligned chest, the body of a Red Mummy stumbling toward its ending.

o

The Black Mummy knows the feel of stitches and sutures, the cutting open of skin, knows how his blood is more like treasure now, but he's never seen Our Mother coated in so much of it. He's never known the smell so resonant, resting on his tongue and teeth and the ceiling of his mouth, and he's never imagined his brother dying with Our Mother's forearms coated, panic on her face, the hallway clock ticking away their lives.

He can't just watch this happen. He can't just stand there, waiting to see if his brother will live, waiting to see what happens. He can't just wait inside such an apocalyptic moment, hoping for the best. He can't just stand there, bearing witness.

Since the beginning they've been two halves of a whole, twins in Our Mother's womb. Together they fed from her and swallowed rain, rolled in a collective crib before taking their first steps, swore pirate curses and dug holes in imitation of Our Father. Together they made maps and watched seagulls transform into bats, the sun into the moon, rain making the clouds ghostly, the soil darkened around them. Together they've waved from the shore, watching Our Father sail away, a pinpoint hazing, left behind to grieve. And together, they've done their best to move on, to assuage the riptide of sadness, to shelter in the arcade, to discover beneath it that complex of caves, to fall in love with the ghost of a girl up the street, to pedal their bicycles in the rain long enough that they become pirates, to sail too from every sadness that is bent on chasing them down.

Now, the Black Mummy doesn't know what will become of any of it.

He has strength enough in his mummified forearms to smash a man's skull, to break limbs, to snap a wrist as easily as a wave touches the shore. He could pull the heart out of a man's chest, push through the skin and muscles and ribcage to grasp the bleating center. The reach of his blackened forearms is infinite, and Mallory, she brightens like a flame whenever he approaches, the ink drawing her like a beacon. She's fallen in love with him. He feels it in her kisses, in her caresses, sees it in the way she burns. Her lips on his, her hands roaming, their bodies combining. He's in love with her too, but there's his twin between them, his brother with pale forearms, skin the color of the moon, and Mallory only in love with one of them.

His brother's chest literally opened, sternum pried, organs slithered into Our Mother's hands, her arms ripe with red, he doesn't know what to do. Is this how he escapes a twin collapse? By watching the other half of himself disintegrate in her hands? Our Mother didn't know he'd been peering around the newel post since she held his brother's heart in her hands, lungs free from his chest. She didn't know he'd been watching as she'd massaged the breath back in, pleading with her eyes, how he'd seen her transparent lips kiss the slick red skin of his heart, begging it to beat again. There'd been so much blood. It pooled across the table and rained down the edges. He'd watched as Our Mother fought to sew him together, mixing red ink to coat his chest, her footsteps leaving bloody marks on the floor, impossible to tell where the rupture ended and the ink began.

Crushing the knob with a black forearm's grip, he left through the front door, leaving the collapsed knob behind him, the mimicry of a wounded heart. Outside, on the porch, the mat still says *Ahoy*, and the township is as wet and spruced as ever.

The Black Mummy rides his bicycle to the once empty house up the street, rides as if there is only this one day left, as if tomorrow he'll be brotherless. He doesn't know how he'll live in that kind of future. It is unbearable to imagine no brother beside him.

A single spine traced in rain as he rides. A seagull hovers. Newspapers mound on the end of driveways as occasional cars spit by, spruce boughs dripping and fern fronds glistening.

When Mallory sees him, she leaps out the front door and down the porch steps, bright all the way to him, hardly noticing the missing brother. Her brow smooth and unknotted, she holds the Black Mummy's hands, runs her fingers over his forearms, and it's as if the stars no longer matter, as if death is only another bout of rain to be endured. She ignores the brother gone, doesn't notice the grief written across the Black Mummy's face.

He doesn't tell Mallory what he's seen of his brother, about the hemostats rising like masts from his chest, his abdomen an exploded womb, the red of the blood and the red of the ink and the stitches welting down his sternum. He doesn't say how his brother's lungs were set aside from his body, how there wasn't a single breath in them. He doesn't admit that he saw his brother's heart beating so softly that it couldn't even compete with the patter of rain, that it stopped, held aloft like a wet jewel in Our Mother's hands, her face buried in its folds.

Mallory's face is so bright. Her fingers in his and the rain falling, the wind soothing. She sits on the seat of his bicycle and wraps her arms around his waist, willing everything to go on like this, just him and her, a glutton for what feels good, here in this wet world.

Without a word, the Black Mummy rides to the arcade, Mallory threaded around him, her chin nuzzled into his neck, the rain wetting their hair. Then they are up and over the curve at the top of this township, heading down the veins of slicked asphalt where the pavement bleeds to dirt near the pebbled shore. The Black Mummy rides them to the arcade, the building cloaked in clouds and rain, all these same forms of abandonment, Mallory's cheek resting on his skin while he tries to forget about his brother thrown open like an abyss.

He leans his bicycle against the siding and they go inside, her hand never letting go. They lift the boards from the cave's entrance and climb into the tunnel's mouth. He leads them with his black forearms, Mallory shining bright as a torch, following the splits of tunnels, walking to where his brother was nearly spiked, where he'd puddled. They stand there, hand in hand, the Black Mummy remembering how his brother had whimpered as no buccaneer ever should. The cave around them makes small noises of scratch and drip, brief breeze moanings, the tunnel's skin iron-colored in Mallory's glow, a complex of caves open in front of them. Neither know what is beyond, but Mallory's hand is enough for the moment. With her there, holding to him, he can pretend to forget about his brother's perils, about the chance that this is the end of the world.

The complex of caves twists and turns and divides. They follow every tunnel in turn, walk until they meet dead ends and have to retrace their steps to the next, pressing and retreating until they are deep into the complex, past numerous other antique traps and pitfalls, other tricks set for prying bodies, for nosy buccaneers. They find curses smeared in charcoal and blood on the clay walls, hold their backs against the curved tunnel to skirt cavernous gapings below, ledges hardly holding up. They grip to handholds and climb piled stones. They hold hands as they cross the partial bodies of others, the skeletons and stains of ancient blood, pistol holes in bone temples and limbs whirled around jettisoned spears. Chains swaying in the tunneled wind, webs of tripping twine rigged and a thousand other forms of deception, none clever or fearsome enough to fully push the images of his brother from the Black Mummy's head, images of his brother's heart in Our Mother's hands, of his red chest devastated and awful. It is too much. Even with Mallory there, it is too much.

No more, he says, and Mallory looks at him, knowing it is a twinship she is undoing. He pulls her by the hand back to where they've come from, across the depths and folds of the cave.

The Black Mummy quickly pulls Mallory up and out into the arcade's weak sunlight, desperate to return home, to find out what has become of the future.

o

Our Father's halved crew is restless and agitated. He told them they were sailing into the moon, and though this is outlandish enough, the real grievance is that they haven't. Our Father only keeps chasing its glowing full figure across the water. It seems like a thousand days ago that he rose from the holds below and leapt up the stairs, a thousand days since he cut off a crewman's ear and tossed it into the sea, a thousand days since he said they would row onto those golden shores. A thousand days and yet the moon is never quite full enough for Our Father.

They've been at sea so long. They've lost so much. They no longer know what to expect from their captain. He said they would sail into the moon. He said they'd moor this ship to its shores and part the radiant sky like a curtain. He said they'd find a treasure beyond any ever dreamt. In the plain sight of retrospect, it sounds more and more like some lunatic lullaby he uses to sing them to sleep.

Our Father says again today, *It's almost time*, and the crew plummets. To them, this moon rising tonight looks the same as all its previous iterations, no bigger or fuller than the one that came before. They see no curtain to part like drapery and no golden shore, no island to sail into. At this point, they are afraid their captain will simply sail them into forever, the water never ceasing, the moon continually reached for until the provisions are decimated and they are weak from hunger and thirst. That mounting possibility is becoming mutiny, which has to be sought before Our Father hurls them any further into slow death, sailing where there is no world left to cling to.

They work on deck rearranging the holds and tucking away the last of the provisions, retooling the riggings as a means to pass the time, to stave off the inevitable. When the work runs out, they thumb playing cards or sing hymns, throw knives at timber or slipknot lassos to mutely seize one another. The sun is setting again and they want to sleep, only mutiny is too near now, their surfaces burbling with a need for control, willing to wrest the helm from Our Father's grip in order to steer this ship back to land, any land. Even the cragged surface of that doomed island seems a welcome change from these endless waters and Our Father's pretend compass-heart, his promises one on top of the other.

Our Father watches the horizon as moonlight deepens across the water. He sees the crew trying to quell their hands, attempting to silence the voices in their heads, longing to ignore their pistols and cutlasses. He sees it coming, prow to the rising moon, face aglow.

There we are, mates, our friend the full moon, almost here.

They've had to wait for their eyes to unblind from the siren island's dreamscape. They've had to forget about their fellow crewmen left to die on that volcanic rock. They've had to keep focus on the promise of legends as the moon rose over and again, never full enough for Our Father's liking, always the same message, *Almost,* the moon never ripe enough for the picking. They are exhausted, and his call tonight is like the hundred that went before it, each promise a star hung helplessly above, a dream gone awry.

The crew is beleaguered. Our Father grins. It's as if he has a hooked hand, as if there's a parrot on his shoulder, as if he has a peg leg steady on the boards. His silver tooth shines. He will sail into the island of the moon, and the shores will be golden, the treasure unlike any they've ever known, and he'll do it with or without this crew. The possibilities are a tethered rope, and he's only waiting to see if the line will hold. There is silence, then wind. They've waited so long. They've endured so much. They never thought this was what Our Father meant when he asked them if they wanted to be legendary. They don't need to know how he'll do it, how he'll sail into the moon, how it could be an island when the moon is so obviously in the sky. They only want something, anything to happen. They only want to board this dream, once and for all, because Our Father keeps saying, *Almost,* and the moon goes on rising, and that's when it finally comes undone.

The crewmen draw their swords, unsheathe their pistols. The night glows up their faces, Our Father looking from the moonlight on the water's surface to the desperation of these halved men, their fraught eyes and eager weapons, the mutiny of their hearts.

Gentlemen, he says, *there is no need*, but their cutlasses are already singing.

The treasure there, he says, nodding to the moon, *is more than you can imagine*, but their pistols are loaded, their fingers poised on the triggers.

Well then, mates, Our Father says, seeing them battened against any reasoning, *I will sail into that island without you.*

The first blade stabs toward Our Father, the crew done with his stories and his beliefs, his legends and lullabies, his voice in the sails. Our Father's sword is brandished, the moon on his face, the ship a melody of weapons through air, Our Father is one hundred men at once, his cutlass stronger and faster and sharper than the rest. He chops a hand, gouges a face, gashes a bicep, pierces intestinal walls and linings, cleaves through a spine, blood soaking doublets. He fires his pistol, exploding someone's head in a fog of red and gush, slashes a throat and clobbers a mate's crown with the butt of his buccaneer pistol, severs an arm, daggers a heart, crashes a brow inward with the hilt of his cutlass, bones splintering through skin, eyes bulging, the rising moon kissing the water.

Crewmen lie bleeding everywhere on deck, waves smearing the blood, red running over the boards. Some groan or whimper, pirates who've suddenly become boys craving motherly arms, the ship swaying and their wounds and cries opening anew with each subtle rocking of the ship.

A pistol is fired from somewhere in the remaining fray and though it's a good shot, a shot that should cut straight through Our Father's chest, there is only a cloud of dissipating smoke and a stunned look on the crewman's face. With the empty pistol still aimed at him, Our

Father threads his cutlass through the crewman's neck, sinking it into the soft spot where chest meets throat. He hardly has to press. Smatters of blood spurt on either side as Our Father drags his cutlass downward, opening wide the man's entire body, organs exposed to the light of the moon, the body retreating, its machinery lulled.

The last men alive are pleading for their lives with interlaced fingers, with harrowed voices. Our Father wraps a mate in rope until his eyes deaden and his tongue unglues, pushes his dagger into the collar of another, settling down until the sternum caves. He slices deep and quick across another's back, kidney to shoulder, a wound expelling rubies across the crewman's clothing, exposing the white of his vertebrae. Our Father reloads and fires, daggering a chest, quieting a heart. Our Father is luminescent. He wrecks bodies until stillness returns to the ship, until the wind appears again in the sails, the boat buoyed by starlight.

And through it all, the moon gently touching upon the horizon, Our Father illuminated by its golden face.

o

The stitches complete, Our Mother waits, gathering her strength to heft the Red Mummy upstairs. His body is sewn. He's breathing again and his heart is pumping. She can feel his thin pulse and the slim exhale of breath beneath the sutures, chest rising and falling under the bright ligature, raised gnarls already deviling with infection, a range running jaggedly. His breath, through slightly parted lips, hardly mounts or abates.

But he is alive.

Our Mother is so ashamed of the brutal work she has performed on this son, so frightened for what he'll be when he wakes. She can't imagine how his body will respond to her rushed and fretful work, the slips of the instruments through her ghostly hands, the hallway clock pouring into her head, the implosion of rain on the roof. This Red Mummy, his chest laden with damage.

His breathing stumbles and rasps. His heartbeat is weary. His ribs are raised in places and sunken in others, as if there's nothing left below the skin. She holds his limp hand at the table, all the belts removed, the Black Mummy somewhere else in this township and the sun nearly gone. There is a sky, though she can't find it through the thickness of the clouds, through the rain and tears. Our Mother holds his hand, remembering all the maps her boys have drawn, all the dotted lines, all the ciphers and omens and signs. She remembers the look in their eyes when they traced those routes, how real the treasure was to them, loaded like pistol shot in their hearts.

When she'd started on this pale son, her hands nervously wrenching, begged into a chest she wasn't ready for, she tried to calm her heart. She tried to tell herself that she'd never feel absolutely ready, that one day she'd have to simply leap from the cliff's edge. She tried to remind herself that she'd pored over a thousand photographs in her reading and rereading, a thousand diagrams, a thousand sets of instructions. But as soon as his chest was open, she was unsure of everything in its gaping cavity, the contents beneath his sternum, the organs and fluids. She'd never opened a son's precious insides. She'd never held one of their hearts in her bare hands.

The wreckage she created was immediate and steady in its complications, the blood running where she hadn't expected, veins she hadn't accounted for, the layers thicker or thinner than she'd anticipated. She'd kept the panic at bay as long as she could, reminding herself of the work she'd already done, how the Black Mummy is stronger now than ever before, how he recovered quickly, how she's watched him beam at his newly tattooed limbs, and how those forearms will never change, will never become any less than she's made them, how they'll remain for eternity. But reminders weren't enough. Her hands went ghostly on the scalpel's grip and she nicked an organ. Her fingers went see-through and fumbling. Her desperation made it worse. She had to blot, to sop, to rearrange. The blood ran, the rain fell, and the worries overcame her. Her hands shook uncontrollably, wracked with frustration and alarm. More than anything else, Our Mother worries, even now, even with his heartbeat restored and his breathing returned, that this can't be undone.

She sits with the Red Mummy, the heat of his body combating the wounds. Rain plucks at the window as clouds pass and reshape. Our Mother's tome never mentioned how many bodies never took to mummification, how many ancient surgeons botched the job, how many operations like this left boys and girls wrecked, broken, ending in funeral pyres. Without the protection of forever, those children would only become bodies burned to ash or buried in the ground to decay and mold, bodies disassembled by blights of nature, by wind and rain and insects in the soil, by the dampness of forever underground. Even in *Chinchorro*'s thousand pages and thousand stories and thousand accounts of conquest, there is no mention of the failures. There was no way to foresee this prospect of catastrophe, this miscarriage. Or Our Mother never understood the possibility until now, the Red Mummy's shallow breathing and faint heartbeat there on the kitchen table, resting while she rests, not yet ready to carry him upstairs to bed.

Our Mother's tears pass through her palms. The ghost of her expands. Through her whimpering she hears what sounds like the Red Mummy waking. She shutters her own sounds to listen, only it isn't the Red Mummy. The rustling persists. It's maybe the wind scraping against the house or a shingle restlessly unhinged, but then she hears it clearer, the bumps and brushes, the quality of its insistence, the murmur of its intent. She places the Red Mummy's arms across his chest, not a tableau of burial but a means to keep pace with his own heart, squeezing his hand, hoping he feels love through his pain and her ghostliness.

Our Mother leaves the Red Mummy there atop the reddened sheet, bordered in panned blood, forsaken and visceral, and she moves cautiously down the hall, past the clock, careful not to get too far away from her boy, to keep him in sight, to be sure he won't simply disappear into the hurt.

The rustling continues.

It could be the softest knocking at the door, faint and ill-timed, but when she peers through the panes, there is no shadow slipping away from the door. She waits and then the sound births elsewhere. She moves back through the hallway, stopping to listen every few feet, hearing the clock mixed with the odd thump and thud, a dense scratching like hands dragging walls.

Our Mother knows, she just doesn't want to admit it.

She creeps back until she's in the kitchen again, the Red Mummy and all the blooded remnants surrounding him, accosted by those remonstrances. There she pins the displaced noise to the bay window, seeing the unfitting darkness pass behind the curtains, a shadow moving sluggishly in stunted motions, the outline crippled and broken, a yawn of menace.

Our Mother draws back the curtain to find Billy's grotesque and disfigured form, his distended arms and hands pawing at the window, wrecking the vigil for her Red Mummy. Billy's face is absurd, his limbs mangled, his self-threaded body pieced together from what she'd buried in a hundred places across the rain and sadness of this township. He is reborn and pulled back to a boyish shape. Our Mother moves to the glass door by the bay window and slides it open with such force that it spins Billy to the ground, his body so poorly assembled he can't immediately rise, like a beetle there on his back, groping at the clouded sky.

Our Mother is on top of him before he has his legs back.

She trounces his chest, pummeling Billy about the face and neck and head, her careful seamstress hands turned to brutal fists. She hits and hammers, breaks what remains of his nose, splits open his brow and blunts his cheeks into ruddy bleeding, his wounds weeping watery, diluted scarlet, rain as much as anything else.

They become a mass of writhing, Billy rolling over and straddling Our Mother with his oddly elongated legs, pinning her shoulders with the gnarled knots of his knees, his limbs not bending properly though still keeping Our Mother's back to the grass. If she could control her transparency, if she could make her body disappear on command, Billy's weight would fall right through her. Instead, the muddy cat trailing bandages ducks around the corner of the house, legs sordid and unhinged, and while Billy's attention is diverted, Our Mother strikes. She wrests her shoulders from beneath his knobbed knees and regains her feet, the cat disappearing into the neighboring spruce boughs, Billy's attention slow to return.

Again she wails on his body, sending him off balance and backward, his unsymmetrical form tipping like a toy ship in a trough. He falls and she drops a knee to his chest, feeling the failed sternum go to fragments under her weight. Billy winces and she continues, kneeing as heavily as she can, his ribs cracking and his body splintering, piercing the organs within.

Thinking of her Red Mummy and how everything went awry, she shreds Billy, her arms treacherous, pressing his face backward into his skull, widening the sides of his mouth, pulling his ears from his head and his hair from his scalp. She works her fingers at the seams of his arms and legs, forcing grotesque gaps in the skin, the blood and bodily liquids spinning out like expelled threads. She rips and splatters Billy, mashes him beneath her palms and heels, rending him with her teeth in unbridled anger, turning Billy back into fragments, ripping and renting until there is nothing left, until Billy is scraps, like fabric winding across the yard.

Our Mother stands in the aftermath, her heart pounding, a dusky rain on her shoulders, and in that moment, she finally believes in seagulls turning to bats, in the possibility of righting this ship.

Above her, above the clouds, the moon rises.

o

The morning sun comes up the next day behind clouds and rain. The Red Mummy doesn't know when Our Mother finished the cutting and prying, the bursting open and gushing out and bleeding of his body. He doesn't know when Our Mother tied off the work of his heart and turned to the suturing and the stitching, to the red tattooing of his chest. He doesn't know when she put him upstairs to rest. The Red Mummy only knows how clear the damage is as he wakes in the lower bunk.

Brushing the exhaustion from his eyes, he follows the line of stitches with his fingers. It runs from below his collarbones to his waistline. His fingers travel every seam, each bit of it burdened with ache, the lines already swollen with infection, agonized, ill-spaced and inconsistently looped, some doubled or tripled yet still weakened by the strain of his taut, bloated skin. It all looks so unlike Our Mother's work on the Black Mummy, her stitching there like stars appearing in the sky, beautiful and glorious. But this, this is barely holding him together. The tissue of his sternum and abdomen are sunken and expanded in turn, the skin loose in places and tight in others, the whole of it hastily lashed into rough shape rather than carefully woven into the forever of mummification. Where his ribs should protect him in a bony shield, they are loose, like splinters pressing inward. His abdomen feels similarly excavated and poorly reset, organs and roped intestines misplaced and wrongly repacked, unspooling inside of him rather than set with purpose. Worst of all, his heart feels dim, quiet as the morning sun on the roof. His lungs seem cautious too, each breath pain, no inhalation ever close to filling him. It is mockery and bleakness. He is tainted. He is wreckage. He is barely alive.

In the bunk above, the Black Mummy lies sleeping, contentment on his face, a bend to his lips like a smile, like a dream fulfilled. The Red Mummy, if he were to see it, that sleeping grin, he'd assume it was in vindication, in happiness at winning this war of mummification, the Black Mummy a victor in this bout of bodies. But the Black Mummy's sleep is smile-infected because yesterday he'd gone to the arcade believing in brotherlessness, worried over his twin's death, sure that the heart Our Mother kissed before placing it back in his chest would be rejected, would turn ghostly inside of him, leaving no twin brother for him. But when he'd returned from the arcade, when he'd dropped Mallory back at her house, when he'd waited outside like a worried father and then stepped over the threshold of their doorstep, hovering on the front porch until the moon was up, he'd found his brother asleep in the bottom bunk, resting beneath clean white sheets. And while his brother's breathing was shallow, the heartbeat faint, it was still his brother, and his sleep was saturated in relief.

Yesterday, he and Mallory had gone far into that complex of caves, sidestepping every pitfall, passing every sprung trap, leaning away from every cavernous edge, working past the jagged blades and the collapsing ceilings, unspooling forward. They'd held one another, fingers intertwined, her skin glowing their way, his strength keeping them safe, but in the end, none of it had mattered. None of it meant anything if he didn't have a brother to share it with. Brotherlessness wasn't worth a single gem, a single gold piece. If he didn't have his other half there beside him, it was no adventure.

There's no sound of Our Mother below, only the ticking of the clock. The Black Mummy eventually shifts and stretches, waking into remnants of yesterday then ducking his head over the side of the bunk to greet his brother below, to apologize for the love he took, for the separation he'd cleaved, but the sheets are rumpled to his waist, the Red Mummy's fingers tracing the grotesqueries of a welt-swollen and sunken torso. The Black Mummy looks into his brother's eyes, this Red Mummy, and sees the damage in his eyes, the pain tormenting him beneath the hasty matte red.

A thousand unsaid vagaries swell between them.

The Black Mummy doesn't know what to do. He rises, dresses, acting as if everything is okay, as if his brother doesn't appear beyond oblivion. The Red Mummy sits up slowly, carefully, awfully. The shirt barely raises over his head. The jeans he buttons and zips are excruciating on his waist. He makes faces of wince and whine, though he keeps the noises in.

There is no breakfast set as they round the bottom of the stairs, looking into the kitchen in T-shirts and jeans, shoes on the rug, one pair still wet from the day before. At least there is no coppery tang of blood in the air, no surgery in progress on the table, no sheet draped or pans palming blood, no scalpels or needles to be threaded.

But the Red Mummy feels faint and has to sit on the last step, hands cradling his head. The Black Mummy moves to the kitchen to find no kettle stirring, no steam rising, no glasses or bowls filled. The back door stands wide in the breeze, the yard fogged in wet greenery, spruce boughs dripping. Our Mother is not there. It is only silence and solitude. The Red Mummy's breathing caves, his body heaving, brutality in each lungful.

Well? the Black Mummy asks, closing the back door, returning down the hallway. His brother holding his head aloft as best he can.

Mallory's, the Red Mummy responds, a fixated burst of determination in his voice and behind his eyes, the exhale making the shape of her name. The Red Mummy's eyes are distant, blood-reddened where there used to be sails, though the Black Mummy can see he will not be deterred.

Aye, the Black Mummy gives back, holding out his brother's jacket from the hook on the wall. The Red Mummy refuses, head bowing again, the last of his strength dissipated for the moment. He can't hide what he's become.

Come on then, the Black Mummy presses, playing at forgetting too, moving headlong as a buccaneer's prow, cutlass raised to fight even in this, the most fruitless of battles. *You aren't on the plank yet*, he says to his brother, a stab at reassurance.

The Red Mummy tries several times to mount his bicycle and ride, but his heart can't kick up to speed, his lungs won't fill, and his balance is off. He can't make it more than a few yards without listing, having to put his feet down as he attempts to coast the driveway. He falters again going over the curb into the street. New blights of pain resound on his body, his skin thin, blood seeping from various wounds and stitches. The Black Mummy sees how simply his brother peels, how readily the diluted blood spills. They've been riding bicycles together for as long as either can remember, yet even this is suddenly out of reach. The Black Mummy hops off his bicycle and walks next to his brother, rain soaking them both, their jackets still on the hooks beside the front door, no lunch sacks gripped to the handlebars.

Newspapers sit at the end of driveways. A widow on a balcony fills her throat with rain. Spruce boughs jostle in the breeze. Fern fronds drip. The soil is black.

They watch Mallory's house glow as they approach, each window in the face of it throbbing with light as they walk their bicycles onto her driveway. The Red Mummy wants to be suspicious of the light pounding there, but he can't muster the energy. His head sags even as Mallory shoots out the front door and down the steps.

Without hesitation she flings her arms around the Black Mummy's neck, kissing him in quick succession, each kiss a pistol shot to the Red Mummy's heart. The Black Mummy's inked forearms gently pry her away, reprimanding her with his eyes, nodding towards his brother whose head is resting on the handlebars. A gust could blow him over.

While Mallory wants to know what happened, the Red Mummy doesn't raise his head, and the Black Mummy can't speak of it. Instead, he lifts his brother's shirt and Mallory gasps, a scream pulled back into her mouth. She is stunned. There is a moment of stillness as she takes in the swells and sunken places of his abdomen, the ruins of his chest, the carnage of his torso. She reaches her fingers to the midsection of the wound, the stitched skin jarring as mountain tops and brightly deviled, a mix of red ink and infection. The Red Mummy doesn't respond to her touch. She used to be electricity. Now, she's an absence of light.

Mallory still wants to go the arcade. She wants to finish the spelunking they started the day before, so many of the traps already mapped in their minds, so much of the complex known to them, handholding the Black Mummy as she did down those tunnels. She wants more. She wants to know what happens when they move past the final traps into the cave's jeweled heart, to find whatever nest egg is hidden there, a stake to start their own life of piracy and ghostliness. But the Red Mummy is in no shape for any of it. The Black Mummy pulls his brother's wet shirt back down, Mallory's fingers falling from underneath, the three of them in a cross-dissolve of existence.

The Red Mummy isn't out of danger, the Black Mummy knows it, Mallory knows too, but there is still life to be had, for all of them. They are here, and hearts want what hearts want. The Black Mummy and Mallory each know what is coming, this inevitable moment, even in the face of this carnage, sometimes especially in the face of such carnage, when it feels like the last day on earth.

They help the Red Mummy away from his bicycle, letting it clatter to the driveway. They support him to the porch, up the few steps and across the threshold of Mallory's front door, into her house. He is weak down to his toes. It is the first time the Red Mummy has been inside her house. He lifts his head for a moment before descending again, his breath steepening in its drag, his heart slumping. How he wishes he could take it all in. How he wishes these were not the circumstances.

Mallory and the Black Mummy set him down just inside the entryway, at the bottom of the stairs. There are no hooks for jackets in the hallway and no clock counting out loud, no framed photographs or furniture. The house is as barren as it had always been, no table or chairs, only those leftover curtains haphazardly hung. The Red

Mummy's chin settles on his chest, every breath setting off a new spike of pain, a steady fisting beneath his seams.

There is no mystery here.

The Black Mummy asks him if they should go home. He thought being in her presence would help, would lift his spirits, but it seems to have crashed him. The Red Mummy declines with a weak shake of his head. Wind thrusts against the side of the house, the rain with it. He can't recover, not even with Mallory's glow so nearby, not even with the sympathy in her eyes or the proximity of her full heart to his crushed one. The Black Mummy casts a shadow in the abundance of her light. Rain falls as they step around him and move upstairs, their hands coming together behind his back. The Red Mummy's chin settles reluctantly downward and without strength, his eyes staring into a single spot of flooring, dim sunlight mapping this exact destiny, what feels like an extinction, an extinguishing.

The Red Mummy listens to them take the stairs. He listens to them travel the length of an upstairs hallway. He listens to a door close. When he can't hear them any longer, he listens to the erratic undertone of his heart, to his rasping lungs and the rain swirling outside. Upstairs, they are exploring a new kind of darkness atop eyelet sheets, ascending into adulthood, the bursting glow of her and the pirate strength of him like pillars of light exploding, rubies caroming in their veins, rain falling on the roof in rhythmic taunts. It doesn't matter. It's what he's already imagined, since the first time he saw them kissing, since he first understood that love doesn't always come back to you.

He listens to the rain falling.

o

Our Father stands on a broken prow, his massive ship exhausted beneath, crushed against hidden shoals. The ship will never leave this place. There is not enough water in the world to put it back to sea.

The hull is smashed, the wood creaking as it continues shifting into splintered beams and broken struts, the tide pressing, nothing left to keep it afloat. The sails are crumpled, unable to harness the wind, masts crooked and battered, wrenched and ready to give in to the next gust. Water gathers in the quarters below, reaching toward the empty hammocks. The ship can't sink because it has run aground, the water already tiding in and out, rearranging its guts of wood and rope and canvas. Yet Our Father is smiling.

With the mutiny over, he'd cleaned the bodies and limbs and blood from the deck and washed clean the signs of treachery, then the hundred versions of Our Father helped remake the riggings and capture the wind, helped sail into the island of the moon rising luminous on the water. Our Father, a one-man crew, guiding the ship through a drapery of moonlight, running the ship aground on its glimmering shores.

Our Father has heard it from every crewmate he's ever commanded. Some say it with the parchment barely out of sight, others wait until mid-journey before they share their misgivings. A few hold off until Our Father is on deck, watching the sky, then their indictments tumble out. All of them, no matter where they were gathered, no matter what oaths they swore or parchments they signed, no matter what bloodlettings they evoked across the seas, eventually they find impossibility in their hearts. Unlike Our Father, they can't believe in forever. They can't believe in a moon opened up. They can't believe in a treasure as big as forgiveness.

Our Father missed his sons' first feedings, missed their first slow blinking into sleep and those newborn dreams, hands and feet twitching as they began to imagine. Our Father missed his sons' first taste of mashed fruit, the sweetness on their tongues, their first crawling and their first steps, the balanced move gaining ground from walking to running. He missed those first pirate curses leading to fistfights, neither son flinching or wincing even as the blood ran. He missed their first climbing of a spruce, the first time they truly saw the rain, the first moment they realized they wanted to be just like him. Our Father missed so much, sailing away as he did.

When the ship ran aground, the hundred versions of Our Father collected back into his body, the brightest spot of moon beaming in front of him as the hull shattered and the ship jammed and water barreled in. For a moment, he wondered if he should have used those hundred versions of himself to tend to his sons, to his wife, to his family. He wondered if he should have spared at least one, even if it wasn't his best self, to be a father, a husband. But he didn't. He shakes the thought off and lowers a jolly boat to the water, rowing ashore, wearing moonlight like a second skin.

Not sons, but this moon still to pursue, to unwrap.

He can't fathom how this moon opened up to the prow of his ship, the hull breaching its golden light, an island pulsing like a ghostly heart. Behind him, the ship's belly fills with water in all its crushed spaces, the mast no longer visible. The longer he rows, the calmer the sea becomes, stretching out into nothingness until there are no waves, no ripples, no wind. Even the wake made by the oars becomes instantly smooth.

This is the beginning of an end: the clear water, the sky bright with moon, Our Father rowing to shore, his sons and his wife running through his mind, the guilt needing to be pushed back beyond the rest, a plague of hope.

When he'd first run aground, the moon's shore looked only like shining sand, but as his jolly boat cuts into it for the first time, the glow becomes more distinct. He reaches his hand over the side and plunges his fingers into the shore. It isn't sand. This is gold. This is an entire beach of gold. The little hills made by his jolly boat running dry would be enough to keep him paid up for the rest of his life. What is mounded across the expanse of this beach would buy a thousand houses and a thousand ships, more than enough to live endlessly. It is more than any ship could ever heft, heavier than the grandest masts could heave across the ocean.

Our Father sets foot on the golden beach, boots crunching, gold grinding and molding beneath his steps. He walks through the shore toward the dark foliage, the shadowy land ahead and the golden lit waters behind. He stops midway and drops to his knees, placing his palms on the beach, resting his forehead on the golden sand. Even with his eyes closed, he can see the bright illumination of the island, the moon glow of its shores. He rests on his knees like a child, gold flecks kissed into his palms and face. The whole world around him radiates. He brushes the grains from his hands and forehead, from the knees of his breeches, the beach stretching into the shimmering distance. Our Father waits for his heart to catch up. The whole of him feels unpacked and reassembled beneath his skin, heavy as a cannonball dropped to the water. He breathes the moon into his lungs and feels the light run through his veins like an electric current.

He rises and hikes the golden beach to where silhouettes meet shore, expecting the dark shades and shadows of a tree line illuminated by the moon, though where golden sands retreat into jungle it is dark as night, a forest of darkness upon darkness. The map in Our Father's heart is bright as ever though, so even in this darkness, he simply walks forward, moves heedlessly into this place of charcoal and lead, a terrain of knotted shadows. It is all that keeps his mind from his family, from his sons and his wife, the three of them waiting for him there, in that township, in the rain. Are they waiting for him still? How long will they wait?

Punching through foliage he can't see, Our Father swings his cutlass at the vines and branches that brush his skin, the golden beach only a strange and distant illumination now, a faint blur in the flooded darkness. Our Father ignores his eyes and hands, ignores the thoughts of family and guilt, his blade singing, his feet pressing onward, paying heed only to the map of his heart, to its pull. There is a treasure here beyond the golden shore, one he has been seeking his whole life, and he has to keep leaning toward it. There are fangs here, somewhere, and the offer of immortality. There is everything he has been wanting, waiting for, sailing to.

Our Father follows the tattooed map on his heart, the compass of his pulse, until he is at the center of the darkness, where the layers of black on black reveal a cave aglow with a dim redness, a magic womb like a dream he's chased ever since Our Father's Father told him of it, ever since the rain has rained down on this township, this legacy of forever finally at hand.

o

Our Mother tore Billy into a hundred pieces, and she left it all piled beneath the spruce boughs of our wet yard before walking back to the house to take care of the rest. There she hefted the Red Mummy from the table and took him upstairs to bed, tucking him into the bottom bunk, where the Black Mummy would find him later, resting. After that she cleaned and stowed the instruments, scoured the kitchen, and went to bed without closing the back door, the curtains left snapping. She felt like she had nothing left to give.

The first morning after, her boys didn't think much about the absence of breakfast, about the lack of bowls or glasses, about the missing sack lunches. They'd only been curious about the back door still open, the rain misting in, and the Black Mummy distraught over the weakness of the Red Mummy, as he'd had to sit on the bottom of the steps, desperate to regain energy, not even enough left to attempt his bicycle.

At dinnertime that evening, there was no food prepared, the kitchen yet untouched, the two of them left to go to bed hungry, their hearts filled with other worries, with all that had happened that day between the three of them, between Mallory and the Black Mummy, between the Red Mummy and the rest of the world.

Our Mother didn't see any of it.

That night and in the days that followed, she only slept, the boys scrounging meals from the cupboards, from the refrigerator, from the pantry. The rebuilding of the Red Mummy had taken so much out of her, and the destruction of Billy had devoured the rest.

She felt holed, transparent. She'd used too much too fast, given everything.

Our Mother slept those days away, so she didn't see how by the second day the Black Mummy was feeding the Red Mummy a spoonful at a time, encouraging him to eat even when he didn't want to, too weak to do anything except push the food away. She didn't see that kind of new brotherhood taking place in the kitchen, only heard the occasional rummaging, the opening and shutting of cupboards, the soft clink of pans on burners or bowls on the tabletop as she rearranged herself back to sleep, rolling over and readjusting, lost in exhaustion, mired in disappointment and shame.

Because she is more than tired. She is more than transparent. Our Mother has ruined her son. She's let herself be pressed into tackling his heart when she wasn't ready, molesting his organs with unsteady hands. She'd sewn and sutured him in the most hustled stitches, hurrying to salvage what she could, her ghostliness rampant, failure hovering only fractions above her skin.

The rain came and went and Our Mother slept. She slept and had a dream about reassembling Billy, about gathering him in her arms, about collecting his smashed and broken pieces and re-envisioning every untenable remnant. In the dream, she felt desperate to remold him, to give some apology. She dreamt of realigning his body, of stitching him back into what he'd been, making Billy purposeful again. In her dream, she made Billy as infinite as the wind, as inevitable as rain spilling over gutters, wetting the streets of this township. She dreamt of coating him in mud, a Mud Mummy to roam the lawns and streets and alleyways, never again to be broken apart, unburdened of any sadness that surrounded his heart.

When Our Mother wakes, days later, it is with that dream on her mind. That dream reaching out to her, telling her what should come next. It is that dream pointing her to salvation. If the cat and the seagull and the bat could teach her enough to create the Black Mummy's forearms, couldn't a remaking of Billy teach her how to undo what she'd perpetrated on her Red Mummy son?

Our Mother rouses herself from the bed to dress. In the kitchen, no dishes out, the table and counters bare, she stands listening to the bleat of the clock, looking through the curtains at the sliding-glass door, out to the spruce boughs and the wet lawn. She can't stop thinking about Billy mounded beneath the sweeping arms of the spruce. Our Mother knows it isn't a dream, it's a forecast. She can save him. She can salvage his body and make him a Mud Mummy. And if she succeeds, she'll be able to clean up the rest of the mess she's made.

She calls her sons' names. There is no answer.

Louder still, and only an echo of her voice returning.

Our Mother takes up needle and thread and walks into the rain, lifts the boughs and enters the sanctuary of that spruce womb where the scatter of Billy is amassed, where she'd pulped him days ago, and where he will be born anew in her hands.

With the dream's tincture coating her heart, Our Mother begins.

Under the spruce boughs, the mash of Billy's parts is slick with rain and blood. The stink is unforgiving. Our Mother kneels. Our Mother works. Our Mother sews. There are parts she can't forge, bits of tendon or ligament or bone so crushed they can't be pretended back into place, parts too dismantled to be remade, skin too blotched and horrific, veins bleeding onto other surfaces, but she deals with what she can, what Billy brought her, what she didn't completely obliterate. She cobbles together an arm, piecemeals another as the wind comes. Our Mother sews a leg, then another, the joints crunching and grinding, most of the tendons unable to pull or retract, twice gutted. This will be Billy's new livelihood, to work for each step he takes. The rain falls outside the spruce haven, making a drone of static in her ears, her eyes pinned to the work at hand.

Billy's head is likewise decimated, opened and skinned and smashed. Our Mother does the best she can to reassemble a boy's face from its detritus. She lifts and tucks and stretches and cuts together the wreckage like a gory quilt, making his passages clear enough for breathing, his ears well enough to hear, his eyes to see. Only Billy's mouth won't work, not a single word to be shaped, because Our Mother can't find his tongue.

When it's done, she is kneeling in a circle of dirt muddied by blood and fluids, surrounded by remnants of skin and hair and chipped bone, haloed in the grotesquerie. The rain is muffled by the boughs above her, Our Mother easing Billy's heartbeat back into him, the blood slowly revisiting his veins. She massages his lungs until they hold breath, presses his ribs into place over them, a fragile shield, tender as stars appearing. Hours later and her scissors haven't slipped once. She hasn't fumbled any organs or dropped a single needle through any transparent fingers. Every swift move of her hands makes this new Billy stronger, amplifies his opportunities for living, taps into whatever came before his sadness, before the isolation crushed his heart. And if Billy can be remade after obliteration, she knows she can save her Red Mummy, can retract her mistakes, can cleanse the dying from his heart and make him anew.

As in her dream, the last step is Our Mother coating Billy in muddy ink engulfing the expanse of his new form, his ragged skin accepting the slick. She paints him into being, giving birth to a Mud Mummy walking crookedly out and into the rain.

o

The Red Mummy is riddled with decay. He can feel it in his chest, where his ribs threaten his lungs. The blood isn't circulating much to his arms or legs, turning each limb heavy as lead. His heart rests reluctantly, as if it isn't there at all. The pain radiates from everywhere, from each piece and part, the whole of it held together by sheer will and nothing else. He feels less a body and more like the last wisps of sunlight as dusk comes on, readying for disappearance.

The night he was ruined, he'd come downstairs when Our Mother and the Black Mummy were asleep. The house was still, only the rain on the roof and an occasional gust of wind. He'd listened to the rhythmic breathing from Our Mother's bedroom and from the Black Mummy in the bunk above him, the clock leveling their lives. He'd worked in the dark of the kitchen, the moon nearly full behind the clouds. He'd waited for his eyes to adjust to the shadow on shadows, then he'd begun. He'd cleaned the kitchen, scrubbed every surface, exhausted his hands scouring over and over, and when all of it gleamed, he'd draped the table in a clean white sheet, reflecting the moonlight like his own pale skin.

He'd found her black kit at the back of a cupboard, opened it to the tools and instruments stowed. The hammer and scalpel and pliers and scissors. The knives. The miniature saw. The forceps and hemostats. The needles and thread. All he had to do was close his eyes and recall his brother strapped to that table, Our Mother's face in surgical concentration. There, in the darkness of his mind, he remembered everything of that moment. He only had to recreate it on the draped table.

Placing each tool and instrument where it had been, he'd followed with the pans to catch the running blood, and when the scene was recreated exactly as he remembered it, he'd readied the belts and lay himself back on the table, tightening each strap as best he could from his prone position. It was no good to be a sad and pale son when his brother was a Black Mummy, when the ghost of Mallory was falling so heartily in love, when his twin had the strength of a hundred pirates and he had nothing but a heart loaded with grief.

Our Mother had woken in the dim light of the morning and had risen to find him there, begging her on. She'd waited, hesitated, almost put a stop to it, but he'd looked at her with his whole heart, made her see the extent of his sadness, and she'd given in. She cut and pried and hewed and tore. She snapped and sawed, his body going awry and him unconscious then, the pain an easy anesthetic.

But when Our Mother's resolve weakened, when her focus waned, his body slipped. It was written all over him: sunken pockets where organs used to be, hills of abdomen and chest where infection and failure mounted, his breathing hindered, his heartbeat strung out, his body wretched.

He wanted a heart that beat like Our Father's, lungs like full sails, abdominal muscles that a pistol could never pierce. He wanted to be a mummified boy like his Black Mummy brother, rubies behind his eyes, Mallory falling in love with him. He wanted to feel blood ripping through his chest, a magic beyond buccaneering, rain pillaging the roof. Then he'd woken from Our Mother's frantic and savage work, risen to wrack and ruin—to arms numb at the shoulders, legs stilled beneath him, blood coagulating and lungs fighting against breath. He'd woken as a remnant, as a wreck, as a ship on the shoals.

He'd dressed that morning trying to pass himself off as energetic and powerful, but then he'd needed a rest at the bottom of the stairs. He'd had to walk his bicycle, legs not even strong enough to walk him through the arcade, scarcely enough blood left in his heart to dream.

So they propped him in Mallory's hallway and went upstairs, and the sounds of their coupling drifted down like fog, everything collapsing around him.

The next morning he could only make it downstairs with the help of the Black Mummy's supportive forearms, and he still couldn't ride his bicycle, and again he didn't have the strength for the arcade or the complex of caves. The morning after that he could only make it to the top of the stairs, shirt half on, no energy left.

Today, the Black Mummy waits for him. It's been days of spoon-feeding his Red Mummy twin, days of cradling his body around the house and through the rain, days spent helping him survive. This morning, the Red Mummy only waves his brother on from the top stair, bowing his head, barely managing the exhaled word *Go*.

The Black Mummy walks up and rests his hand on his brother's shoulder. The Red Mummy shrugs it off and waves again to the front door. The Black Mummy concedes, slowly, going down one careful step at a time, pausing at the bottom without looking back, not wanting to see his brother dying there.

In this township, brotherhood is such a delicate balance.

The Black Mummy doesn't want to go on without him. Our Mother has taken to sleeping instead of nursing her Red Mummy son back to health, going ghostly instead of correcting the sutures or rebuilding his organs, instead of reclaiming her motherhood by recasting his frame. Meanwhile, he's been left to help his Red Mummy brother dress, to balance him up and down the stairs, to feed him one mouthful at a time, to walk him beside his bicycle and help shake the rain from his heart. He doesn't want to leave his brother, but it's too much. He can't stay any longer in this house of abandonment. He can't watch everyone fall away.

Instead, he retreats to the only person left, the one waiting with open arms, the one still capable of loving him back. He goes to Mallory's house, to her room behind those gauzy curtains. There, he doesn't think of his Red Mummy brother or Our Mother endlessly sleeping. He doesn't think of Our Father out to sea. There, they kiss, Mallory's lips a whisper of caves, a salt breeze that expands his chest. There, they continue to map each other's passages, moaning.

The Black Mummy pulls Mallory's body over his own, loses himself in her. With Mallory, their hearts and tongues and breath, the groans undone from their bodies, the Black Mummy works to remember what it means to live.

o

For Our Father, it started when he was still a boy in this township. Our Mother was a girl there too. Our Mother's Mother had long given in to the ghostly, and Our Father would ride his bicycle up the street to that house. Our Father, young, and Our Mother too, they played marbles together, chased stray cats, the rain wetting their hair, streets blistered with water. They floated makeshift boats and chalked the sidewalks into weeping colors. They ate sack lunches under the boughs of a spruce, seagulls floating, love unburied from the soil.

Later, it was Our Mother in his arms, her hair laid its length, bare bulbs strung above and the rain ceasing for once, stars showing on the black curtain of the sky, their hearts knotted. They danced and the sky opened its wide starry mouth, spilling. The stars were reflected in her eyes as he dipped her back, as he dove into her body, longing for eternity, longing to live a thousand lives inside her heart. That night, Our Mother shone. Their bodies pressed together, the stars pouring onto their faces, piling in their throats.

They were in love, Our Mother's skin then stretching so tight across her belly, her body making two more bodies, twin boys prowling her insides. She hadn't known there were two of them until they arrived, born ready for swordplay and piracy, born to a double risk of drowning, a double danger of abandonment, double the eyes to be filled with sails, double the mouths for this rain, double the hearts to be infected by the spoils of growing up. Twin boys, and then Our Father gone to sea while they rooted at her chest, the sky clouded over, breath like wind across their future bows.

Or another night, another kind of love, when the four of them had sat and watched the bats at night. Our Mother stretched a blanket across the lawn, partially shielded under the eaves of the house, protecting them from the mist. Our Father rested in the shape of a crucifix. She put her head in the crook of his arm, leaning into him while the boys stumbled into the rain and back again, hands held to the sky. They opened their mouths to the clouds before returning to nuzzle their parents, dusk coming on and the bats with it, swooping shapes in fading light, when their whole boyhood was still intact.

Now, on an island in the moon, staring into the pit of a cave, a silhouette is visible to Our Father there in the deep darkness. He can already picture the glint of fangs in her mouth as this womanly figure stands in seduction, a rapture. This woman is not Our Mother. She looks like the woman from his latest port, though he can't be sure, the darkness blurred and unforgiving. The woman beckons him, but Our Father doesn't move. Desire mounts in his blood while his feet are rooted in memories, his mind run aground in thoughts of his family, of his twin boys, of his wife, of all the mistakes he's made. He stands there, lashed by waves of remembrances In front of him, the woman calls his name with a voice like a gown of wind, while in his heart, Our Mother calls, her voice bright as a star. He stands, staring into the darkness of the cave's mouth, the glow of treasure he can see and feel there. Our Mother's radiance comes from her heart, from the constant and pure rain of her love. Behind Our Father's eyes, the seas of these memories are high and arcing.

He remembers his sons making a pirate headquarters under wringing boughs, remembers their tiny lips and tongues suckling even in sleep, remembers these newborns in Our Mother's arms, in their house in the rain. He remembers standing at the shore with them, small hands holding his large, buccaneer ones, those twin boys waving goodbye as he sailed away. He remembers rowing with his eyes forever upon them, then the times after when they couldn't even look at him, the weight of their sadness too overwhelming. And Our Father remembers the last time he left that shore, how they didn't even wait for his ship to leave the bay before they were back in the jeep, tires sighing up the pebbled beach and back to the wet asphalt beyond.

Our Father is legendary, but he could become a man without end. He could become a buccaneer, swathing through the centuries, collecting every treasure that's ever been buried. He'd own the sea. He'd be boundless. He'd build and rebuild his ship greater and stronger with every passing decade, never to be breached on any shoals. He'd learn every language, every dialect and variation, every syllable of every word ever uttered. He'd wear his sash for so many thousands of years it would disintegrate around his waist, the blade of his cutlass worn so thin it'd be transparent. He'd heave up from the world every treasured chest. He only has to step forward, step into that darkness. He only has to open up his veins.

Our Father hears this woman who is not Our Mother calling to him again, a voice threaded with the rush of tide. He has made the journey, defeated the mutinies and commanded his ship across the sea, made it past everything, past ghostly ships and siren crags onto the moon's golden shore, this one night in a thousand. Our Father has come here to conquer life, to turn blood to magic, to live past living.

Yet, he hesitates.

If he turns to this woman who is not Our Mother, to her fangs and her mystic blood, to the belief he has held since Our Father's Father said it, since the first bats came looping down through the dusk, he'll never be able to return to his family. He'll hold all the glory, all the riches, all he's ever sought. He'll be the greatest pirate who ever lived, endlessly living, but he'll never be able to return to that township. No one wants a father who outlives them. Trading his blood for this tincture will make him eternal, but it won't make him a better father, a stronger husband. It will not erase his faults or fix the years he's spent sailing. It won't negate the losses he's already handed down. For that, there is no magic.

To be a husband, Our Father only has to return to that shore. To be a father, he only has to stand in the rain alongside his family. Transfused blood will do nothing, and a few nights will never be enough. He'll have to remove the rubies from his heart, rid himself of every mast and sail, soak in the falling rain. He'll have to forget this longing for the magical. He'll have to follow the truth buried in the dark folds of his heart, the truth he has ignored for so long.

He loves them. Those sons. Our Mother. He wants to be with them, no matter how many wrongs he's committed, no matter how hard they hate him. They might not accept him, might not have even waited for him, all this time he's wasted buccaneering, putting treasure above their hearts.

Our Father looks to the stars instead of the cave's mouth, and remembers falling in love. He closes his eyes. He will go. He will return to them. He will attempt to live as he should have, so long ago.

When he opens them again there is no cave. There is no woman who is not Our Mother. There is no glow of eternal treasure. There is only the possibility of salvation, if he isn't too late.

o

Our Mother finds the Red Mummy laid out at the top of the stairs, fallen back from a seated position, his shirt askew and his red torso exposed in all its infected incisions, the welts and stench of the stitches bursting, arms splayed as in penance.

Billy restored her faith in mummification as he hobbled away through the rain of this township, a new boy made from fragments, freed from a life of sadness. He was broken and slick with hurt, yet she made him into a Mud Mummy, a new kind of boy to leave slick footprints across the alleyways, endlessly chasing that bandaged cat up and down the wetted streets.

Now she is ready to make amends with her Red Mummy.

From the top of the stairs she can't tell if it's night or day, the rain and the light faltering. The hallway clock runs. She lifts the Red Mummy's desiccated body, light as a newborn, cradling his head as she moves downstairs, through the hallway, to set him on the kitchen table, his heart scarcely beating, a single pallid and final breath left in his lungs.

The laughter of her sons used to light this house. There was the tiny glow of her sewing machine, a halo around its hum, and the lamplight from the bedside where Our Mother lay with no one to hold, with no love to keep her warm. There was the dimness of the porch light outside the bay window, the ocean beyond it, and there was the small light above the stove, blushing on Our Mother's kettles. But all these lights were nothing in comparison to the radiance of her sons' laughter, before the sadness crept in. When the rain was only rain above them and not rain in their hearts, when Our Father was only a pirate they looked up to, when Our Mother wasn't yet a ghost, when her twin boys still found so much in this world to love, they lit up this house. Then the sadness rolled in, at first only in small waves breaking on their pebbled shore. Our Father out to sea again, Our Mother's limbs wavering, their futures looming and no cutlass sharp enough to cut through, no pistol shot or cannon fire strong enough to obliterate the loss of family.

Our Mother doesn't bother with the straps or the sheet, the Red Mummy too weak to open his eyes, so little blood left in him. She sets out her instruments, places the pans to catch what remains, ready to pour it back when she is done because he can't afford any further losses. She knows now that she can bolster his heart, can sift love back into him. It is the strongest magic she has, and it is simmering. Her hand hovers above his sternum rot and as she makes the first cut, her hand goes see-through, the scalpel slipping. But instead of lamenting, instead of being rattled, Our Mother only picks it up, wipes it clean on the tongue of her apron, takes a breath, and continues. Our Mother is ready for the fight.

Working through the layers and the ghosting, she cuts into the Red Mummy, quickly reaching his chest for the second time, ready to make amends. She works his organs, rearranging and refurbishing and resetting. She reroutes the veins and arteries, reconnects them to make his heart pound, stitching the nicks she left last time, fixing the small ruptures she caused, the tears and tumult left on her last hurried voyage over his body.

Her work is patient, diligent, until she hears a dragging on the bay window, behind the curtains. There is a rasping breath, like a mouth full of lost words, stunted hands pawing at the window. It's the Mud Mummy coming back as he will, to his birthplace. She doesn't have to pull back the curtain to know he's there, and she doesn't need to stop working. The Mud Mummy is a part of this township now, and his noise to her has become as reassuring as the rain. Our Mother continues while the Mud Mummy scratches across the siding, redefining the Red Mummy's organs, reengaging his blood, running it like rivers to the shore. And Our Mother doesn't stop there. Like the rain, she is insistent. Like Our Father, she knows how to follow the pull of her heart.

Leaving the Red Mummy at the table, Our Mother walks outside, past the Mud Mummy hiccupping near the door. She gathers a bundle of spruce boughs and wet grass, rain and sodden black soil, blooming flowers and a handful of stones, even a smear from the Mud Mummy's arm, lovingly touched as she heads back inside. From the house, Our Mother gathers arcade coins and marbles, the last ruby Our Father ever brought her, and a strand of her hair, nearly invisible in her fingertips.

Our Mother will make the Red Mummy more than just a salvaged boy. She will completely exhume his sadness. She will make him a boy unlike any who has ever lived.

Back in the kitchen, she bends the spruce boughs around his heart, rests the grass and pours the rain there too, brushes the black soil in and places the blooming flowers beside, tucks the stones nearby, lovingly dots the mud. Our Mother sets the arcade coins around his heart as well, and the marbles, and the ruby, and the strand of her ghostly hair. The rest of his chest she molds and mounds as it once was, making sure he is no longer caved, not sunken like a scuttled ship or swollen with blight and bloat. This time, she is careful with every stitch, perfectly seaming rows, laboring with precision and pride, knowing his heart will soon thunder through him, the sadness quieted. The sutures align flawlessly down his chest, the skin immaculate, no redness or welling, no temptation to burst.

Lastly, she coats his torso in a remade ink, a stronger red, closer to blood, a vibrant and unmistakable torrent. She paints his torso from shoulder to shoulder, down to his waist and around his ribs, across his back and up his spine. The ink seeps into his skin, bleeds into his new body, his heart ready to beat until the last stars come back, beyond any new grief that can ever be done to him.

o

He'd left the Red Mummy at the top of the stairs, heeded his final, exhausted orders as if they were a captain's command, took the stairs as he had a thousand times before, back when they were still pirate twins. Only this time, he didn't look back. His brother was in such a state of rot, such duress, he couldn't bear to witness it one more time. This was worse than Our Mother's ghost, worse than Our Father never home, worse than a family riddled with sadness. This was the grief of a brother dying.

There was nothing he could do but follow his brother's order: *Go*, and he did, walking the plank into Mallory's glowing arms, diving into her light, their bodies crashing together and the sparks so devastating that sometimes the room was lightning. Mallory's heart never went dark like the soil, never clouded over as the sky, was never hidden like the stars above. In her arms, he could forget everything.

The Black Mummy and Mallory had fallen in cavernous love, a boy for forever and the ghost of a girl, attempting to erase all that had come before.

In her bed, Mallory's arms wrapped around his waist, her hands caressing his forearms, the heat smoldering between them even under the heaviest rain.

Later, clothed and returned to the outside world, they wound their way up and over the soaked streets, past the gauze of curtains hiding the other lives of pirates and ghosts and fishermen and widows, past the sons and daughters abandoned in this township, until they arrived at the arcade, its brash bell resounding above the door, the machines chirping their return. There, they uncovered the cave's mouth and joined up to the complex of caves, ready for whatever fate was buried there, whatever was at its heart, whatever future was at stake.

With his bicycle leaned against the arcade's siding and the machines electrically murmuring, with the cave's mouth opened wide, they went about exhausting the recesses of this complex of caves, Mallory's heart a torch and the Black Mummy's strength protecting them from every trick of the tunnels, every pitfall.

In this way, Mallory and the Black Mummy spiraled deeper and deeper through the ore-colored passageways, unstopped by the revelation of skeletons jabbed through, skulls caved by pistol shots, the ground coming loose beneath them or echoes in the darkness, unstopped by the sporadic wail of wind or the flutter of wings somewhere above, only holding each other tighter, every path one path closer to the cave's center, closer to the final tunnel, closer to their next beginning.

Eventually, there came a faint sound of rushing water, and they followed it until Mallory's glow was reflected in misted air, the tunnel suddenly humid with droplets. Lengths further, they saw the water falling into darkness, rushing into the unknown. The waterfall ran turbid and white, the sides of the cave slicked, the ceiling dripping, their shoes struggling to tread the dampness. The tunnel became a ledge and the ledge a lip and where the lip disappeared, the water fell to black. There, the water unspooled, the cave unspooled, and they could hardly hear their own hearts beating.

On that ledge, Mallory and the Black Mummy stood, watching the water spur down, a cool breeze pressing their faces. They closed their eyes to dream one last time, each making a wish of life before they leapt.

The Black Mummy dreamt of wind in sails, of captaining, of jewels clinging to islands, of a lifetime of the moon's glow on his blackened skin. It was a retribution for his brother's death, which he was sure was occurring right then, above them, in this township's rain, at the top of the stairs.

Mallory dreamt of the Black Mummy by her side in the once empty house up the street, walls decorated and rooms furnished, rain falling on the roof and his hands so charming and wonderful in hers, dreamt of raising a family there with him, of becoming what she'd never had: a mother.

The waterfall careened and Mallory did too.

I'm pregnant, she said, but the Black Mummy only heard water and wind. He was still dreaming of piracy, of building an armada to avenge the wrongs committed on his twin brother.

I'm pregnant, she repeated, pushing the words above the noise of drowning, the Black Mummy's eyebrows knotting. He watched her lips move, leaned his head toward her and pulled her closer, putting his ear so near her mouth she could see the tiny cave there where her words rushed. She spoke into the chasm, her lips brushing his skin. His hands went limp. His pulse bottomed. The water fell.

She watched the Black Mummy's eyes for understanding, trying to imagine what thoughts billowed now in the wet air between them. She was longing for forever, but he only stood there as if he hadn't heard anything. His eyes sparkled with the glimmer of bounty and waves, of masts and sails, cutlasses and pistols, of a sash tied blood red at his waist, of a grizzled beard and the musk of mutiny. Even in the cave's darkness, she could see what was coming.

We'll jump, he said at the loudest rim of his voice.

What? she asked.

We'll jump, he said, and he regripped the tunnel wall, this complex of caves that had finally brought them to the heart of it.

Love, then, seemed not like love at all.

The first day she'd seen these two brothers appear in the street, her body had shone. She'd given away her existence in trade for a buccaneer, not understanding then how piracy was impossible to hold, how her life would be immediately latched to its anchor. She wanted to say something else to him, but her voice was as dim as the sun in a rain-covered township.

They jumped.

The air shucked away their breath. The walls were wide, the tunnel plunging, ore sides raining down and Mallory's glow not enough to illuminate anything anymore. This was their love, falling bodies, the smashing of a ship on the shoals, the span of too much too impossibly pressed together. Their collective hearts were bursting, shadows wicked from the walls, the fall taking the words from their mouths and the dreams from behind their eyes.

When it was over, they were standing waist deep in a dark lagoon, the ceiling a dozen stories high, the walls steep and black, lit only by the wet candle of Mallory's body. The echoes of their breathing reverberated, the lagoon shivering amidst the plunge of water. They were soaked and there were streaks of mud across their clothing, thin red openings on their exposed skin, the muddle of forthcoming bruises. Mallory's lip was bleeding, and the Black Mummy put a finger to it, as if to push the blood back in. They poised themselves on the silted shore sloping toward the center of the steely lagoon. The water rippled with their movements, the Black Mummy's heart gravitating to the pooled darkness. This was the map of their future, the stake for their piracy, the beginning of his buccaneering.

Mallory stood holding the Black Mummy's hand as he stared at the water, as he edged into it. Her palm fit beautifully in his, a cloud gloved over the moon, the lagoon revealing his true, black-gemmed heart. Mallory could hear the hum of a sewing machine in her veins, could taste the kettle steam in her mouth, could feel two tiny heartbeats beneath the pulse of her own. Her smile went see-through, like curtains breezing out. The imagined weight of gathered treasure was already slung around her neck, haloing her in coming sadness.

Far above, the rain continued.

Far above, Our Mother finally went fully ghostly, down to nothing, completely gone.

Far above, the Red Mummy was waking, restored, one more adventure to burst open.

o

Our Father looks up at the rain falling for the first time in so long, wetting his face and his shoulders and his hair, clouds blanketing the sky. He is standing in the middle of the island of the moon, and he needs to get back to the beach, to his jolly boat moored there, to save himself from being stranded on this island, to keep from becoming a part of the stars, drifting forever in darkness.

Our Father has decided, and he won't look back.

There is only this moon to escape and then he can row himself into another life.

Our Father moves swiftly, afraid the dark might swallow him, boots hefting over the rocky landscape, cutlass sashed to his waist and pistol sheathed, knowing he'll never use those weapons again. There is no sword sharp enough to cut through his failures, no pistol shot strong enough to explode the wrongdoings mounded in his heart. They are useless instruments now, accessories of a previous life, and as he walks, he puts his hand to his throat to feel for his pulse, to assure himself that this once malfunctioning heart is throbbing now in his chest, mapped anew, bringing him back to where he should be.

Our Father does not have a peg leg or a parrot on his shoulder, an eye patch or a hooked hand. He runs his tongue over his silver tooth and brings his hand to his neck, so much altered blood taking hold in his veins. It didn't come from the fangs of a vampiress but from realizing how much he's missed, how much of this life has already passed him by. This new blood scares him, Our Father hoping to capture as much as he can of what remains.

Here on this island, suddenly, it is all shadow. His feet are sore, his hands raw. The shades widen around him, stars wavering between clouds, behind rain, honesty such a newfangled feeling for Our Father, hope too impossible for him to hold, grasping it like a cat by the tail, the whole thing scratching and clawing in protest. He knows this is how it should be, how it must be.

Before long he's sure he's seen these same trees silhouetted, this same jab of rock beneath his boots. He feels so close to the shore yet the beach remains distant as ever, the glow on its surface no closer than the last time he scanned the horizon. Our Father furrows his brow, attempts to make the shore stay where it is, to undo the circles he's been walking, to cut a straight trail. The world swims in a blur of darkness and swelling clouds. He is lost. He wants to raise his pistol to the sky and unload a shot, to rouse a crew sleeping anchored in the bay, but his ship is broken on the shoals and the crew is dead. There is no one left to command. Our Father is alone, and how quickly the moon has receded. The world pulls hard at his chest and for once, Our Father feels like an aged and fallen man, scarred with piracies, atrocities accumulated in his limbs. All he can do is keep walking, wend his way toward the shore as the silhouettes steepen, as the stars blink away, an enormous sackcloth pulling over the sky.

The foliage swirls around Our Father in shapes he doesn't recognize. The darkness menaces, full of regrets. It no longer matters if seagulls change to bats at dusk. It no longer matters what Our Father's Father said to him those few nights in every thousand, immortality sung like a lullaby. It no longer matters if his boys are boys or if the house is draped in rain. All that matters is to return there, to them. All that matters is making it back to his sons and Our Mother, to that township where he desperately hopes they are still waiting for him.

Our Father wants it with all his heart, a heart beating savagely through the night.

There are no stars left now and no glow in the distance.

Too many lifetimes have passed.

Too many moons crossing above his head.

Our Father closes his eyes and dreams of Our Mother, dreams of his sons, dreams of their house, dreams of the curve of the bay and the hum of Our Mother's sewing machine. Our Father imagines his sons riding bicycles up and down the wet streets, imagines the chance he might still have, his heart throbbing with love, the feeling almost unrecognizable amid his pirate rot.

He hardly has the strength to carry this new love, but when he opens his eyes, it is with vigor and purpose. He cuts across the rocks, trounces through the darkness, the landscape pressing into his soles, his chest expanding broader with each breath.

He will no longer strap those pouches around his neck, tucked beneath his doublet. Instead he will watch his sons become men, show Our Mother he can still love, and maybe, with enough time, the skies will open, will part to reveal the stars or the sun.

The shore of the moon is black when he arrives, its golden sands no longer luminescent, no longer gold, only a beach like a dark smudge where black water laps. He kneels in the darkness, feeling the sand of this island for the last time, the stars hidden behind clouds. His ship is broken on the shoals, but the jolly boat is beached there, oars shipped, the horizon a thin, hovering line. The tide tongues his boots. He shoves the jolly boat into the water and steps aboard. As the moon fades from view, the sky above profound and starless, Our Father heads home.

o

Our Mother is so weary of the rain, of the ache across this landscape. Her heart with nothing left to offer. She no longer cooks, no longer sews, no longer looks to the bay for Our Father's ship, no longer cares for the difference between the sun and the moon. For Our Mother, the stars have become pointless fixtures.

When he isn't roaming the alleyways of this township, the Mud Mummy paws at the house, heart magnetized. The spruce boughs hang in the yard, the soil black as it has always been. Cars pass, nights and days too. Then more rain and more suns and more moons, the township going forever on, lingering, while Our Mother disappears. If one of her boys was to look in on her here, in this bedroom, in this bed where Our Father once lay land-sickened, wet rag on his forehead, emaciated by this family, they would see only a pocket of covers where she once was. They'd see only the vague outline of what used to exist.

Our Mother hears the clock go silent, finally run out of time. She hears their jackets dead-hung on the hallway hooks, hears no coins jangling in their pockets, hears no boy footsteps running down the stairs. She hears no heartbeats either, not of the Red Mummy or the Black Mummy or Our Father, not even her own.

Our Mother imagines herself rising from bed, walking the short hallway to the kitchen to find her boys there, eating a breakfast she's made. She imagines hearing their pirate curses across the table amidst two black forearms and a red torso, the life she's given back to them. She imagines how they'll live forever, the sadness culled from their bodies, youth and joy brought to the surface, strength and courage and resilience amplified, the bright strain of boyhood bursting from their seams. She imagines Our Father opening the door, backlit by the entryway, the boys rushing to him, her gracefully sidling up too, the four of them holding one another, a family remade and the rain washing everything else away.

But Our Mother never rises from that bed.

She held a vigil with the Red Mummy at the kitchen table until he finally woke, his torso beaming red. The ink was bottomless atop her repairs, his heartbeat and breathing regulated and sturdy, but when he sat up and looked into her face, it was with a dumbfounded kind of gaze, a hollow smile she'd never seen before. And though she smiled back, his staggered grin continued no matter how she stared or knitted her brow or even frowned. He smiled as if she wasn't there. He smiled as if Our Mother was already a ghost. Then he raised his hand and waved, his face remaining absurdly smiling, branded in an overpowering, blank innocence, a simplicity, a loving emptiness.

She'd made his heart beat again, preserved his blood, restored his lungs and sustained his organs. There was no swelling, no signs of infection. The stitches weren't welted and the incisions were clean, his ribs held and his chest not caved, no strange paunches mounding under his painted torso. But his sadness had been replaced with an unfocused euphoria, a haze of unthinking, a ridiculously undiscerning grin that looked like it might never go away, no matter what took place in the world around him.

Our Mother used to see sails in his eyes, big and billowed as his brother's, used to see rubies secreted away, the want for cutlasses and captaining, the splash of enemies thrown from the plank. Now, in this Red Mummy's eyes, she sees nothing. There are no sails or ships, no tides or islands, no swords or pistols or planks. It is only the vacant stare of grinning oblivion, because Our Mother packed his heart with too much, and it has overtaken him. He is overfilled with affection, with fervent and unguided love, with unbound and directionless joy for anyone or anything.

After he smiled at her, after he waved at her, Our Mother left him there on the table, dumbly staring, his arm still waving even as she turned to the stairs, even as she took to her bedroom, even as she crawled under the covers and disappeared completely. She'd broken both her boys. She'd stopped the sadness, but replaced it with either too much or too little. She'd placed too much of herself around the Red Mummy's heart, and too much of Our Father in the Black Mummy's forearms. She'd given so much love to the Red Mummy that he is left with mindless affection, with no defense against the rain, no guard against the wiles of the world, no shield from mutiny. And she'd given the Black Mummy too much strength, too much piracy, until he'd surely become a charmer, a magnet, obsessed and single-minded like Our Father, and capable of all his same abandonments.

She'd wrecked them both in the remaking.

In bed, under the covers, Our Mother feels her fingers and her toes go first, then the transparency creeps up her legs and arms, parading like an army to her chest. She can feel the ghostliness, cool and unforgiving, sapping what is left of her, unchallenged by her veins or her blood, unchallenged by her heart. It is ghosting. She disappears, grieving her own failures, her own losses, her own trajectory, until she is nothing.

Outside, the Mud Mummy paws at the house, tongueless mouth moaning. There is a seagull gliding in the sky, a bat swooning. There is rain. There is a widow on a balcony, drowning in the downpour. This as the last of Our Mother's life weeps out, her body evaporating.

o

Our Mother doesn't hear the Black Mummy return, doesn't know he's on the front porch, turning the crushed knob of the door, sharply inhaling as he finds the Red Mummy at the kitchen table, sitting up, grinning and waving, his newly reddened structure lit by slim light through the bay window. She doesn't hear the Black Mummy's footsteps as he strides closer to his shirtless brother, his chest an even brighter shade of tattooed red, doesn't see the Red Mummy's hollow smile or the Black Mummy's realization of the empty gesture, one brother waving at the other, grinning.

Our Mother doesn't see the Black Mummy gently press his brother's arm down, the smile on his twin's face never changing, the rain and wind sounding like a hand dragging down the walls. She doesn't see the Black Mummy sweep aside the curtains to find the glass smeared with mud, streaked with handprints, doesn't see how he stands and watches the yard where Our Father dug holes forever ago, where he and his brother played pirate under the spruce boughs, where there were never any stars.

Our Mother is not in the yard or the kitchen. She is not at her sewing machine, her hands streaming through fabric under a halo of light. The Black Mummy looks into her bedroom to find only a crumple of sheets on an unmade bed, the outline of a body but no body there. He looks in the living room and the hallway and the kitchen again, tracing routes over and across the empty house and its empty rooms, retracing, the Red Mummy smiling and waving each time he passes. Rain falls like a thousand hearts breaking, until the Black Mummy knows that Our Mother will never appear again, and he takes the Red Mummy's hand.

The Black Mummy walks his brother upstairs and helps him dress, putting no coins in his pockets and no marbles either, the time for boyishness gone. He walks his brother down the stairs and out the front door, onto the driveway, leaving their jackets on the hooks in the hallway and their bicycles against the side of the house, nothing left anywhere except the rain.

o

Mallory was left waiting for the Black Mummy to return. It was the first of a thousand times she would be stranded by the pirate in him, on a shore awaiting his return. He'd said he would never go back to Our Mother's house, but he couldn't excise the thoughts of his Red Mummy brother. He had to know what happened. He said he would go see about him and come right back, then he'd never leave her side again.

Her love masked reality.

On his return, she was only expecting news of grief, of demise, word of a single twin becoming the ashes of a decimated family, because the Red Mummy had looked so exhausted the last time she'd seen him, the stitches down his chest raging with infection and his head unable to balance on his neck. Only when she sees the Black Mummy walking up the street, it is with his Red Mummy brother striding beside him. Mallory is aghast. Even at a distance, she can see the Red Mummy's bright torso, and a smile on his face like she's never seen before, as if he is completely unshrouded.

Watching them walk up the street, Mallory can see a new and darkened lifetime spanning in front of them, the three of them, and as she reaches for the handle of the front door, moving to greet them, her hand goes clean through. Her heart thuds in her chest while she reaches again, slowly, palm striking the handle this time. Mallory has always been a ghost of a girl, always doing her best to pretend it is nothing. The rain soaks hard into her dress as she moves down the porch steps.

The Red Mummy's shirt billows and deflates in the wind as he continues to smile at Mallory. Then he waves at her, his face beaming. She wants to confess how she's fallen in love with the Black Mummy, fallen in love with his tattooed forearms and the blackness of his buccaneer ways, how she's drawn absolutely to the piracy of his body, the charm of his lips, the magnetism of his command, but she can already see how the Red Mummy wouldn't understand, would only smile and wave. He is vapid. She wants to admit how they've coupled in every possible way, how her heart is a part of his, how there are other heartbeats inside her too, but she can see it won't change the grin on his face. He is stuck this way, minted like a coin. He has nothing left to offer except love, even in the rain of this township, even in the face of brother mutiny. The Red Mummy is only and ever this. Even if she confessed, he would stand by her side, smiling, offering every bit of his heart, his love a sprawling sea.

The Black Mummy's forearms glisten with rain and Mallory sees his future abandonments enlarged in the ink. Words soak into the ground around them, each silently looking into one another, Black Mummy and Red Mummy and Mallory, the wind sighing.

Together, they leave her once empty house up the street and walk among the other houses nestled in spruce and rain, past the alleyways and the families either gone or disappearing, the clouds compressed in the sky. They pass the boarded doors of empty buildings, the dirty windows, the cars parked on the wet streets, the waterlogged newspapers at the end of driveways, Billy's bicycle still rusting at the corner store and the shore there too, the bay beyond, the cliffs too low to suicide from. There is a seagull overhead. There is the flutter of a bat. There is the tail end of a bandage fleeing around the side of a house and muddy footprints straggling with it. Their hearts are there, beneath muffled layers of drenched clothing, the arcade bell chiming, their dripping path leading to the mouth of the cave, its darkness wicking the world.

At the arcade, they descend into the complex of caves, new lives blooming in shadows as Mallory lights the way, her heart a faded torch. The Black Mummy leads them both down into the tunnels, steers them through the pitfalls and traps, the deceits perpetrated in these tunnels. The Red Mummy follows, grin aloft on his face the whole time. He smiles as they sidestep skeletal bodies, as they skirt protruding blades, as they scramble over boulders and leap cavernous gaps. He smiles as they pass the tunnel where he found the hovering jawbone, where he whimpered and moaned from the floor, where he wet himself and became everything other than a buccaneer. He smiles, with no recognition of that past. For him, everything is now, and he finds it all lovely, wonderful, worth savoring. They course through this complex of caves, his smile never ending. Even when they tell him to jump down beside the falling water, to bound into the unseen below, he does so grinning and waving.

Mallory and the Red Mummy and the Black Mummy tangle, plunge into the dark gradient of the lagoon's shore, standing waist deep where it weeps into that endless center. The Black Mummy is eager to show his brother what he's found there, though the Red Mummy only dumbly returns the look. The Black Mummy thought this lagoon's secreted treasure might spark his brother back to buccaneering, might make him a pirate again, set him in the direction of captaining, but the Red Mummy is only heart. No piracy will ever undo it. He wants to ask his brother if he feels anything under that red torso: the magnetism of gems, the glimmer of want, the lust for treasure. He wants to say to him, tattooed and grinning, *Use your heart*, though he can see there are no sails left in his brother's eyes, no masts aboard his body.

Bowing his head in loss, the Black Mummy reaches out to hold his brother's hand, and as he does so, the Red Mummy turns to him, and waves.

When Mallory first saw these two brothers, these twin boys on their bicycles riding up the rainy street, turning circles in front of her house, bats at dusk, she knew they were her future. Later, when they called her name, she went brighter, watching them cross the threshold of the driveway to peer into the windows, trying to glimpse her body behind the curtains. She remembers wanting to keep her heart hidden, though it turned out to be impossible. She imagined how terribly wonderful it would be to fall in love with a pirate. She dreamt of the way a sashed cutlass looks, how tall the masts are, how full the sails. She dreamt of them holding loaded pistols to the sky and wearing captain's tricornes, the exotic feathers plumed there. She dreamt of the planks, water washing across the deck, a crew of inked and muscled men following their every command. She imagined herself in the middle of them, ghostly between their bodies, no doublets in the world thick enough to keep their skin apart. How perfect her smile was in those dreams, how beautiful the radiance of her ghostliness in those imaginings. Now, standing waist deep in this lagoon, her light nearly deadened, her greatest regret is falling in love with a pirate. She's learning that a gem and a heart are not the same thing.

The Black Mummy will sail, will return only a few days in every hundred. His ship will caress the bay like a tenuous fog, swearing the treasure of the world is collected in its belly. He'll say he loves her. He'll say she is his armada, then he'll give her a palmful of rubies, every ruby as red as blood.

Water drips from her body, those secondary heartbeats swelling within, her arm linked with the Red Mummy's. She closes her eyes. She breathes. *I'm pregnant*, she says, her voice small in the Red Mummy's ear. The Red Mummy smiles back at her, bright as ever, the skin of the water distended around them. There is only love in the Red Mummy's eyes, no jealousy or pity or grief, no anger, no envy of his brother's conquests or of his own body's failure, no hatred for her choice. He is only happy for her, eager to stay by her side, ready to help raise this family as if it were his own.

o

The moon gone, stars shrouded in clouds, Our Father pulls his jolly boat finally onto the pebbled beach of this township, onto a shore full of rain, where Our Mother and his sons aren't waiting for him. There is no jeep parked askew on the stones, no doors flung open or arms wide to embrace him. It is only the tide beneath his feet as he beaches the boat and ships the oars, only the dim gray of morning and a few seagulls above, slim grass wavering where gravel meets roadside.

Our Father removes his tricorne and headscarf, closing his eyes to the rain. He thinks back once more to the glow of the moon's golden beaches, to the dark heart of its center, and how his name fell from otherworldly lips. But it was not his wife. It was not his sons. It was not his family. Every stroke of the oars he rowed to regain this shore was worth it. This is more valuable than any horizon he crossed to get here, any treasure he ever set his fingers on.

Rain falls across his face, wetting his cheeks.

If he was weeping, it would be impossible to tell.

Our Father didn't expect to find Our Mother breathless here, waiting, the jeep's engine muffled beneath the sound of waves, his sons running toward him. He knew none of this was what it used to be. He knew he'd finally been gone too long, absent during the most important moments.

He breathes, his lungs saturating with this township's wet air. He steps past the hull of the jolly boat, boots committed to the shore. Our Father expects the land-sickness to pounce, rolling nausea and aches to travel his chest, his hands to tremor and his legs to melt, though as he stands, the usual bleats of pain and sickness are absent. His stomach is easy, his head level. He is standing on this shore with firm legs and solid feet, with his back straight, a new future etching itself into his soles one step after another. Our Father is ready to be father and husband.

There are no lights on when he arrives home, no motion behind the curtains, no evidence of anyone within. It's like an empty house, a vessel of once-was. Our Mother isn't peering out, his sons aren't waiting behind the panes. Not even a tiny halo of light emits, not a single ounce of living.

He opens the front door, ready to step back into this life he's ignored. The handle is dented. Rain drips from his shoulders onto the floor, puddling beneath him in the hallway, silent and gray. Even the sound of the clock is gone. He calls their names. There is no answer. He calls again and the air around him refuses to respond, the entire atmosphere stilled. He looks down the hallway, into the living room and the kitchen, to the empty table there. On the sliding-glass door he sees the muddy smears of what looks like mangled hands pawing, dirty streaks the size of a boy's hand, printed in mud. The rain picks up on the roof.

Our Father moves to the bedroom, where he'd been laid up in so often with land-sickness, dizzy and fevered and nauseous. The covers are a jumble, as if a body could be shrouded beneath, though he sees nothing there beyond the indentation of Our Mother's fetal curl. He rushes to the boys' room, hurling their names as he goes, finding a sea of clothes and scattered piles of arcade coins. The rest of the room is hollow, emptied of its lives. It's as if his boys are no longer boys, as if they don't exist anymore.

He comes crashing down the stairs, ready to stalk this township, hair soaked, half-crazed and grizzled as he runs into the puddled streets, desperate for his family.

He scans the porches and alleyways. Wet newspapers sit at the end of driveways, widows stand on their walks, telephone poles boast seagulls. He combs down one street after another, manic, raving up and down the rain-streaked asphalt, spruce boughs dripping. The clouds bunch, rain running from Our Father's beard. A cat darts around a corner, trailing some kind of shroud, its body muddy, its head loose.

Doused in rain and swollen with longing, Our Father ends up near the once empty house up the street, shrouded in fog, where he finds a family playing in the rain of their front yard. It is a young mother with ghostly limbs watching twin boys trundle through the soaked lawn, splashing. The boys stamp their feet and clap their hands, swallow mouthfuls of rain as it runs over their faces, their young mother holding hands with a man who looks unlike a pirate or a fisherman, a man with a chest tattooed red from collarbones to waist, a solid line of threaded Xs visible through his wet shirt. The man's face catches in Our Father's throat. He seems almost like one of his sons, almost like one of those boys he abandoned in this rain, except this man wears a smile unlike any he remembered his sons ever wielding, open and pure and honest, full of love, a look Our Father can't parse.

He stops, not wanting to go any nearer, not wanting to disrupt a family like the one he could have had if he'd only been willing, if he'd only stayed, if he'd only listened to his heart instead of pretending his life away playing at piracy, chasing down treasure when so much was already at hand.

Backing away, Our Father leaves the ghostly mother and red-inked father and twin boys playing in the rain, happiness on their faces.

Mist engulfs the township and Our Father doesn't know what else to do, so he returns to the shore, the only place that has ever made sense to him, the only place he understands.

Back there, boots crunching on the shore, he listens to the ocean calling, his heart no longer a pull to the water. He waits with one hand on the prow of his jolly boat, looking past the bay where there is no ship for him to captain, no crew to command. Everything is gone, even the magnetism of his heart.

Rain runs from his hair while he nudges the boat back into the water. He sits there, holding the oars, bobbing in the shallows, tossed in its tidal motions, the waves on repeat. Before he can row out, he suddenly feels nauseous, dizzy, parched, and fevered. The roll of the waves bunches his stomach and blurs his vision, makes his arms and hands tremble so violently he can't hold the oars. His entire body aches, seasickness coming on so harshly he can't do anything but hold tight to the hull, wishing his feet were on solid ground.

As soon as he grounds the boat, as soon as he steps over the hull's rim back onto the beach, the bleat in his body recedes, the blur diminishes, the nausea passes.

Our Father collapses in the surf and stones, too late for everything.

o

Our Mother didn't hear the dented handle turn, didn't hear the door open, didn't hear Our Father's footsteps down the hallway, calling each of their names. She didn't hear because she wasn't there to call back, the hallway clock no longer keeping time. She wasn't there to hear his boots thud across the floor, to hear his steps in the living room and the kitchen, wasn't there when Our Father saw the Mud Mummy's prints smeared on the glass, left behind like a muddy map. She wasn't there when he stood in the bedroom, searching for her ghostly body, his beard wet and grizzled. She wasn't there to see him looking less like a buccaneer than he ever had.

Our Father's heart opened, finally, and Our Mother wasn't there to love him back, wasn't there to throttle him either, to choke him, to destroy him with her bare hands for all he'd ever done to her, to them. She wasn't there to ravish Our Father for his voyages, for the word *armada* on his lips, for the jewels in his eyes, for the other women, for leaving his brood to soak in sadness while he roamed the world. She wasn't there to say the words she'd been holding in for a lifetime.

She wasn't there when Our Father came downstairs, rushing out into the rain to find those boys who weren't boys. She wasn't there to follow quietly behind as he roamed the streets, bareheaded, chasing every alley and silhouette until he was swallowed by the rain.

And she wasn't there when Our Father finally reached the once empty house up the street and saw that young family playing in the rain, a ghostly mother and a father widely grinning, twin boys learning to taste the rain. She wasn't there to see him not recognize his own son, the red of his chest through a wet shirt, the seams down his torso, never believing one of his sons could house such love. She wasn't there to see him never meet Mallory, her motherhood worn as easily as a second skin, his twin grandsons stomping puddles, their arms already pretending cutlasses, mouths already making the sound of cannon fire, and how they looked just like their Black Mummy father.

She wasn't there either as Our Father headed back to the shore, walking beside gutters rivering, returning water to the sea, the only place he had left. She wasn't there to see the piracy sag in his shoulders, the waves receding behind his face, and how old he looked, a husband and a father arrived too late, so little heart left in his chest.

Our Mother wasn't there among the rain and the waves to say, *I loved you since the first time I saw you. You were on your bicycle. You took me up and down the wet streets of this township. How much has passed since then, since I saw you there, looking at me like I was the most beautiful ghost you'd ever seen. Your hair was wet and mine was too. It felt like you could reach through my ribs, to my heart beating there, the sails in your eyes.*

She wasn't there as Our Father pushed his jolly boat into the surf, the ocean swirling about his legs, unable to say to him, *We couldn't stop touching. Our hands and arms and legs. Our bodies. Then I told you there was a baby coming and the clouds parted, and we saw the stars. How a chasm opened between us then, and nothing could hold you back.*

Our Mother wasn't there to watch the rain fall on his face and arms and back, the small waves lapping at his thin hull, his face blanched. She wasn't there to see how, before he could even raise his oars, his limbs went limp. A gauze fell over his eyes. She wasn't there to witness Our Father's shame, his failures trapping him here, pinned to the shore in grief and regret.

Our Mother wasn't there to say, *I still love you.*

Instead, it was only the wind that whispered as he collapsed under the weight of everything.

o

It was raining when they left the arcade and its complex of caves, the lagoon at its heart and the tunnel's mouth buried by floorboards. It was raining as the three of them went up and over the curved streets, passing the boarded doorways and the houses with their worn paint, weathered by the wind, seagulls drifting and the silhouettes of widows on their walks. They watched the tail end of a cat's muddy body through the bushes, and they saw Billy too, a Mud Mummy now clamoring through the alleyways, a groaning hollow where his tongue used to be. It was raining as they approached the once empty house up the street, Mallory's house, their house now, the three of them, this new kind of family. And below the houses, nestled across these spruce-lined hills, the waves fell on the white and gray pebbled beach, a horizon over which the sun and moon floated, where ships sailed.

Time distended. Mallory's hands began to ghost, the Red Mummy's eyes grinned, the Black Mummy went hunting treasure.

There were two extra heartbeats in Mallory's life. The Black Mummy had sailed away, and the Red Mummy was a fixture at her side. Mallory's skin radiated a different light. Mallory's twins, the Black Mummy's twins, the Red Mummy's twins, they were pretending to walk off planks, making their hands in the shape of pistols, practicing their buccaneer gutturals. When Our Father returned, he'd already missed their first steps, their first words, the first glint of rubies in their eyes. When Our Father returned, Mallory was telling stories of Our Mother, how she'd sewn boys into fathers, into pirates, how she'd culled the sadness from their bodies, reformed them as best she could. When Our Father returned, there was an insurmountable divide.

They saw him only once, standing on a rise of wet pavement down the street. Mallory and the Red Mummy were playing with the twins in the yard, rain sweeping across their heads, the boys eating up the sky. She'd been laughing and the Red Mummy smiling when the clouded figure of Our Father appeared in the street. He stood and watched from a distance, and Mallory saw how much he looked like the Black Mummy. The twins didn't notice him any more than they noticed wet grass, but Mallory waited to see if the Red Mummy would raise his hand and wave. He didn't. He only smiled his always-smile and went to looking after the twins.

Our Father stood there for a long while, watching the twins and the Red Mummy son he didn't recognize, a love between them more than any he'd ever known. He stood there, then he backed slowly into the mist.

The Black Mummy said he'd return more often than Our Father, promised he'd be more of a father than Our Father had been. He said he'd always love Mallory, said he would never abandon her on this shore, in this township, weeping like a widow for the remembrance of what had been. At the very center of his ruby heart, the Black Mummy believed in those possibilities. Mallory let the wind speak for her, the rain falling around them, holding the Red Mummy's hand, one brother becoming a pirate and the other a father, the thin difference between sky and sea, each draped in so much longing, in so much want.

o

In this township, the rain runs like blood from a body, wetting the houses and lawns and streets. In this township, rain collects heavy in the sky, pooling and puddling down into the black soil beneath ferns and spruce, over the eaves, gutters spouting rivers that converge on every street, running down seaside cliffs and back into the ocean. In this township, clouds are sutured to the sky.

In this township, an abandoned house is a seething cavity. There is no sound in its hallways beyond the rain on the roof, no hum of a sewing machine and no kettles with tremoring lids. There is no blood dripping from the kitchen table, though sometimes, a cat hunkers near its siding, bandages trailed like tendrils unspooling from its haunches, sky visible between its neck and head. And sometimes, a muddied visitor paws down the walls, smearing palms across the glass door, a story caught in his throat. Sometimes, a candle-width of glow appears impossibly in its window.

In this township, above the shadows of the spruce boughs and the wet noise, above the black soil and the lawns seamed with reburied holes, the thinnest sliver of a moon appears, dousing the world in a strange light. Those nights, there are no widows drowning in the rain, no sons or daughters throwing hopes down cave mouths, no pirates begging for golden shores. Those nights, there are no mothers recanting love, and no fathers returning too late. Those nights, an abandoned house will sit like the skeletal remains of a young heart, while up the street twin voices mingle, sharpening like cutlasses in the dark.

In this township, seagulls sit atop wooden posts like guardians, dispatched to the roofs and the telephone poles, adorning the corners of porches, preening. They descend sporadically to spoon and peck at the streets, to trod their webbed feet in the gutters and puddles, to wing back to their positions as the occasional car passes, or a bicycle treads water up a boy's spine. Their feathers are tipped black, eyes beady as pitch, the rain deflecting down their bodies. They flank the shingles like omens, calling to the mothers and widows, to the sons and daughters, to the fishermen and the pirates and the monstrously otherwise. And when dusk comes, drying like blood in the sky, the seagulls turn into darker silhouettes, trading feathers for black wings.